~*ANGELS IN

ANGELS IN LEATHER

Copyright © 2014 Bella Jewel

ANGELS IN LEATHER is a work of fiction. All names, characters, places and events portrayed in this book either are from the author's imagination or are used fictitiously. Any similarity to real persons, living or dead, establishments, events, or location is purely coincidental, and not intended by the author. Please do not take offence to the content, as it is FICTION.

~*ACKNOWLEDGEMENTS*~

There are so many people I would like to thank; it's quite possible I could take up two pages with it. In all my time writing, the support I have received has been utterly mind-blowing. I've had so many kind people offering to help, from blogs, to fans, to people I don't even know. You're all amazing, each and every one of you.

Now, to the personal thanks.

To Sali Benbow-Powers—my crazy, enthusiastic reader. Your notes kept me going. You ripped a smile out of me every time, without a doubt. Your personality is like a breath of fresh air, as I've told you before. You're the kind of girl people go to when they're feeling down because you're bound to make them smile! You know you rocked my book, so you know I'll rock you back!

To Bella Aurora, my sissy, my sunshine. You're one of the most beautiful people I've ever had the pleasure of meeting, and I'll never regret making a friend out of you. Your help with this book really made a difference to me. You took the time out, even in all your crazy fame, to talk to me and get me through this one. I'll adore you forever, twinsie.

To Lauren McKellar, for editing this book for me. You took the time out, chatted with me the entire way, and were so damn sweet about it. You're utterly amazing, and I feel so lucky to have snatched you up. No doubt there are many out there who would like to grab you and keep you. But they can't, you're mine, muahahahaha!

To Jennifer Tanner and her gorgeous model Miles Logan for taking the picture on this book cover for me. Jenn, you have been so kind to me, helping me out and getting exactly what I wanted. And Miles, you did an amazing job on this cover, even though you were sick. I appreciate this more than you will ever now. A big thanks from all the way down here in Australia.

To Ari, from Coverit Designs. Girl, you rock my covers. Seriously, you're the best cover artist ever. You just get an idea, and you make it amazing. Without you, this book wouldn't look pretty, which means no one would buy it, so girl, you get half the damn credit!! I love your work!

To Love Between The Sheets for all the time and effort you have put in getting my name out, and organizing my tours. You ladies got my name out there, you helped me grow and expand. You're absolutely amazing.

To my fun-loving admin, MJ! You're freaking amazing, your witty comments bring a smile to my face all the time. Thanks, girl, for running my page for me when I'm sleeping here in Aus-land! You rock it!

And, of course, to all my fans—you know without all of you, this wouldn't be possible. So to each and every one of you reading this right now, THANK YOU!! Keep doin' what you do best, and that's reading!!

~*LINKS*~

Please come and join me on my Facebook page, Author Bella Jewel.

Just click here → and click like. Author Bella Jewel

You can also add me as a friend, by simply searching Author Bella Jewel.

~*OTHER BOOKS FROM BELLA JEWEL*~

Hell's Knights – MC SINNERS book 1 – Available on Amazon, Barnes & Noble & Kobo now!

Heaven's Sinners – MC SINNERS book 2 – Available on Amazon, Barnes & Noble & Kobo now!

Knights' Sinner – MC SINNERS book 3 – Available on Amazon, Barnes & Noble & Kobo now!

Bikers and Tinsel – MC SINNERS book 3.5 – Available on Amazon, Barnes & Noble & Kobo now!

Enslaved By The Ocean – Book one in the Criminals of the ocean series. Available on Amazon, Barnes and Noble & Kobo now!

~*COMING SOON*~

Number 13 – March 2014 (See Excerpt at the back of this book)

Where Darkness Lies (April 2014)

PROLOGUE

MEADOW

I'm not broken, just defeated.

The wind whips my face as I lower my head, staring down at the water below me. My heart clenches, and my entire body is trembling. The sick feeling in my stomach can't be described. My skin is covered in a fine sheen of sweat, and my heart is pounding. Tears leak from the corners of my eyes, and I know they're likely the last tears I'll ever shed. The thought doesn't even scare me; it brings me comfort.

I'm going to jump.

I don't really remember the moment when I ended up here, but it creeped up upon me so quickly it was like a hurricane. I knew my life wasn't ideal, but more often than not, I dealt with it. Then I began dating, and my heart got broken, and things just spiraled downwards. Without a mother to support me, I quickly crumbled. My father, while loving, is always so busy with his life. He didn't notice me sinking.

Depression snuck upon me, slowly eating me away until nothing seemed beautiful anymore. I no longer looked at trees and saw their beauty, or found happiness in the smallest of life's delicacies. Nothing was pretty. Nothing meant anything anymore. I was empty, and slowly but surely, that emptiness consumed me until I ended up here.

Alone.

My fingers tremble as I climb over the railing of our local bridge. It's quiet tonight, because the small town we live in has their annual bash going on, and no one is out. I picked the perfect night. The wind is non-existent, and I can hear the distant hum of beetles in the trees. That's the last sound I'll hear.

I swallow, and begin to cry harder as I climb over the railings, and clutch them. It only takes a second to let go; yet it takes so much more to get to this point.

I feel my body begin to sway as I begin to heave.

This is it.

My freedom.

"What the fuck are you doin', Cricket?"

That voice. I close my eyes, so sure it can't be real. I haven't heard that voice since I was twelve years old. I slowly turn my head, and blink through my tears to see Axel Wraithe standing on the other side of the road, staring at me, cigarette hanging out of his mouth. He's not a young man anymore; instead, he's grown into an older, far more handsome version. I blink again, making sure I'm seeing this correctly.

"Axel?" I rasp.

He drops his cigarette, and walks across the road, stopping behind me. "I'll ask again, Cricket, what the fuck are you doin'?"

I should just let go. It would be quick, and he wouldn't be able to stop me. I don't want him talking me out of this. He'll never understand why I'm here. He left a long time ago, when he and my father had a falling out. He never came back to visit, and he never called. I adored him once, not in the romantic kind of way, hell I was only twelve, but as a friend. When he left, I began to fade.

I don't answer his question because I can't. Even though I'm sobbing, my throat is dry and scratchy. I keep my gaze on the water below, and I know I have to let go. If I don't do it now, then he'll talk me out of it and then leave. Where will that leave me? I can't put myself through the pain any longer. I can't do it. I don't want to have to answer to him, or anyone, again.

I let go.

I begin to fall, and my heart feels like it's going to leap out of my mouth. A strangled scream leaves my throat. I can't swim. I know I can't swim. It's why I chose the deepest water I could find under the highest bridge.

It takes only seconds for me to hit that deep, never-ending water. I land so hard, and my entire body stings all over. I open my mouth to scream again only to have it fill with water.

I choke, and my arms and legs flail around. I'm suddenly desperate. People often wonder if those who commit suicide question themselves right at the moment before they die. I realize, some of them probably do. My body is filled with panic, and the desperate need to surface. My lungs are screaming, and my body is becoming weak, but I start kicking frantically. It's at that moment I realize . . .

I don't want to die.

My vision begins to blur as my arms slowly lose all their movement. My body sinks lower, and my lungs no longer hurt. I feel…peaceful. Maybe this was the best choice. Maybe this is where I'm meant to be.

My eyes close as I sink further and further down into the darkness. I don't feel scared anymore.

Maybe this won't be so bad after all.

~*~*~*~

MEADOW

Heavy hands press down onto my chest over and over, pumping. My head spins when it's lifted, and a mouth is shoved against mine, breathing into my aching lungs. I begin to cough so badly I struggle breathe through it. My body is jerked upward, and I throw up until I'm dry-heaving. Everything aches, and my head is pounding. I open my eyes, and blink rapidly. My vision isn't great as I try to take in my surroundings.

"Keep breathin', Cricket. Don't you close those eyes again."

Axel?

I slowly remember how I ended up here, and I begin to panic. I gasp for air, and grip anything I can for comfort. Axel's shirt is what I take hold of. It's wet beneath my fingers. As my vision begins to clear I look up at him, and I realize he's soaking wet. He came in after me. He saved my life?

"Why did you save me?" I croak.

He wraps his big arms around me, holding onto me tightly.

"Why did you jump?"

"I can't answer that," I whisper, feeling his body beginning to warm my skin.

9

"Then neither can I," he murmurs into my hair.

"I..."

"Don't," he says, pressing me further into him. "I know how it feels to be surrounded in darkness, Cricket. But don't you ever...ever let it consume you."

"I have nothing," Trembling, I whisper a hollow, "There's just nothing left."

He reaches down, lifting my chin, and forcing me to meet his eyes. "There's always something left. You just have to fight to see it."

He's right. I know he's right. I stare at him, and I know he's given me a second chance, even when I thought I didn't want it. It wasn't until the last moment that I realized I didn't want to die. I couldn't die. I had to fight. The way I was taught to. This isn't me, and I'm ashamed that I let myself sink so low. What is it they say? You have to hit rock bottom before you can get back up again? I'm at rock bottom, and Axel has picked me back up again. I say the only thing I can.

"Thank you."

He pulls me closer, rubbing his hands over my back.

"You're welcome."

AXEL

I can't fuckin' breathe. All I can do is close my eyes and hold my breath, hoping it ends soon. It's always too long, always too much. I can't fuckin' deal with it. I can't tolerate the little whimpering sounds coming out of her mouth. She's gasping and squirming, but her hands are tied behind her back.

I can't function, I want to be sick, but they won't let her stop until I am done. I hate them for that.

"Please," the girl gasps, turning her eyes towards the dark-hooded man in the corner.

"Keep fuckin' sucking. Don't you fucking stop until he comes."

I shake my head from side to side as her mouth touches my flaccid cock again. Bile rises in my throat, and it takes everything inside me not to break. They want me to break. That's their goal, that's their punishment, and it's all his fault: Mitchell Haynes. He set me up. The one man I trusted, and he fucked me over. He sent me on a suicide trip, and now I'm here, getting abused by a club that wants their revenge.

The girl gags, and I want to reach up and rip my own eyes out; anything to take this pain in my chest away. Her lips work harder and faster, trying to get my cock to play the game. It's the only way she can stop - if I come. It's sick, and fucking twisted, and it's burning into my mind, taking a part of me that I know I can't get back.

The girl reaches up, and her finger slides into my ass. I can't stop her. I'm chained up, and there's nothing I can do to stop the assault.

I want to throw up. I hate it, because my cock hardens.

They know how to get a man over the edge, even when the man is disgusted.

She sucks harder, and the bastard in the corner watches, probably with his own erection. I'll get my hands on him one day, and I'll fucking kill him. I'll gut him and string him out to dry.

11

I won't show him it feels good. He gets off knowing he's forcing me to come against my will. It's satisfying to him. I meet his eyes, and I don't move them as my cock jerks, and I come into the girl's mouth.

A small smirk appears on his lips.

It's victory for him once again.

CHAPTER 1

MEADOW

You are my undoing.

Blood trickles down my fingers as I lift my shaky hand to my face, staring at it. So much blood. So red. So sticky. I lower my eyes to where my father slumps against the seat, panting, gasping for air, reaching for me with a desperation that I don't quite understand. How did we get here? We were just heading to the bank, or so he said. Then, out of nowhere, they appeared: Axel and his gang.

Axel, who was once my father's friend.

Axel, who once had saved my life.

He shot my father in cold blood, nothing but emptiness in his eyes. Like he never mattered to him. Now we're in an alley he pulled over into, just barely. His skin is going a funny shade of gray, and his breath sounds wheezy. My heart is beating so heavily I can hear it in my own head. My entire body is tingling with fear, a fear that I can't shake, because I don't understand it. I know what my father is. I know he's a bad man, but I didn't know he was in this kind of trouble.

I reach down, taking my father's hand and lifting it into my lap. "Dad?" I rasp. "Dad, what's happening?"

"Baby," he chokes. "R-r-run, you need to run."

I shake my head. I'm confused. Why do I need to run from Axel? He used to swing me around when I was a little girl. He stopped me from ending my own life—why would I have to escape him? Where are my dad's guys? Why aren't they here? Why aren't they backing him up? If they knew he was in trouble, they would be here. Wouldn't they?

"Meadow." He almost snarls, shoving something tiny into my hand. "Take this, run...deliver it to the police department in Los Angeles to a man named Raide. Don't give it to anyone else. Promise me, please. Don't let Axel get hold of you. H-h-h-he's not who you remember. H-h-h-he's fucked up now. Promise me," he begs, ending in a coughing fit that has blood splattering across my shirt.

"Dad, I can't leave you," I whisper frantically, ripping my shirt off and pressing it to the blood leaking from his body.

His eyes dart around and he shakes his head, coughing more blood from his mouth. No. No.

"Dad, please, let's get you to a hospital and..."

"No!" he breathes, and his eyes begin to grow heavy. "Promise me, Meadow. Promise me you'll take the case, and you'll get it to Raide? Change your name. Leave the club. Leave this place. They're dangerous; they'll kill you. Promise me you'll do this for me. It's all I've worked for...Promise...Meadow..."

Who will kill me? I don't understand.

"Please," I whimper, feeling warm tears touch my cheeks as they slide from my eyes. "Don't make me go. Don't make me leave you here."

He begins to gasp for air. "I'm g-g-g-going to die, baby. P-p-p-promise me...you'll do this..."

I look into my father's eyes, and I realize I'm about to lose the only family I've ever had. Without him, I have no part in the club he associates with. He's been all I've had since my momma killed herself four years after I was born. He's been my friend, my dad, my hero, and everything I've fought for…and now he's going to die. My vision blurs as I take his hand, pressing it to my heart. You can't stop death, but you can make it easier. I give him the one thing he needs from me, and I swear in that moment I'll make sure I do it for him.

"I promise, Daddy." I disguise my trembling with the firmest voice I can muster. "I swear I won't let you down."

CHAPTER 2

ONE YEAR LATER

You can run but you can't hide, I know what lies deep inside.

I lower my glasses and rush across the road, head down, hoodie covering my hair. A small woman standing outside the door watches at me as I dart around behind the gas station, backpack tightly wrapped around my shoulders, clipped at the front. My sneakers are worn, and they squeak on the pavement as I scurry into the ladies toilets. I rush into the small, crappy room, kicking in the doors, and when I realize it's empty I lower my hood.

My long blonde hair tumbles out as I remove the cap from my head that was sitting firmly under my hoodie. It's my usual look these days: jeans, sneakers, singlet top, hoodie, and a cap. It's the easiest way to disguise who I am when I'm forced to get out in public. I lower my face, and turn on the tap, filling my hands with water and splashing it on my skin. I close my eyes, letting the cool calm my nervous, frightened body.

They've found me.

It's only the third time Axel Wraithe has managed to catch up with me in just over a year, which isn't bad considering he's got sources, and I don't.

He's the President of the MC club Angels In Leather, and he's been chasing me since the moment my father sent me running with information on a USB drive. I've never plugged the drive in to see what's on it. I've never had the chance. Whatever is on it, though, I imagine is extremely important. He wouldn't be chasing me like this if it weren't.

Axel wouldn't have killed my father if it wasn't something he needed.

Would he?

I still don't know what went down that day. All I know is that whatever my father has on this drive, Axel wants.

Axel used to be a part of our family, so to speak. He used to come over, and talk to my dad, and hang out with me when I was a little girl. That was until one day, when he went missing for about six months. When he came back again, there was something different about him. He was darker, angrier, and he hated my father with a wild passion. They became sworn enemies, and were constantly at war. He stopped speaking to me, and I rarely saw him. Until the day he saved my life.

Just after I started running, I heard that Axel had upended the town looking for me. Any friends I had, he went to them. Any person who knew me, he harassed. He was looking for the information. The information I've been running with for just over a year. The information that's clearly been more important than anything else that's come up in that time, because Axel hasn't stopped looking for me.

Which means I haven't rested.

There have been times I've wanted to just give in and let him take it from me, but then I think of my father's face the day he died in the front of our SUV, and the desperation when he made me promise to run, and deliver this USB. If I let him down…I'll never live happily. This is my mission, and sadly, it's become my life. I don't have anything else.

Without this, I'm nothing. I have nothing…no one.

I have been struggling to find Raide. He's not at the police department anymore, and without resources, I don't know where he is. No one will give me any information. So here I am, in a women's bathroom, trying to calm myself down and figure out a way to escape Axel a third time around.

He's not an easy man to escape. He's a goddamned genius, and he's managing to get closer and closer to me no matter what I do. I have to think of something new.

I pat my face dry with my sleeve, and stare in the mirror at the empty blue eyes looking back at me. Most girls my age would be out partying, falling in love, enjoying their life, their jobs, their friends…but me, I'm running, living a criminal life that I never chose. On the rare days I get when I manage to relax, I find myself imagining what it would be like to just be normal.

I shake my head. It's never going to happen.

I hear the distinct rumble of Harley-Davidsons outside, and I know they've stopped. I feel my palms become clammy, and my heart speeds up. I have to get out of here, and into the trees behind the gas station. They're thick and lush, and I can run for miles through them.

The problem is getting out. This was the closest place I could find to gather myself, and it took Axel a matter of minutes to locate me. It's never a coincidence with him. Never.

I swallow, and lift my hair up onto the top of my head again, tucking it under my cap. I pull my hoodie back over, and grip the straps that are sitting around my waist. My bag is strapped on as tight as I can get it, because I don't want it to be taken from me. If that gets taken, then all this has been a waste of time, for me, and my father.

I pull my sunglasses down over my eyes, and I peer out the window. And there he is. I feel my body tingle with fear as I lay my eyes on Axel. He's standing out the front of the gas station, speaking to the young woman, flashing a photo at her. I know it's a photo of me. She nods, and points to the bathrooms. Goddammit. Axel lifts his head, and he turns his eyes in my direction.

I gasp.

Axel Wraithe is a gorgeous man. He always has been, but he's got a heart of steel. I remember as a young girl, in the years before he and my father had a falling out, I used to think he was one of the most handsome men I'd ever met. He was just a young man back then, but he had the kind of face that women would drool over. Now...now, he's older, and more defined, and even more breathtaking.

He has this thick black hair that sits messily on his head. His body is huge, tall and well-built, yet unlike most bikers' skin, it's not covered in tattoos. He has a few, but not many.

His shoulders put most body-builders to shame. His eyes are the color of turquoise water, and are the prettiest eyes I've ever seen. He's got a few days growth of stubble on his face, and his ears are filled with silver hoops.

His body is covered in all black clothes. Large, chunky black boots. Black jeans. A black shirt, covered with his black jacket that I know has a large angel surrounded in fire on the back. Their club's patch. He wears chains around his neck, and leather bands around his wrists. Hanging off his jeans he has silver chains, topping off his look.

Axel is about thirty-two years old, and while he was my father's friend, he was younger than him. Axel is ten years older than me, but even when I was just a young girl at ten, and he was twenty, we always got along. He was so carefree back then, so beautiful. Now he's a monster with eyes that make you want to shrink inside yourself with fear.

He's deadly.

He's standing, staring at the bathrooms, with an empty expression on his face. Sweat trickles down my face as I turn, peering around the room for an escape. There's a small, narrow window above the far toilet. It's not locked, and I could squeeze out of it with enough effort.

I glance back out the front window and see Axel still staring at the bathroom, nodding to the lady as she speaks.

I have minutes.

My adrenalin spikes as I rush towards the toilet. I peer up at the window, and use the toilet and basin to launch myself upwards. I take hold of the windowsill, and use my free hand to rattle the glass pane. It's rusty, but it dislodges itself easily enough. I shove it out, and it lands with a crash on the ground. My heart begins to hammer.

I unclip my backpack. There's no way I can get through with it on my back. I peer out the window, and when I see it's clear, I shove the bag through and let it drop down onto the ground. That's when I hear the rattling on the toilet's main door. My heart lurches, and I feel my jaw begin to drop.

"Hiding in a toilet won't stop me from finding you, Meadow."

Axel's voice has me freezing, but only for a split second. I've been running long enough now to know how to keep myself from freezing for long enough to cause a problem. I lift my leg up, and try to be as quiet as possible as I jump three times, and shove my body through the small gap. I lose my balance when I push through too hard, and land on the dirt the other side with a thump. I roll, gripping my bag and throwing it on quickly before leaping to my feet.

And there he is.

I scream, and leap backwards as he appears around the side of the building. Up close, he's powerful, huge, and dominating. He has a tattoo of a bird on his neck, and it seems to be staring at me, taunting me. I lift my eyes to meet his, and I gasp softly. Beauty—it just doesn't cover what he is. He can't be classed as beautiful. There is only one word I could ever use to describe him, and that is…devastating.

"Hello, Cricket," he growls, using the nickname for me he used when I was a little girl. "Long time, no see."

I swallow, and grip my backpack. "Axel."

He smiles, but it's empty. There's something missing in his eyes, something that got taken from him a long time ago. Something that turned his heart into ice. "And here I was thinking you'd forgotten about me. I mean, you've been running from me now for…how long has it been?"

"One year, three months and six days," I whisper, shuffling backwards.

His eyes pin mine, even though I'm wearing sunglasses, and they're so intense I struggle to hold his gaze. "And you know I was going to catch up to you eventually, so we could have avoided all this if you had just

21

given me what I wanted back then."

I don't say anything. I just tighten my fingers around my pack straps, and let my eyes dart around behind my sunglasses to look for a way out. I see a thick mass of trees behind him, probably about fifty meters. If I could get to them, I could hide myself…I also see a pile of rusty metal poles in the corner, leaning against the wall. I turn my body slightly toward them, and begin very slowly backing up. Axel steps forward, suddenly gripping the side of my face. His other hand wraps around my backpack.

"We'll not continue to fucking play this game, Cricket," he hisses, jerking me hard.

I bring my leg up, hitting him in the thigh. He snarls and steps backwards, shoving me as he goes. I stumble back into the wall with a wince. He crosses his big arms, and he looks like he's trying to control his panting. Suddenly he doesn't look beautiful anymore, instead, he disgusts me. His eyes burn into mine, and I know it's taking all his strength not to throw me down and tie me up. Both of us know that in a place like this, he'll never get me away.

"Don't call me that, and we will continue to play this for as long as I need," I growl, clenching my fists.

My body is trembling inside, and I'm getting hot in this hoodie. I want to lower it, but at the same time, I don't want him seeing my face. Not now. I feel myself becoming flustered, though, and I know I don't have a choice. If I pass out, he wins. And he needs to know that, no matter how hard he fights, I'll fight harder.

"Why don't you lower the hoodie, Meadow?" He purrs, but it's in no way sexy. "Let me see you. It's been a long time. Don't you at least have the guts to look me in the eye?"

The asshole is challenging me. Straightening my shoulders, I decide I'll let him see me, so he can see what kind of damage he's doing to a young, innocent girl.

I take hold of my sunglasses and I pull them off, then I lower my hoodie and rip my cap off. The breeze feels cool; I was so hot. I inhale deeply, needing to feel the fresh air filling my lungs. I turn my eyes to Axel, and he's staring at me, his face expressionless. I thought I saw a glimmer of something in them, but right away they're hard again.

"Well haven't you grown up," he leers, letting his gaze travel slowly down my body and back up again. "Filled out real nice."

Pig.

I cross my arms, giving him a hard stare.

"Are we goin' to stand here all fuckin' day, or are you goin' to give me what I need?"

"Do you think I'm stupid?" I say, trying to stop my voice from trembling.

He glares at me, and his jaw ticks. "You are fuckin' stupid, because you've been wastin' your time running for me for the past year. I will get what I want; I always do." His eyes crinkle, and a cruel smirk appears on his lips. "Just accept defeat graciously, like a lady. Give me the USB, and go back to living your life like a normal girl."

"You know nothing about me, Axel. I'll never be a normal girl. And if you think I'm going to believe your promises of freedom, you're wrong.

I've been around bikers before, remember my father? The one you killed? I know how it all works. I won't let you get your hands on me, not now, not ever."

He flinches at the mention of my father, and his eyes harden. He takes a step forward. I brace myself to run.

"Smart mouth for a girl trapped against a toilet wall with nowhere to go."

"Again," I say meekly, reaching around behind me, and gripping the long metal poles I've been edging closer to. "You don't know me. If you knew me, you'd know that I know what I'm doing by now, and no one traps me against a wall."

I swing the pole. His body moves to block it, but it hits his hands so hard he goes reeling back with a roar. I swing it again, connecting with his kneecaps. When he drops to the ground, I run. It's one thing I do know how to do. I put my head down, my arms by my side, and I run as fast as I can move.

I hear Axel's bellow, and I know he's calling for his men. I have seconds. I hit the trees just as I hear the shouts beginning to grow louder behind me. I skid to my left, running through a narrow set of tall trees in an attempt to get into the thicker shrubs. My sneakers crunch, and I know there's no way I can pull this off quietly, but I will pull it off.

I hear the sounds of boots crunching in the distance, and I have no doubt Axel has his entire group of men spreading out to chase me. My adrenalin spikes, and I pick up my pace, ignoring the sweat pouring down my face, and the branches scratching into my skin. I won't let him beat me now, not after everything I've fought for.

I pick up my pace when I come to a clearing, running hard and fast. It's never good to be caught in a clearing; I've learned that. I put my head down, and run as hard as I can.

I can hardly breathe through my panting. It's so intense. The sweat begins to fill my eyes, and it burns. I blink rapidly, lifting my hand to swipe it quickly across my brow, trying to remove some of it. It only makes it worse. My chest heaves, and my lungs burn.

"I will fuckin' catch you, Meadow, give it up," Axel thunders viciously, and I know he means it.

I look over my shoulder to see him and six other men running towards me. My adrenalin spikes, and I focus my attention in front of me. The only thing I can see is a large river off what looks like a small ledge. My heart skitters. Can I jump off that?

"Stop now, and I'll make it easier for you."

I don't have a choice.

I have to jump.

I run to the edge, and skid to a stop as I look down at the flowing water. My entire body stiffens and my breath hitches. Memories of that night on the bridge flash through my mind. My skin begins to prickle, and it becomes even harder to breathe. It's not the same. You can swim now, and the water is nice, clear and safe. You won't die. You just have to get over the other side.

"She won't jump," I hear Axel yell.

"Hurry it up!" someone else bellows.

I hear the sound of boots crunching coming closer. God, if they get hold of me now all this has been for nothing. I stare down at the water, and goosebumps break out over my skin. I can't breathe. I can hardly concentrate. I know they'll get me any moment. I close my eyes, taking a deep breath.

"Promise me, Meadow…"

My father's words spring back into my mind, and I know I have to do this. So, without opening my eyes, I jump.

It happens in what feels like slow motion. My entire body plummets to the water below. I hit it flat on my stomach, knocking the wind out of me. I sink quickly, even though I can swim now. The panic has my body stiffening in fear.

I begin to struggle. My backpack is too heavy. I shake my head from side to side, keeping my mouth clamped shut, kicking my legs as hard as I can. I feel a set of hard arms go around me, and I seize. I'm slowly being pulled to the surface, and when I surface I'll be taken somewhere I don't want to go. At the realization of that, I start kicking harder, until I hit the person holding me.

When I surface, I gasp a breath of air in, and I kick hard towards the other side of the river. I hear Axel's crackled voice sound out behind me. "Stop moving!"

I kick harder, using everything inside me to get to the other side. I reach the bank and launch myself up, gripping the sides with my hands. I'm about to pull my body up, when those arms go around me again, and yank me back down. With a scream, I go crashing back into the water. Axel has me, and he spins my body around so I'm facing him. Up close I can see his eyes, and right now his beauty only makes me hate him more.

"Quit this fuckin' bullshit, and just give in."

"No," I growl, shoving at his chest.

"I won't play this game with you any longer, Cricket. If I have to, I will hurt you."

I lean in close, almost nose-to-nose, and sneer, "Does it look like I care?"

He growls, and pins me tighter against his body. When I'm this close to him, and my body is pressing against his, I can feel every part of him. His powerful form is twice the size of mine, and a good solid foot taller. His arms tighten around me, and I know I have to think quickly. I stare up at him, meeting those shattering eyes.

"I'm a bad man, Meadow. You're pushing a wild animal, and eventually that animal will lose it."

"You don't scare me," I rasp.

His eyes lower, and meet mine. The intensity in them scares me, and I can see something dark behind them. Whatever happened to Axel, it was bad. "Well I should."

I turn my eyes away from his, and I have to think quickly. I do the only thing that comes to mind. I drop my mouth onto his shoulder, and I bite so hard I feel his skin pop. A metallic tang fills my mouth, and I resist the urge to gag.

Axel roars and stumbles backwards, his hands slipping from my body. I take the opportunity to spin around and launch myself up onto the bank. I graze my knees as I scurry forward. I get to my feet, and I run...fast.

"I'll find you, Meadow," Axel roars. "Mark my fuckin' words."

I have no doubt he will.

But like always, I'll find a way to escape him.

CHAPTER 3

AXEL

Let your demons beat you, so I can defeat you.

"Motherfucker," I bellow, driving my fist into a nearby tree over and over until my knuckles bleed. She got away again.

I spin to Cobra, my Vice President, and I can feel water running down my back. She made me fuckin' jump in after her. I'm getting desperate; time is running out. I need that information, and I need it fucking now. I managed to slip a tracker into her pack, but the water might have stopped it from working. I need to find out.

"Get me the program for that tracker. I need to find her."

"Got it in the van, boss."

With a growl, I storm back towards the roadhouse and over to where our bikes are parked. My entire body is swelling with rage, and I'm beginning to lose my control. I wanted to lay my hands on her, to hurt her. I wanted to put my fingers around her throat, and strangle her until she gives me what I desire. I want her to suffer the same way she's made me suffer this year.

I'm all kinds of fucked up.

I stalk towards the van, and slide the door open. Cobra is tapping in some information on a tiny laptop. He narrows his eyes, and bites the rings in his lower lip. Then a smile appears on his face, and he turns to me, giving me a look full of victory.

"It's working. She's heading on the highway, south."

"We'll wait until she stops. If she hears us coming, she'll run. Get the boys ready. I want them all. I don't want her escaping again. Give me drugs, whatever I have to use to stop her. I'm done playing nice."

"On it. You want injected drugs?"

"Yeah," I grunt.

He nods. "I'll let you know when she stops."

I stare out the window of the van.

This ends tonight.

MEADOW

"Yes ma'am, that will be eighty for the night," the too-friendly receptionist says as I check into a motel four hours later.

I'm still damp, and shivering. I didn't get a chance to dry; it's not warm enough out. I ran until I couldn't possibly run anymore.

I didn't get as far as I would have liked, and I didn't really want to stop, but I had no choice. I'm exhausted.

I dig through my purse and I give the lady the amount she needs. The only reason I've been able to keep myself going is because of cash jobs. There's a lot in this area.

"Thank you." She smiles, and hands me a key. "You're in room 303, out this door, to the left, and up the long corridor."

"Thank you." I force a smile.

"There's room service if you're hungry."

I nod, keeping that fake smile. "I appreciate it."

I take the key and turn, leaving the reception. I let my eyes scan the street before slowly following the directions she gave me.

When I find my room, I unlock it and step inside quickly. My entire body is aching, and my mind is spinning. Axel isn't the man I remember, and the idea of being caught by him is beginning to scare me.

I flick the light on, and peer around the room. It's small, but very clean and tidy. It's one-bedroom, with a bathroom and toilet off to the side. A small two-seater sofa sits in front of a tiny box-television diagonal from the double bed. It's nice, and it'll do just fine. I turn and lock the door, before dropping my backpack down and shrugging out of my hoodie.

I head straight for the shower. I don't hurry it, I just enjoy the feeling of warmth that slides through my body as I stand under the misty spray. I finish up by washing my hair and shaving my legs with the complimentary items, and then I dig through my backpack and find some clean clothes. I am thankful in that moment that I purchased a good, waterproof backpack. It took me a good two months to save for, but it was more than worth it.

I find my brush and drag it through my hair before dropping down onto the sofa and sighing loudly. I need to find a way out of this mess. I believe Raide is still located in Los Angeles, and it's not cheap to get there. He's been next to impossible to track down, but the only leads I have are in L.A., so that's where I need to get to.

I lift my fingers and rub my temples, massaging them to try and ease the throbbing behind my eyes. God, this can't possibly go on forever. What could be on that USB that Axel wants so badly he'd kill my father for it? I don't understand. I peer down at the bag, and I lean down, taking hold of it. I zip it open, and find the tiny device. I need to hide this. If I don't, my life remains in danger. If someone catches me and I don't have it, they're likely to keep me alive.

I stare around the room. Maybe I could hide it here? In the roof, perhaps? I look up to the ceiling and glimpse a large hole that leads up into the roof. One they use for repairs. No, it's too risky. What if someone went up there? I groan loudly, and drop back into the sofa.

That's when I see it. From this angle, I can see a tiny device in my pack. I sit up quickly and lunge towards it, pulling the tiny silver circle out. It's no bigger than a twenty-cent piece, in fact, it look remarkably similar.

I know what this is.

My blood runs cold.

It's a tracker.

I leap to my feet, letting my eyes dart around frantically. All along, Axel was baiting me. That's why he didn't just throw himself on me and tackle me to the ground; he wanted to track me. He's smarter than I thought, and the hunt is getting a whole lot more interesting now.

I need to hide this USB. Having it on me is getting more dangerous. I stare around the room. Maybe I can leave it here? I can't see any hiding places, until I look up at the hole in the roof again. It looks like it's going to be my only choice. No one would look there, and it would be safe until I could make a decision about my next step.

I take hold of the sofa, and drag it directly underneath the hole, then I climb on top of it. I wobble a little, but manage to get my footing by reaching up and gripping the handle on the large hole. I tug once, and it doesn't budge. Come on. I pull hard four times, and finally I hear a creak. Another few pulls later and it swings open. Dust fills my eyes, and I cough and splutter, waving my hand around. I guess people don't go up there that often.

When the dust has cleared, I reach up and I pop the USB into the large space. It's warm up there, the heat from the roof trapping itself. I move my hand to the left, and make sure it's set on the wood of the roof and won't fall, then I shove the door closed and lower myself down. I hope I've made the right choice. Until I can find Raide, I think this is my only option. I can't be carrying that USB around. If Axel gets hold of me now, he might not hurt me since I don't have what he wants.

Someone knocks on my door.

I stiffen, and turn, facing it. Has he found me? I swallow, and tilt my head to the side, peering at the windows. They're not big enough to get out of, and they're locked. The front door is it. Another knock sounds out. If it were Axel, he'd be yelling at me…wouldn't he? He never comes unannounced. He's always loud and boisterous. I can't risk it, though, not after that tracker. I stare at the window again. Maybe I can get a look.

I tiptoe over, and lower myself to the ground, crawling the remainder of the way. I gently lift the curtain, and I peer out. There he is: Axel, and about ten bikers. My heart leaps into my throat. Shit. Fuck. How the hell am I going to get away? If he knows I'm in here, he won't let me go. They're probably surrounding the entire building. I frantically turn and

33

crawl back to the sofa, taking hold of my my pack.

"I know you're in there, Cricket. The nice lady at reception told me so. Open the fuckin' door, I'm not playin' anymore."

I feel myself begin to shake. There's no escape. Not here. I can't. I close my eyes. Think, Meadow. Think. Then I look up at the roof. If I'm quiet enough, I can get in there. I gently crawl over, and climb onto the sofa. I stare at my pack, realizing it's better to leave it down here. Axel will think I've gone out. He will take it, thinking the USB is in there. I dig through and take my cell, and my purse - the rest I leave.

"Three seconds, and I blow the fuckin' lock off."

Shit.

"One."

I leap up onto the couch, and I'm thankful when it doesn't squeak. I grip the handle on the hole, and luckily for me it comes open easily. I take hold of the ladder and pull it down. It squeaks. I stiffen.

"Two."

He didn't hear me. Thank God. I begin to climb until I'm up in the dusty, no doubt snake-filled hole. I pull the ladder up, and then lean down, pulling the door closed. I have to put my hand over my mouth to stop myself breathing in the dust and coughing. I find the USB, and I tuck it into my pocket.

"Three!"

I hear a shot, and then I hear the door being kicked open. I close my eyes, and try to focus on anything but the small, dark space I'm cramped in. If he sees any dust, he might figure it out. I hear him order the men to search the room, and I hold my breath, praying he doesn't find me. Minutes feel like hours as I hear them shuffling through my room.

"Here's the bag, boss," I hear someone say.

"She's taken all her fuckin' stuff," Axel barks. "Fuck her!"

I hear something smash, and I slowly let my breath out. He doesn't know I'm in here.

"Let's go, she can't be far."

I hear more shuffling, and then my door slams. I wait for a long ten-or-so minutes, before swinging the door open and glancing down. They're gone, but I have to get out of here. I realize my backpack is gone, and I curse. Dammit. I was hoping he wouldn't take it. I climb out of the small space, and close it up. I have to get out of here—I just don't know where I'll go. I need to figure out a way to keep myself hidden. I don't know how to do that.

I'm so tired of running.

I'm so tired of being hunted.

CHAPTER 4

MEADOW

I am the devil's friend. I'll be there to the end.

"Where are you headed, darlin'?" the old truckie says when he pulls over to the side of the road early the next morning.

"I'm heading to San Diego," I say, hoping he can get me that little bit closer to L.A.

"I can take you there. It's on my route." He nods.

He looks friendly enough. In case not, I purchased a good knife that's tucked into my jeans. I open the truck door and climb in, sitting as far away from him as I can. I clutch the USB stick like it's my lifeline.

"What's a young, pretty girl like you doin' catchin' rides with strangers?" he asks as he pulls out.

"I'm just in a bit of a pickle, that's all. I'll see my family in San Diego," I lie.

"Oh? You got folks there?"

"Ah, yeah. A mom and dad."

Another lie.

"You goin' to school?"

"No. I never really had an interest to do anything professional."

He nods as if he understands. "Fair enough."

I peer around the truck, and see empty packets of food, drink cartons, and smoke packets everywhere. Gross. Then I spot the laptop tucked into the side of the seat. Oh God; maybe it works?

"Does that laptop work?" I ask.

He nods. "Yeah, have a look if you need."

I grip the computer and place it on my lap, turning it on. I wait for it to load up.

"Does it get service?"

"Yeah, got me one of those fancy-ass little sticks that give me Internet."

I nod, forcing a smile. The computer connects to the Internet, and I begin researching Raide. I have only had limited access to the Internet, so it's not been easy trying to locate him.

I start searching all the Raide's in L.A. Turns out the name is actually quiet popular, and there are thousands of them. I add in a profession, which is police officer, and narrow it down to about thirty of them.

Some are too young, or too old, so I rule them out. Some are retired, so they're gone. I narrow it down to three, and I pull out my cell and write down their numbers. That's when curiosity sparks. I've always wanted to know what's on the USB, but I was scared of being tracked. I won't be in this truck long, so the chance of tracking me is slim. I pull it out of my pocket, glance at the truckie who is whistling and focusing on the road, and then I put it in.

It takes a long time to load. When it finally pops up on the screen, I glance at the hundreds of files. What is this? I click one, and narrow my eyes. There are loads and loads of pictures of drugs, all tightly packed in what seems like a warehouse. The next lot of pictures has my stomach turning. Oh God, they're dead bodies, like police shots. Why the hell does my father have police shots?

The information is extensive. There are drug locations, and information on all the massive motorcycle clubs, but there's a lot in there about Axel's club. I don't get a chance to read the rest because truckie is glancing at me, and I don't want him to get suspicious. I eject the USB, and tuck it back into my pants.

He shifts, and the seat squeaks loudly. "So what's your name, girlie?"

"Laila," I lie.

"Pretty name."

"Thanks," I mumble.

I can't concentrate. What does all that information mean? Why was my father gathering information on clubs when he was running one himself? Is that why he and Axel had a falling out? Was my father working for someone else? I don't understand it, and the confusion is making my head feel likes it's spinning. Is this Raide guy safe? Or am I running into a trap?

I don't know, and it scares the hell out of me.

~*~*~*~

MEADOW

"Thank you," I say, jumping out of the truck at San Diego.

"Any time." The truckie smiles before pulling back onto the road.

I glance around, trying to get my bearings. I've been here before, but I need to find somewhere that's safe, somewhere Axel wouldn't think to look for me. I have no doubt he'll catch up to me—he always does—but I am hoping I might get a night's rest. I need it. If I don't get it, running will become difficult.

I walk out onto the road and flag down a cab. I need money to be able to survive all the way to L.A. I have enough from my last cash job to get me through a few more days, but I'm going to need to find something low-key to make sure I can get through. A bright yellow cab screeches to a halt beside me, and I climb in.

"Nearest hotel," I say.

"You got a price limit?" The older, gray haired man says, staring at me through the rear-view mirror.

"Nothing expensive. Something cheap, under one hundred if possible."

He nods, and puts his blinker on before pulling out into the busy traffic. I stare out the window as he drives, and wonder how long it will take Axel to find me here. Will I get enough time to get myself a job, maybe some extra money in case I can't find Raide? I hope so. I'm running low. I close my eyes and rub my temples, feeling the urge to throw up.

I need to change my look.

The thought hits me very suddenly, but it's a brilliant idea. It might buy me a few days. Axel is looking for me. He knows what I look like, and if I change it up, he might be thrown off my trail a little. I lean over the seat and say to the cab driver, "Never mind the hotel, take me to a salon. Again, preferably a cheap one."

39

He raises his brows but nods, and turns into a small side street. He pulls over on the curb, and nods toward a bright pink store. "They're said to be good."

I smile, and hand him a twenty. "Thank you."

Another nod.

I get out of the car, and he drives off. I peer up at the large, overly pastel store, and then I grip my hood and lower it. I pull off my sunglasses and grab the handle. A little bell jingles as I pull.

When I step inside, it smells like hair products, and is buzzing with people. A young, very attractive blonde girl saunters over, smiling at me. She has massive hair, all piled up on her head. I could never achieve that if I tried.

"Hello, how can I help?" she says, stopping at the desk.

"I...need a change. A big one."

Her eyes widen, like I've just made all her dreams come true. "Oh?"

"I need to look different. I'm tired of this color and this style."

She nods, and walks over. "May I?"

I bob my head as she reaches out, takes my hair between her fingers, and begins inspecting it. She lets it out, and loosens it, before circling me.

"I think dark. You have the skin tone for it, and your eyes are stunning. I'm thinking a dark chocolate brown, if you're willing to do a change that drastic?"

I nod, liking the idea. "Sounds good to me."

"I say we take some length off too, and shape it. Is that okay?"

"Yes," I say. "That's great."

"Well, if you will just come over to the sink, I'll wash it for you."

I do as she asks, and settle myself in the large, leather chair that she points to. I tilt my head back and let it fall into the sink, and she begins washing it for me. My entire body breaks out in tingles. It's been so long since I've felt something so good. I want to moan, only I don't want to come across as creepy so I put a lid on it.

"Okay, all done, come over to this chair and we'll sort this out for you."

The next few hours pass by in a blur. She colors my hair and then trims it, and by the time I walk out of the salon, I don't recognize myself. I stop in at a cheap travellers' store, and I pick myself up a new pair of jeans and a tank, deciding to ditch the hoodie. Axel is looking for that. I get a new pair of sunglasses, and then I flag down another cab.

He takes me to the nearest hotel, and I book myself a room for three nights. It was cheaper than I expected, so I'm able to give myself a little extra time. The room I'm in is basic, modern and comfortable. The hotel doesn't look like it's been around long, so everything is fairly new.

As soon as I settle in, I let myself relax just a touch, and my body slumps in exhaustion.

I need to rest.

I stare over at the bed, longingly. Can I afford to rest? Or should I be out looking for a job? Glancing down at my watch, I realize it's early enough for me to get a good few hours of sleep. I drop my clothes until

I'm in only my bra and panties, and I crawl into the bed. It's a soft mattress with feather pillows, and within minutes of my head hitting them, I'm out.

CHAPTER 5

AXEL

Let your true feelings show, I'm a part of you, more than you know.

"You've got to be fucking kidding me," I snarl, clenching my fists. "How can she just disappear?"

"She's not been seen in the past day. She's hiding well," Cobra says.

"She's fuckin' smarter than I thought."

"Maybe there's a way to get her out, draw her to you. Didn't you say you used to know her when she was a kid?"

I think back to the girl I remember, with her blonde hair, her blue eyes, and her beautiful laugh. She was the only sunshine in my world back then, but when I finally escaped the clutches of Hell's Reign, she became the enemy. Her father put me there. Her father ruined my life. I can no longer see her beauty; all I can see is revenge.

Now the need is intense.

I need to make someone pay for what happened. And the urge to make that person her is stronger than I am.

"She doesn't trust me, and I don't trust her," I say, reaching into my pocket and pulling out a cigarette. "The only way to get her now is force."

"And you're willing to use that kind of force, even for a girl who used to mean something to you?" Cobra says wearily, with his brow arched.

"Fuckin' oath I am."

~*~*~*~

MEADOW

Later that afternoon once I've woken from my nap, I set off down the street. I need to find a job, and bars are the best place to look, so that's where I'll go first. They're often looking for girls to serve, and they're always good for cash jobs.

The first bar I come across is only two blocks from my hotel, and is quite flashy. I grip the door handle and step inside, staring around at the impressive space.

It's got large wooden booths running along two of the walls. A bar runs along the front, and in the middle of the room there are a few pool tables, a jukebox, and some space for a dance floor. I walk over to the bar, and take a stool, waiting for the younger man who is serving to notice me. When he does, he turns and flashes me a dazzling smile.

"Can I help you?" he says, as he stops in front of me.

He's a handsome man, with light brown hair, big brown eyes, and a chiseled face. His body is tall but extremely muscled, and he boasts some impressive tattoos. He has a ring through his lip, and one in his eyebrow. He has that bad-boy look, only his eyes are gentle.

"I was wondering if you happened to have any fill-in work going? I'm in town for a little bit, and I need a job to get me by."

He nods, smiling again. "You're in luck. I just fired my last girl

44

yesterday."

"Y-y-you're the boss?" I say, shocked. He's so young.

He chuckles. "Call me an overachiever."

I smile. I can't help it.

"My name is Colt, and you are?"

"I'm...Meadow."

He raises a brow. "Interesting name."

"Thanks, you can blame my parents for that." I flush.

He grins at me. "So, Meadow, have you worked in a bar before?"

"Yes, many times."

"You want to tell me the reason you're jumping from bar to bar?" he asks, lifting a glass and wiping it.

"I'm actually travelling," I say, and am surprised by how easily the lie slipped from my mouth. "So I'm usually only in one place for a few days to a week at a time."

He grins. "Good plan. I did that when I was twenty."

I feel my body relax. I like Colt. He's got a gentle, warm feeling about him.

"Oh, how'd that turn out for you?"

"I got a chick knocked up, nearly married her out of guilt, got into at least four fights, and lost about ten kilos from eating bad food. I'd say a successful trip, yeah?" He winks.

I chuckle. "Well, I'll make sure to check everything I eat."

His smile widens, and he leans down and presses a button, starting a dishwasher.

"So, you said you have something?" I add, hesitantly. I don't want to sound pushy, but I only have a few hours.

He nods. "I have shifts I need filled for the next three to five days. They're from about lunchtime until midnight, can you cope with that?"

I shrug. "I like late nights."

"Then we'll get along just fine. It's a quiet enough bar, but we do get our busy times. You'll be okay."

"When can I start?" I say, almost too eagerly.

"Now, if you'd like? I'll just get some information from you, and then I'll show you the ropes. It's just you and I on tonight."

"That's fine with me." I smile.

"Okay, well, come out back and we'll get you some paperwork and a uniform."

An hour later, and I'm dressed in a black top, and black pants, and my hair is tied up above my head. Colt is updates me on pouring drinks, and so far I've not spilled anything. The customers have started coming in, and I feel like I'm flowing quite well, serving them quickly.

"You're a natural," Colt says from beside me as I pop the top on a beer.

"I've done it a bit," I admit with a sheepish smile.

"Nothing to be ashamed of. Bar bitches are hot."

I laugh, and continue serving.

"Well hello there, lassie." A husky voice comes from in front of me. I look up and see an older man, smiling over at me. He has beautiful sky-blue eyes, and a charming smile. "You're new."

"I am." I beam.

"The name is Old Jon, and I'm Colt's father."

I smile, and turn to see Colt rolling his eyes. "Well, he's a lucky man, then. What can I get you, Old Jon?"

"I like this one, Colt," Jon yells. "She's got them real good manners."

"Noted, Pops," Colt yells with a laugh.

"Now, about that drink. Colt says I have too many, so I'm limitin' myself to beer."

Giggling for the first time in a long while, I hand Jon a beer.

"So where'd he pick up a pretty one like you? All the others are dragons."

I laugh loudly, and shake my head, waving my hand. "I'm only here for a few days."

"Aw, well, that just ruined my night."

"You're flattering."

He chuckles. "It's where my son gets it."

I smile, and get back to work. By midnight, I've made more than $100 in tips, mostly from Jon. I wait around with Colt as he closes up the bar, and then I get changed and tuck my tips, plus my first night's pay into my pocket. All up, I have over $200. Colt didn't question why I needed cash-only jobs, but I'm grateful for that.

"You need someone to walk you home?" Colt asks, walking out with a set of keys in his hands.

I stare around the empty bar, and I yawn. It's probably not a bad idea. I'm exhausted, and I'm in a strange city.

"That'd be great. I'm only two blocks down."

"You hungry?"

My stomach grumbles at the thought, and I nod, sheepishly. Colt laughs and we leave the bar, stepping out into the warm night.

"I know an awesome place that's open twenty-four hours. It's only a few blocks away, too."

"Sounds good to me," I say, letting my eyes scan the roads. No Axel. Just breathe.

Colt and I begin walking down the street, the opposite direction to my hotel. We pass bars and clubs that are still pumping. Girls stop and grin at Colt as he passes them, and I roll my eyes. Not that I can entirely blame then; he's a good-looking man.

"So, you got yourself a boyfriend, Meadow?"

I snort, and shake my head. "No, they're too much hassle right now."

He laughs. "I agree. When I was travelling, I didn't like having something holding me back, either."

"I don't imagine you'd ever have a time when women weren't throwing themselves at you?"

He looks at me with shock. "Are you saying I'm beautiful?"

I laugh loudly, and it feels good. "Stunning."

He chuckles, and grips my hand suddenly. I turn to him, confused, but he nods his head to the left. "This is the place."

I lift my eyes, and see a big flashing sign hanging above a small shop. The smell coming from it has my stomach twisting with need.

"It smells amazing," I groan.

"It is. You like burgers?"

"I love them."

"Sit, I'll get us something."

I shake my head. "You don't have to do that, Colt. I have money."

He waves a hand and turns, not letting me argue. I find a table and take a seat, letting my eyes scan the streets again. It's habit; I can't just shake it off. I'm always watching, even when I'm relaxing.

I'm deep in a daze by the time Colt comes back out. I hear the seat skid, and I squeal, leaping out of mine.

"Whoa there," Colt says, putting the plates down. "Just me."

"Sorry," I mumble, shaking my head. "I was off in a world of my own."

"Can see that. Here."

He slides a plate toward me, and I stare down at the large cheeseburger and fries. Oh, yum. I lift the burger and I take a bite, groaning loudly as the flavor dances on my taste buds.

"Oh my God, it's so good," I moan between mouthfuls, looking at Colt.

He laughs, shaking his head. "Damn, girl's got an appetite. Not often

49

you find a chick who can eat and is good looking, all in one."

I flush. "Sorry. I must look like a starved animal."

He shakes his head, biting his burger. "Naw, you look kind of cute."

I roll my eyes, and take another bite. We eat in silence, and I am enjoying every single bite of this delicious burger. When we're done, I take my can of soda and Colt and I begin the walk back to my hotel.

"So, where to next, after this?" he asks.

I shrug. "Wherever the road takes me."

It's not entirely a lie. I really don't know where I'll go. I'm supposed to be heading to L.A, but I don't even know if what I'm looking for is there.

"You got any friends to meet up with on the way?"

I shake my head. "I meet new people all the time. That's the beauty of doing it alone. It's my own hours."

God, I'm such a bad person. I'm lying as if it's second nature to me now.

Colt nods in understanding. "I met some crazies on my journeys."

"Oh? Tell me the best."

He chuckles. "I met this man who'd had his penis cut off in an attempt to become a woman."

I giggle. "Nice."

"He…or she…was the funniest person I'd met in my life. To this day, we still talk."

"So he's a she now?"

He laughs, and runs his hand through his hair. "Yeah, he's a she. Bert is now Berta."

I laugh loudly, and notice we're already at my hotel. "This is me."

Colt looks up. "Good choice."

"It's not bad," I say, turning to face him. "Thanks for giving me a chance."

He shrugs. "No problems, any time."

"I'll see you tomorrow."

He winks at me. "Later."

Then he's gone. I smile, and walk into the hotel, feeling good for the first time in a long while.

I made a friend.

~*~*~*~

AXEL

"We'll take a few days here, and then we'll hit the road again," I say, unlocking the door to the compound.

We've been based in San Diego for the past six months. It's a central location for us, and there are no other clubs dominating the area at this point. The compound is just out of town, and we own four warehouses, as well as the main house where I reside. This is my home now. Even that doesn't bring me any comfort.

"I'll keep the checks running," Jax, one of my guys, says.

"Yeah," I grunt, walking inside the compound to the beer, women, and chaos.

"Yo, Pres," one of my boys yells. "Any luck?"

"None," I say, shoving my way into the kitchen.

I find the fridge, swing it open, and see it's empty.

"Stupid fuckers," I grumble, spinning and slamming into a small, big-breasted form.

I step back and see April, my weekly fuck, staring up at me with doe eyes, and a sweet-ass expression. She holds up a beer. "I heard you come in."

I grunt at her, and take the beer, swallowing the cool, crisp liquid.

"You look like you've had a hard week," she croons. "Do you want me to come back to your office?"

I stare down at her. Why the fuck not?

"Yeah," I say, turning and walking into my office.

The minute we get in, I spin toward her, and she screams, scurrying toward the bed. "Don't hurt me!"

"Get back here, bitch," I growl, slamming my beer down and charging toward her. She knows how I like to play my games. She's always been the only girl who lets me play it my way. She gets that I need her fight to be able to fuck her.

I stalk toward her, knowing my eyes are cold and empty. I clench my fists and grind my jaw, hissing through my teeth. "You fuckin' run, I'll make it hurt."

She edges backward, her eyes wide. "Please, don't hurt me."

I see a glimmer of true fear in her eyes, just for a split second as my hand lashes out and curls around her shoulder. She plays this like a game, but sometimes I see genuine concern in her eyes. I feel my insides swell with want. Something about having her afraid of me, even if it's just a touch, has everything in me growing hungry and depraved.

I throw her down onto the bed, and cover her body with mine.

"Fight me, bitch."

And fight she does.

~*~*~*

MEADOW

I sleep in until ten a.m. the next morning, and then spend the next two hours finding somewhere decent to eat. By the time lunch rolls around, I've only just gotten my breakfast. I start work in an hour. It's a super-long shift tonight, but I need it. I gobble down my breakfast before practically running towards the bar.

The minute I step in, I run into Colt. "Whoa there, steady on."

I pull back, knowing that I'm flushed. "Sorry Colt, I kind of couldn't find anywhere to have breakfast."

He gives me a confused look. "You should have called me. I would have made you some."

I smile. "Anyway, I'm here. Where do you want me tonight?"

"Tables. I have Selena, another one of my girls on the bar."

I nod, and duck past him, heading out back. There's a girl with dark black hair and pale, beautiful skin, standing and applying make-up in the small mirror. She's got a pair of tight jeans on, and a red top. "You must

53

be the new girl," she says, applying a layer of lipstick.

"I am, and you must be Selena?"

"The one and only," she says, turning and giving me a once-over. "I'd say it's nice to meet you, but they never stay long."

I raise my brows. "Oh, well, I'm only here three or four days, anyway."

"You're better off," she says casually, gripping her hair and tying it up.

"How so?"

She walks past me, and I get a strong scent of perfume. "Well, it's basic, really. Colt woos them, he fucks them, they get clingy, he doesn't do clingy, and he fires them."

Oh.

I never saw Colt as that kind of man. Though he did kind of woo me last night. If I hadn't been thinking of another tall, dark stranger, I would have probably fallen for it hook, line, and sinker.

"Well, I don't even have time to bother getting interested."

She smiles at me. "Well, good. Come on, I'll show you how to wait the tables."

I spend the next hour with Selena, and she shows me how to wait on the tables. When she leaves me to it, I take over without a problem. The afternoon is a busy one, and the tables fill quickly, but that's okay; the tips are huge so far. I'm already up to $150.

My feet ache as I rush backward and forward, collecting glasses, delivering drinks and snacks. In the late afternoon, when Selena is finished her break, she waves me over. With an achy body, I go. Colt is at the bar when I arrive, and he flashes me a warm smile.

"Sore feet?"

I shrug. "I get used to it."

"You want a break?"

I nod, walking around the bar and pouring myself a glass of water. I grab a packet of chips off the counter, and hand Selena some money for them. I sit on a stool, and sigh loudly.

"You're earning some good tips out there," she says, pouring a colorful drink for a young, annoyingly loud girl who is standing at the bar staring at Colt with a silly expression on her face.

I eye the girl, before looking back at Selena. "Yeah, they're good this afternoon."

"It's those pretty-as-hell eyes," Colt says.

I shake my head with a grin. "Or, maybe they just like me."

"Maybe." He grins.

I lean back, and close my eyes, taking a few moments to myself when I hear the distinct rumble of Harley-Davidsons pulling up outside. I feel my heart begin to hammer, but I know it's just me being dramatic. Hundreds and thousands of people own Harleys. Stop being so paranoid.

"That'll be your main man. He's pissed, I hear," Selena says to Colt, sliding an empty beer bottle across the bar.

Colt grunts. "Yeah, he's always pissed."

"Is that a friend of yours?" I ask, hoping for a little information.

"Yeah, actually. He's the president of the club I'm with."

"You're a biker?" I say, shocked.

He grins at me. "Don't look so shocked."

"I thought bikers just hung around each other, and didn't hold jobs."

He shakes his head. "Well, this one wasn't going to do that. I do what he needs, but this is my main job. Besides, the guys love it."

"What's your club's name?" I ask, standing and picking up and towel and a glass to dry, making it look like I'm doing something productive instead of just prying.

"Angels In Leather."

The glass slips from my hand, and smashes on the ground. My head spins, and I take a step back, putting a hand against my chest. This can't be happening.

"You're...you're...one of Axel's boys?"

Colt's eyes widen. "You know Axel?"

Selena stares at me. "Oh, are you one of his fuck buddies?"

"No...not exactly. I...we don't get along very well. It's a long story."

She nods, as if in understanding. "He is such an ass. I wanted to fuck him once, but he's so broody and angry. He told me to fuck off, and didn't even give me a second glance."

Colt ignores her, and narrows his eyes. "Are you okay? You look like you're about to pass out."

"I just...thank you, Colt. For all this. But I can't stay if you're involved with him. Believe me, we don't like each other. It's not worth bringing into your life," I lie.

"Meadow," he says, firmly. "You don't need to run. I don't have to tell him you're here if there are issues between you two."

"You d-d-don't?" I whisper.

He shakes his head. "Nah, just go on home, and I'll make sure he's not here for your next shift."

I quickly untie my apron. "Thank you, Colt."

Before I can turn and rush out back, the door swings open. I quickly drop to the floor behind the bar; it's the only thing I can do. My heart leaps into my throat as I hear boots crunching across the wooden floor. I scoot backwards, pressing myself as close to the bar as I can.

"Colt," Axel's voice booms out. "Get me a beer."

Colt peers down at me, and I give him a pleading look. He must take pity on me, because he shifts the bin under the counter, and points to the space. I crawl in, and tuck my knees up to my chest. Selena smiles at me, a knowing smile, and gets on with her work. Why the hell is Axel in San Diego? Does he live here? If Colt is based here, maybe he does. Only I could pick the one city and the one bar that he's associated with.

"How's it, boss?" Colt says, his voice gruff.

I hear the sound of Colt popping the top on a beer and sliding it across the bar. I hear a stool being pulled out, and I realize Axel is right there...just above me.

"It's fuckin' crap, that's what it is."

"Didn't find what you were lookin' for?"

Axel makes a growling sound. "Nah."

"What is it you're lookin' for exactly, boss? You've been on it for months. I'm thinkin' I could use a break. Might come with you."

"I'm takin' you on the next run. I need someone that can run fast."

Run fast. To catch me. Oh, God.

"Run fast?" Colt questions, shifting closer to me and reaching for a glass.

"I'm after a girl. She's got something I want, but she keeps fuckin' out-smartin' me. God help her if I get hold of her now. I'm fuckin' mad."

Colt's hands slide into his pockets. "What's a girl got to do with anything?"

"Open your fuckin' ears, boy, I said she's got somethin' I want."

"What's she got?"

Axel shifts. "Nothin' that's of concern to you. I suspect she's around this area, so keep a fuckin' eye out."

I don't feel so good. My hands begin to tremble, and sweat trickles down my forehead.

"What's her name?" Colt asks, cracking another beer. "I might have heard of her."

"Meadow."

I see the exact moment Colt stiffens, because his legs go rigid. Shit. Shit. Shit.

"Here's what she looks like. You see her in here, you call me."

Oh God.

Colt's silent, and I suddenly don't feel like being here is a smart idea. If he decides to tell Axel I'm here, I won't be able to get out. I have to run, and I have to run now. I crawl quietly from my space, and as soon as I'm near the back door, I stand.

"What the fuck? Colt, were you gettin' your fuckin' dick sucked while I was talkin' to ya?" Axel bellows, slamming his glass down onto the bar.

He doesn't recognize me. Oh God, he doesn't recognize me because I changed my hair. My heart pounds, and a moment of hope rushes through me. I reach for the door, ready to run, when Colt murmurs, "Meadow, pretty sure there's somethin' you haven't told me."

"Meadow?" Axel rasps.

I turn, and I meet his shocked expression. His eyes widen, and he skids his stool back. His powerful body launches up and over the bar, sending everything within reach flying. The shrill sound of glasses smashing fills my ears.

That's when I run.

"Don't you fuckin' dare," he bellows, but I'm already out the door.

I push through the offices out the back, slamming and locking as many doors as I can. My adrenaline spikes, and I duck through the back kitchen and out the back door. I hear Axel's roar of frustration, and the sounds of smashing coming from inside. Shit. I run across the staff parking lot, and duck into the nearest alley.

"You fuckin' stop, now," Axel yells, rounding the corner and charging down the alley after me.

I pick up my speed, running as fast as I can. I reach the street and I skid to the left, shoving through the ocean of people as I try to escape the angry, determined man behind me.

"South of the city, she's on foot, dark hair. Get moving!"

Axel is ordering his men in. I close my eyes, drop my head, and just run as hard as I can manage. I charge around another corner, and across the road. Cars beep and screech to a halt as I dodge my way past them. I stumble as I hit the gutter on the other side, and I go down with a pained cry. My knees scrape across the gravel and my hands go instinctively out in front of me to stop me from landing on my face.

It's the moment Axel needs. It's the moment he's been waiting for.

He's behind me before I can even get to my knees. People on the street don't even stop to see if I'm okay, they just keep about their business. Axel's hands go around my body, and he hurls me up, pressing me into his chest. He spins us both around, and begins pulling me toward the closest alley. I dig my heels in, not willing to accept defeat. Not willing to give in.

"Let me go," I cry, squirming.

"Stop doing that," he growls.

I decide to try pleading. He's not listening to anything else. "Please, just let me go, Axel, you don't have to do this. Just stop. Please. For whatever friendship we had all those years ago…"

He flinches, and his entire body stiffens. "I said fuckin' stop squirming. If you keep it up, so help me God, I'll put you on your knees and fuck you until you can't breathe."

I stiffen, and my entire body slackens. What did he just say? I blink rapidly, trying to process his words. Why would he say something like that? Why would he even think it? He drags my body into an alley, because I can no longer make my legs work. They're weak, and I'm exhausted.

"You wouldn't hurt me like that," I rasp, quietly. "Would you?"

He stops, and spins me around, staring down at me. His eyes are hard, and I can see deep in their depths that he would hurt me like that. My entire body breaks out in fear. "I'm a fucked-up man," he growls. "I'm not the person you remember. You don't know me anymore. You don't know the kind of shit that's in my head now."

I twist one more time, feeling panic rise in my chest. He's right. He's not the man I once knew, and I can't risk staying with him. If he finds out I don't have the USB, there could be a big problem. I put it in a bank yesterday, in a safe locker where no one could touch it. Axel is taking me, but he has no idea that it's for nothing.

"I said stop fuckin' squirming," he roars. "Goddammit, stop!"

I stop, but not before I feel his cock brush against my ass. It's hard against his jeans, and my body shivers. I'm not sure if it's in response, or out of pure fear. My struggling arouses him, and that both scares and excites me. It sparks something inside my body that I don't quite understand, and right now, I don't want to understand it.

"No," he whispers, his breath near my ear. "Not possible."

What's he talking about?

He shifts his hips, and tightens his hold on my body. "Don't fuckin' move."

I whimper, and he growls deep in his throat. "Fuck," he murmurs. "You like it."

What?

No.

His fingers slide down my over my shirt, and his finger grazes over the swell of my breast. Fear courses through my veins. He wouldn't rape me...would he? I swallow, unsure of the feelings running through my body right now. Beneath the pain, and the hesitation, there's something else. A slight want that I can't make sense of. I turn my head, and Axel's eyes meet mine, and the cold, deadly depths devour me. I look away; I can't face this. I can't face this uncertainty that I'm feeling.

I can't be as twisted as him.

I can't be enjoying his body against mine...oh god...can I?

"Boss!"

I lift my eyes to see four men in black leather jackets walking down the alley. Reality hits me like a brick, snapping me out of my haze, and I kick back, giving Axel a shock attack. My foot connects with his shin, and he bellows, releasing his arms. I spin, and my fist flies up, upper-cutting his nose. He roars in pain, and his hand goes over his face to halt the spurting of blood. His eyes meet mine, and they're filled with uncontrollable rage. Blood drips through his fingers, and I shiver with fear. I'm not sure that was a good move.

I turn without giving it anymore thought, and I run toward the other end of the alley. I'm nearly there when three other bikers step in front of me. I turn quickly, ready to go back, but I see Axel and the other guys standing, panting. Axel has a needle in his hand. There's blood running down his face now, and dripping off one of his hands. I begin shaking my head, putting my hands up as panic fills my chest, and my legs grow wobbly.

"Please, Axel," I implore. "Please don't do this."

He walks toward me, nodding at the men behind him. One reaches for me, and I dive forward. Axel catches me, and his large arms wrap about my body. I can feel his breath on my ear as he leans down, and plunges the needle into my arm. Warmth shoots through my body, and I reach up, taking Axel's arms as my legs give way. I can smell the coppery scent of blood, mixed with his own manly scent.

"Easy," he murmurs as everything fades to black.

AXEL

"She's still out, boss," Cobra says, walking into my office.

"She chained?"

He nods. "She's chained, and the door is locked. She ain't gettin' anywhere."

"You find out where she was stayin?"

He nods again. "I'm on it. I found her room and sent Jax and Pick over to get her stuff."

"Fuck, she'd better have that USB there."

"It ain't on her," he adds, lighting a cigarette. "I checked her body thoroughly."

My eyes widen, and a cruel smirk appears on my lips. "Yeah? You stripped her, eh?"

"Yeah, boss. Nice pair of tits that girl has on her. Don't worry I left the bra on. I'm not that much of a pig."

I grunt, and nod, dismissing him. Lucky fucker got to be the one to strip-search her. I reach over, picking up a smoke. I light it, and inhale deeply. A moment of calm washes over me as the nicotine fills my veins—but the moment doesn't last long. What the fuck happened out there earlier? I got a fuckin' stiff, and she liked it. She liked the fight. I've never met a woman that liked it. Most of them pretend to like it because they want my cock. I close my eyes, and rub my temple. Fuck. This is all too fuckin' hard.

My frustration fades for a second, replaced with complete exhaustion. This has been going on far too long. I get to my feet, shoving the chair back, and I walk out into the hall. I'm midway down when April saunters up, stopping in front of me. "Hey you, I heard you got what you needed?"

I glare down at her. "Club business your business, April?"

"Well, no, but…"

"Then mind your own fuckin' business, or I'll mind it for you," I hiss.

I step past her, and head toward my room - the room where I have her chained. My body stiffens at the idea of her being restrained in there, unable to move, unable to get away, desperate…my cock flinches, and I curse under my breath. I'm a sick fucking bastard, because the idea of her not being able to escape me…no matter what she does…no matter what I want to do to her…it feels fucking good.

I reach the end of the hall, and turn left, walking into the only room in

64

this section of the three-story house. I turn the knob and step inside the dimly-lit space. Meadow is sprawled out on the floor, her now brunette hair fanned out around her. She looks peaceful like that, almost as if nothing in the world could hurt her.

Except me.

I can hurt her.

I walk over and sit on the bed, staring down at her. She's got chains around her ankles, and around her wrists. They're chained to shackles on the wall. I have had to explain to many women why I have shackles on my wall, but most don't understand. April is the only one who plays my game, so she's the only one I keep around.

Meadow stirs, and groans deeply. God damn her for looking as beautiful as a fallen angel.

"Axel?" she murmurs in her haze. "I'm sorry."

Sorry? What the fuck is she sorry for?

She shifts, and goes to roll, only to feel that she can't roll. She's chained. Suddenly her body jerks and she bolts upright, screaming. I drop down to my knees, and I grip her shoulders, causing her to scream even louder.

"Enough," I order, giving her a little shake.

"Axel?" she cries. "What have you done?"

"What I had to do," I growl into her ear, and she tenses. "Now, we can do this the easy way, or the hard way. Where's the USB, Meadow?"

"Why would I tell you?" she cries, her voice frustrated. "I can't stand you."

She notices then that she's wearing different clothes to what she came in, and her face pales.

"Y-y-y-you stripped me?" she screams.

I meet her gaze, giving her a deadly smirk. "Needed to make sure you didn't have the USB on you."

"You fucking piece of shit," she screams. "You're useless!"

My body jerks at her words, and I shake her harder. "Don't fuck with me. I don't have time for this shit. You tell me where that USB is or so help me God, I'll do whatever it takes to get it out of you."

"I hope God helps you then," she whispers.

"What?"

"I'm not giving it to you, Axel."

I snarl, and slam my fist into the wall beside her. She cries out, and shifts her body away from mine.

"Fine," I hiss, standing. "We'll do this my way."

CHAPTER 6

MEADOW

Chains and whips excite me.

I yank the chains around my wrists, and let out a frustrated cry when all they do is dig into my flesh. I throw my head back and yell loudly, fighting the desperation building in my body. I can't get them off, and Axel isn't going to move them any time soon. He walked out about ten hours ago, and he hasn't come back since. I've heard the music and partying outside, but no one has come in this room.

It's dark now, and I can't see anything. It must be midnight, if not early morning. I'm starving, thirsty, and fully aware I won't get a lot until I co-operate. I also know, they won't let me die without knowing where that USB is, so for now at least, I know I'll get fed eventually. I close my eyes with a sigh, and hang my head.

"I'm sorry, Dad," I whisper. "I tried."

I hear the sound of the door, and I quickly lie down. I don't need to argue with Axel any further. I manage to get down and onto my side. I peek through my lashes as the door swings open. Axel all but stumbles in, gripping the table by the door for support. Great. He's drunk. He slams the door behind him, and walks over, staring down at me.

"You ain't asleep," he grumbles.

I open my eyes and stare up at him. "I'm sure you're proud of that clever observation."

He grins, and it's shocking. Axel Wraithe doesn't grin. He glares. He smirks. He smiles a smile that's empty and broken, but he doesn't grin. His eyes scan over my body for a slow, agonizing moment before lifting and meeting mine. His grin turns lazy, and I realize the only reason that grin is even on his face is because of alcohol. I hear it numbs even the worst hurts. He kneels down in front of me, and takes the chains, rattling them.

"Not so smart now, are you? I told you I'd catch you…"

"Fuck off," I growl.

He chuckles softly. "When did you get a backbone?"

"Probably the same time your heart froze."

He narrows his eyes, and studies me. "What would you know about my heart?"

I shake my head sadly. "You were the one who jumped off a bridge to save my life, were you not?"

He narrows his eyes, and we stare at each other for a long, silent moment. I feel my skin prickle, and my entire body becomes aware of the large, beautiful man in front of me. After that moment is over, Axel turns his eyes away, and I watch them grow into those empty stones once again.

"I know what you're trying to do, and it ain't gonna work."

I sigh, and shake my head. "And what is it you think I'm doing?"

"Tryin' to fuck with me."

I snort angrily. "Don't flatter yourself, Axel. I already know a heart like yours can't be warmed."

His face changes at my statement, and he almost looks offended by my words, however he quickly wipes the look and replaces it with that empty, blank look he carries around each day. I shake my head, proving to myself that Axel isn't going to break. He's managed to gather some kind of darkness in his soul, and he's not willing to let it go.

He rocks back on his heels after a moment, and gives me another empty smirk. "You got some sort of hero in your life that's goin' to come and foolishly try to rescue you?"

I lift my eyes, and meet his. I know my expression is hard. "Heroes are for the weak, Axel. If I escape, it will be all on me."

His eyes sparkle with challenge. "Well, you'll need all the luck you can muster up if you think you're getting out of here."

"I don't need luck," I say, sitting up and crossing my legs.

"So confident, aren't you?" he murmurs, still kneeling in front of me, rubbing his big hands together.

"What happened to you when you went missing for all those months?" I blurt suddenly, and then cringe at how forward I'm being.

I've never seen someone's body stiffen so quickly in my entire life. It's almost as if he jerks, he stiffens that intensely. His eyes seem to glaze over, going off into a different place. His breathing deepens, and his hands form fists. I narrow my eyes, watching him closer, taking in every movement on his face as he goes through the motions. When his eyes finally lift to meet mine, they're wild with rage.

"What happens in my life," he snarls, baring his teeth, "is none of your motherfuckin' business."

"You made it my business when you killed the only person I had left in my life. You made this my business when you decided to make me run across the country!" I protest angrily.

His eyes widen for a split second, showing his shock. But in true Axel form, he covers it quickly.

"You're walking a fine line, Cricket," he says, baring his teeth.

"Before all of this, before you killed my father and I was sent running, there was something between you and I. A connection. An understanding. Hell, a friendship. Now, though, you're empty. Something eats at you, and the person I knew has been replaced with this…shell."

"I've changed, and you're pushing me over a very, very weak line right now," he rumbles, and I catch a glimpse of his trembling hands.

"People don't change, Axel, they simply take paths that lead them down roads which are sometimes damaging. It doesn't change who they are, it merely adds to it. You're there, somewhere, past all that darkness and brooding."

"The man you knew is gone," he says, so firmly, so icily, that I shudder.

"I don't believe that."

He gets to his feet, staring down at me. "Believing something is just a way of trying to convince yourself that something you so desperately want is real. You can't make something real just by believing in it, Cricket. This," he says, pointing to his chest, "is damaged, and there ain't no glue in the world that can put it back the way it was."

Then he turns, and he leaves the room, leaving me to stare at the empty door with burning eyes and an aching heart.

~*~*~*~

AXEL

I slam my fist over and over into the punching bag in the garage. They burn and ache, but I can't stop the rage. I drive my fists into the hard leather until they're busted and bleeding, then I slump down onto the ground, gripping my head and smothering the angry roar that's creeping up my throat.

I need to regain my control. I need to put her back in her place.

She's trying to fuck with my head, and no one, no one fucks with my head. I drive my fist into the bag again, and my knuckles split, sending bright-red blood down over my wrist. I snarl and hit it once more, sending a delicious burn up my arm. I won't back down now. I'll give her a reason to hate me, and I have the perfect way to do that.

My feet move, and I find myself heading out into the main room.

When I see Cobra, I do the only thing I can. The only thing to put a distance between us. The only thing that will stop her looking at me like she can fix me.

"Cobra," I rasp. "It's time to scare her into giving me the location of that USB. Prepare her. We're going to the local bridge."

CHAPTER 7

MEADOW

Capture my heart, lock me in the dark.

I open my eyes when I hear the sounds of boots squeaking across the polished wooden floor. I see one of Axel's men, Cobra, I believe, edging towards me. His eyes give me nothing. He's staring at me as if I'm no more than a pathetic toy his boss is playing with. It's a shame too; he's an extremely sexy man. He's got this longish blonde hair that falls over his forehead, and his eyes are a piercing blue. He's got lip rings, and an eyebrow ring. All this combined gives him a dangerous look.

I see a set of handcuffs in his hands, and my entire body stiffens. What is he doing with those?

He leans down, unchaining me. He's an idiot. There's no other way to put it. The moment my feet are unchained, I lunge forward, punching him in the groin. With a bellow, he stumbles backward and roars in pain. I don't wait around. I leap to my feet, and I run out the door. I get to a long hall, and I skid quickly to the left. Hearing the sounds of voices, I tuck myself into a room, breathing hard and fast.

"Yeah, I'm hearing you," a female voice says. "He's in a mood all right."

"Fuck him," another female says as they fade into the distance.

I peer around the door, and I hear Cobra bellow out Axel's name, and something about escaping. Shit. I run back out into the hall, skid around a corner, and come crashing into Axel. His hands instantly curl around my upper arms, so tightly I'm sure I'll bruise. He turns and slams me against a nearby wall. His eyes are wild with rage, and he's panting. I guess he heard Cobra's yelling.

"You just don't fucking give up, do you?" he roars.

"No," I snarl, bringing my knee up and hitting him in the groin. He bellows in pain and stumbles backwards. I duck around him to keep running but he lunges at me, using the power of his body to drop me and crush me against the floor.

I don't stop fighting. I grip the carpet with my fingers, digging my nails in, and I pull myself forward, all the while kicking and twisting furiously. Axel's body is heavy, and solid, and there's no escaping it. He reaches up, gripping my wrists and bringing them back forcefully behind my back. I wail in pain, and snarl curses at him as I continue to twist.

"Hand me the fuckin' cuffs," he growls.

A moment later, the cool cuffs are snapped onto my wrists. Axel moves his body off mine and reaches down, taking hold of me and hurling me up so hard a sharp, shooting pain radiates through my back. I scream and kick out again, hitting him in the shins. He spins me, slamming me against the wall, and leaning in close.

"You're goin' to fuckin' regret that."

"Bring it on," I spit.

His eyes grow wide with something, I don't know if it's hate or desire, but I'm almost sure I just made the wrong move challenging him like that.

~*~*~*~

MEADOW

My lips are trembling, and I can't breathe. I want to open my mouth and scream, but nothing comes out. Even if I wanted to speak, I couldn't. My words are caught in my throat, no doubt trapped behind the protests. Axel has me pushed against the railing of the biggest bridge he could find that wasn't in a public place. I can see the water below. I can hear it splashing against the rocks along the side.

"Didn't wanna have to do this, but you're not understanding me, Cricket. I need that USB, and I need it now. If I have to toss you off this bridge a hundred times to get it, I will."

I open my mouth to beg, but nothing comes out. I'm frozen with shock and fear. My entire body is stiff, and tingling all over. My heart feels like it's going to launch out of my chest, and my stomach is coiling tightly. Desperation fills my body, and I want to beg frantically, anything to stop Axel from putting me over this bridge. But I can't speak. I'm trying. I can't.

"Answer me, goddammit," he snarls.

I close my eyes, and angry tears slide down my cheeks. You're stronger than this, Meadow. You can beat this fear. You can swim now. Let him throw you over the edge…let him…my eyes snap open…if he throws me over, I can swim to the side and run…I can escape. My heart rate picks up, and my body fills with that familiar adrenalin.

"Last chance. Answer me, or I toss you over."

I clamp my mouth shut, fighting with fear and terror, fighting with my own head. This might be my only chance. I focus on trying to breathe as

74

I feel Axel grip my shirt, shoving me forward. I swallow a scream, and my hands clench together. You can do this. You can swim now. It's going to be fine. It's all okay. You're stronger, braver, better…

"Fine, have it your way," Axel hisses, and then he shoves my body forward and I fall over the side of the bridge with a scream so loud it echoes through the night sky.

I land in the water with an almighty crack. My skin burns angrily as I struggle to resurface. It isn't easy when I'm cuffed, but I manage to. I blink furiously, kicking my legs and using my combined fist to shove the water from my eyes. I see Axel's men standing at the left and right sides of the bank. They're watching me with smirks on their faces. I scream help, and begin flailing around, pretending I can't swim. Then I take a deep breath and go under the water, heading straight under the bridge and out the other side. I ignore the tingling all over my body, and the slap-like pain that's radiating off my thighs.

I reach the bank, and I can hear Axel's men yelling and cursing at each other. They probably think I've drowned. At least, I hope they have. That was the point. I launch myself out, hitting a bunch of thick, spikey shrubs. I scramble, struggling to get to my feet without the use of my hands. My body is filled with a strange kind of power, and the fear of jumping from that bridge is gone. Instead, it's given me a sense of strength.

I duck down, and I shove through the trees. I have no idea where I am, or if I'm going to end up over the side of a cliff running into the night like this, but it's a risk I'm willing to take. I can't hear Axel, and I wonder if he's still making his way off the bridge. That, or he's slowly murdering his men for being so stupid.

When I get past the shrubs, I begin running gently, cuffed arms out in front of me to navigate my way through the trees. I glimpse a light to my left, and my heart leaps into my throat. Seconds. Seconds. I turn to the right, pushing on, distancing myself from the light as much as I can. I can hear voices yelling in the distance somewhere, but I don't want to stop and hear what they're saying.

I hit what feels like pavement, and I almost sigh in relief. A road. I peer left and right, and the lights of the cars begin appearing both ways, burning my eyes. I squint and take a step back, debating which way to run. The road was behind the bridge, I believe, so I'll go left, the way that leads away from him.

With bare feet, I start making my way down the road in a light jog. My legs are aching, and an awful tingly feeling is creeping its way up my body. My body is stiff and sore, and my head is pounding, but I don't stop. Nothing can make me give up right now.

I don't even want to consider how close Axel might be. I didn't hear him yell. Maybe he thinks I didn't surface.

Then I hear the rumbling of a Harley-Davidson, and my body stiffens. I slowly turn, and see one single light hammering toward me. With a scream, I leap off the road and begin running through the trees again, hitting them and scratching my body with their twigs. I see a light flash, and then I hear the sound of boots crunching. I pick up my pace, and end up running directly into a large, thick tree. I am launched backward with a scream, and blood spurts from my nose. I cry out loudly as I feel my body sink to the ground in shock.

Then I feel arms, wrapping around me and dragging me back out through the trees.

"Let me go," I scream.

"That was fuckin' stupid, but smart. You're fuckin' clever, you little shit," Axel growls.

"My...n-n-n-nose..." I choke out, pressing my hands over it as Axel drags me.

When we step onto the road, Axel lets me go and flashes the light across my face.

"The fuck did you do?" he asks.

"I ran into a tree trying to escape you, you stupid fuck!"

He snorts, and then turns to his bike, opening the side panniers to get an old, oily slither of material. He lets me go for a split second, so I turn and attempt to launch my body back toward the shrubs. If I can run further, maybe a car will see me with blood all over my face, and stop.

Axel growls and runs after me, his boots crunching loudly on the gravel. He reaches me before I even have the chance to get fifty meters down the road.

My body is exhausted.

I'm exhausted.

His fingers curl around my arm, and he spins me towards him with a feral hiss. "Fight as you may, you will not escape me. I'm not going to be making such a stupid mistake again. You're cluey, girl. Smarter than I'd thought. Your dad would be real proud."

"How dare you?" I seethe, tugging my hands, but he's got them firmly clasped in his.

He steps back, keeping one hand on the chain of my cuffs. He takes his shirt, and pulls it up, unhooking one arm before switching hands and unhooking the other. My eyes widen in shock at the sight of his excessively large, muscled body. Jesus. He walks toward me, and curls his fingers around the back of my head, pressing his shirt to my nose. I'm grateful he decided not to use the scrap of material, but the pain of him pressing it against my face has me crying out in agony.

"Stop fuckin' movin'," he orders. "I have to hold this here until the bleeding stops, because clearly you can't hold it."

He rattles my handcuffs, and I want to cock-punch him.

"You fucker," I growl, but it comes out as a muffled sound that even I can't understand.

"I can't understand you," Axel says, and his tone is amused. "But by all means, keep cursing me. I imagine that's what you're doing behind my shirt right now."

Asshole.

He stands there for a solid ten minutes, neither of us speaking. When he's satisfied the bleeding has stopped, he pulls the shirt away and tucks it into his jeans.

"On the bike. We're goin' back."

"I hate you," I mutter, gripping the bike seat and throwing my leg over it.

"If you gave me what I wanted, we wouldn't be going through this constant 'me cat you mouse' bullshit."

"I'm not giving you anything until you tell me everything," I say defiantly.

"Ain't nothin' to tell."

"That's a lie, Axel, and you know it."

He glares at me, but takes a helmet and shoves it toward me. I'm thankful, in that moment, that it's an open-face helmet and not a closed-face one, or I'd be in a world of pain right now. I shiver as a gust of wind whips past me, causing my damp clothes to feel cool against my skin. Axel climbs on the bike in front of me, and then turns back, uncuffing my wrists and pulling them around his waist. Then he cuffs them again. He's not stupid. Then, without warning, he pulls out onto the road.

I close my eyes, unable to stop myself, and breath in the fresh, crisp air. Being on a bike is like being free. There are no words to describe the intense feeling of joy that swells in your chest as you soar through the wind, nothing surrounding you, nothing holding you down. It's just you and the bike. Or, in my case, you, the bike, and the biker. I concentrate on the moment of freedom, instead of focusing on the way my lips are trembling from the cold, or the fact that I'm cuffed to a man that despises me.

Worse I'm trying to ignore the feeling of his warm, hard skin against my hands.

By the time we get back to Axel's compound, my nose is pounding, and my head feels heavy. Axel helps me off the bike, and leads me directly to his room where he spins me around and uncuffs me before taking the hem of my shirt, beginning to raise it. I screech loudly, and he snaps his hand back.

"What the fuck?" he growls.

"Don't touch me!"

He narrows his eyes. "You want to stay here, in wet fuckin' clothes?"

"No, but I don't want you touching me."

"Fine, I'll go and get Cobra to do it. He did enjoy it last time."

My mouth drops open, and I clench my fists. He knows he's giving me a choice, and he knows I can't refuse him. I'm cold, I'm wet, I don't want to be in these clothes all night, and I certainly don't want Cobra taking my clothes off again. God only knows what he did last time. Lowering my eyes, and clenching my jaw, I lift my arms.

Axel rolls his eyes angrily, as if my hesitation was stupid, and then he takes my shirt, lifting it over my head. I keep my eyes downturned as he moves his large body down mine, and grips my pants, lowering them too. I don't want to look at him, or recognize that my body is having some sort of reaction to him being so close. My feelings for Axel confuse me, and I don't know that I'll ever begin to understand them.

When I'm in my underwear, he stands and tosses me a shirt. I pull it on, and it goes all the way down to my knees. It's one of his. My heart stammers, and again, it makes no sense to me. He's a monster to me, and yet my body is reacting every time he's this near. I stand still as he chains me back up on the floor, and then he turns and I hear him ruffling around. A hand is shoved in front of my face a minute later, and I see he's got some painkillers and a power bar. Shock fills my body as I reach out, and shakily take them.

Then he leaves the room without a word.

Just for something different.

~*~*~*~

MEADOW

The next few days are spent going over the same bullshit. He asks for the USB, I deny him, we get into an argument, and he storms out. By day four, I'm tired of the same crap. I've contemplated just giving it to him and leaving this place, but I'm not entirely convinced Axel will let me go once he gets what he wants. He's a whole other person now. Someone I don't know.

And yet he's drawing me to him like a magnet. I want to know what went down. I want the story. I want answers. I need my closure. I don't know what happened to Axel, or why he needs this USB, but I want to. I should hate him for killing my father, and part of me does, but part of me knows there's so much more to it than I could ever imagine.

And until I can understand that, I don't want to leave.

So I keep playing this silly little game. On the night of day four, I'm curled up in my little spot in the corner, ignoring the ache in my thighs and legs from sitting too long. Axel gets me up, and moves me around, but I spend most of my time here, chained up, as if I am a wild animal. He's trying to break me. I'm not stupid. My wrists are chaffed from the cuffs, and my body is weak with dehydration. I feel exhausted, and yet sleep most nights is non-existent. Instead I listen to Axel sleep, and dream.

He dreams a lot.

I hear the door creak open, and I move my eyes up to see Axel walking in with those lazy, heavy eyes. I slowly lie down and close my eyes, once again too tired to deal with his shit. I hear him shuffle across the room, and then I hear him stop in front of me. I peek through my lashes to see him kneel, and stare down. His eyes hold something I've not seen before. It's compassion. A certain level of gentle I didn't think he had left.

God, what is he doing?

He leans down, stroking a finger across the hair covering my face. I try not to shiver. Why is he touching me like that? I swallow, and try to keep as still as possible. Axel leans over me and I hear him rattling the chains. He unbuckles them, and hooks his arms under me, lifting me off the ground. I barely have the strength to open my eyes, but I do, staring up at him. His are heavy and sleepy as he looks down at me.

"What're you doing?"

He doesn't answer me. He just walks me over to his bed and pulls back the covers, putting me in. He grips my wrists, unchaining them. My chest swells with hope until he takes my hand, and pulls a set of cuffs out of his beside table. He raises my hand above my head, and cuffs it to the bed. He leaves the other free. Then he moves down to my feet, and he untangles them from the chains.

I watch with complete confusion as he walks around to the other side of the bed, and removes his shirt. I feel my lips part, and suddenly they feel dry. His body is amazing. He has a tattoo across the top of his back, and one down the side of his ribs. Otherwise, his skin is clean and perfect. He lowers his pants until he's wearing only his boxers, and he climbs into the bed beside me.

Why is he doing this?

"Axel?" I whisper.

"Hush," he orders, and moves closer to me, so our bodies are just touching.

I'm pretty sure he's lost his mind.

I wait, sure he's going to realize what he's done and throw me out, but instead, his breathing becomes deep, and I realize he's drifting off to sleep. The moonlight from the window behind his bed shines in, illuminating him, and he looks so breathtaking it makes my heart ache for him. He's beautiful in the kind of way most people aren't. His beauty is dark and broken.

I feel my eyes growing heavy, and I fight to stay awake, scared to fall asleep next to a man who I know hates me. I can't fight it, though. After days of being on the hard floor, the soft mattress is heaven. It's those little things you take for granted, and sooner than I know, my eyes are closed, and my own breathing is becoming shallow. I yawn, and find myself sinking into the pillows. Maybe I'll give in…just for one night.

~*~*~*~

MEADOW

"Fucking stop!"

I hear the pained bellow beside me, and I jerk awake. What the hell? I feel Axel's body thrash beside me, and I turn my head to see him convulsing in the bed. His jaw is tight, and his body is covered in sweat. His back is arching, and…oh…oh my God. He's got his fingers wrapped around his cock, and he's stroking, hard and fast.

"Don't," he growls. "Don't cry, I'm fuckin' sorry…"

His hand works faster, and my eyes widen. I can't move my eyes from the thick length in his hand. He has four piercings going around the base

83

of his head, and his shaft is thick, long, and straining. I bite my lip, but his cries have my eyes moving back up to his face. Something is destroying him. A dream. Something dark inside his soul.

"Don't make her," he roars. "Don't...oh God..."

"Axel?" I whisper softly, knowing that you're really not supposed to wake people during a nightmare.

I reach over with my free hand, and I place it on his chest. His skin is smooth and bronze, and it's covered in a fine layer of sweat. His hair is stuck to his forehead, and I can hear his teeth grinding, he's got his jaw so tense. His hand works faster, and the muscles in his arms strain and pull. I run my hand over his chest, feeling the tension there.

"Axel," I whisper again.

He groans when my fingers glide over his skin again. His hand is jerking so hard that his body is bowing.

"Axel," I say, a little louder.

"Fight me, goddammit, fight," he moans throatily.

Fight? What is he dreaming about that would involve fighting and...sex? I hate to think of the reasons why he might be so traumatized, and I know, whatever it is, it's not simple. I can see it in his eyes when he looks at me. He's empty. I move my hand down his belly further, and he groans deeper. "Yes, oh, God, yes."

I clench my legs together, and guilt swells in my chest. He's having a nightmare, I should be waking him up, not touching him...but it seems to soothe him. His body isn't rigid anymore, and his hand has slowed down. I move my hand in a small circle over his belly, feeling the hard bulges of muscles beneath my palm. His body relaxes even further.

"Please," he rasps.

Is he awake? I peer over, and see his eyes are still closed. I slide my hand further down, biting my lip as I feel his hand graze mine. I also catch a feel of the silky head of his cock sliding past my hand as he slowly jerks it. Guilt swells in me again, and I shake my head, pulling my hand back. What the hell am I doing? What sort of sick am I?

Axel's hand lashes out suddenly, and he takes my wrist, pulling my hand back. I flinch, and struggle against him.

"Yes," he rasps. "Fight me."

Is he still asleep? I don't know. I can't tell. I pull my hand again, and he groans. He likes me fighting him. I feel a bolt of pleasure shoot right into my pussy at the thought of that. I don't understand it, and I'm not even sure I want to. I can't face that I might be as crazy fucked up as this man is. He tugs my hand toward his cock, and I squirm beside him.

"God, yes," he says with a ragged breath.

He puts my hand against his cock, and I feel the pulsing length against my fingers. It's rock-hard and warm from his own hand working it. He twists my wrist, and places my hand around his cock. I curl my fingers around the length, and I squeeze. He hisses, and his back arches. Oh God. I shouldn't be doing this. What if he's still asleep? That would make me twisted…

Wouldn't it?

He wraps his hand around mine, and he begins stroking, up and down, using both our hands. The pulsing between my legs is verging on being painful, and I so desperately want to release the pressure. Axel begins moving our hands fast, and his back starts arching again. I smother a moan as his cock tightens in my hand.

"Fuck, oh God, fuck," he roars as the first spurt of his release hits his belly. I watch the white strands settle there, and more pleasure shoots to my groin. I squeeze and then release, and a warm trickle slides down my hand.

God, this is so wrong. So wrong.

When I feel Axel's cock beginning to soften, I try to move my hand but his grip tightens. Oh God…he's awake?

"Axel?" I whisper.

He doesn't answer me, and it's then I notice his breathing is deeper again. Oh. My. God. He's asleep. He's…not…awake. I try to gently pull my hand away, but he won't let it go. He moves our hands off his cock and up onto his chest, and there he holds my hand, refusing to release me. I realize it's comforting him somehow.

So I close my eyes, and I let him keep it.

CHAPTER 8

AXEL

I'll haunt you right until the end, you'll never escape me, my friend.

I shift, and groan. That's when I feel the warm flesh in my hand. I open my eyes, and turn my head to see Meadow cuffed to my bed. I've got her hand firmly in mine, and it's pressed to my chest. What. The. Fuck? I slowly uncurl my fingers, and she groans, turning her head and letting her lips part with sleep. She's so fuckin' perfect.

I move my hand, and it swipes through something damp. My heart stammers and I look down to see a damp patch of seamen on my belly. What…the…hell? I move quickly after that, jerking out of the bed and stumbling as I land incorrectly and go crashing into the bedside table. Where are my fuckin' pants? Oh fuck. I had a nightmare. I put her in my bed, and I had a nightmare. Fuck…I came on her.

I storm into the bathroom, but not before glimpsing her on the bed, eyes open, watching me. Nothing is showing on her face: it's blank and emotionless. Maybe she was asleep when…it…happened? I glare at her, and then I slam the bathroom door, and start shoving things off the counter, sending them smashing onto the floor.

What the fuck is wrong with me?

I grip the sink and drop my head, panting. Why the fuck would I pull her onto the bed? Why the fuck would I do something so stupid? God, I was probably high. I don't remember how last night went down. I went out, I had a few drinks, a joint, and then I woke up with her in my bed. Fuck. I lift my hands and tangle my fingers in my hair and pull. The sharp pain snaps me back into reality.

No more.

~*~*~*~

MEADOW

I tuck my knees up to my chest and peer at the bathroom door, wondering what he's breaking in there. I've heard things smashing, I've heard him cursing, and then it all fell silent. Did he realize what he did? Did he remember? It's obviously affecting him quite badly, so maybe it's best if I play dumb, and don't let him know that I was fully aware of what happened.

I hear the bathroom door creak open, and he walks out, bare-chested. I feel my eyes widen slightly, hating that I want to look, yet not being able to stop myself. I slowly move my eyes down his body, then back up again until I meet his seething eyes. He's angry, again. It's nothing new to me, but I thought…I guess I'd hoped…God, what was I hoping? That he would wake up after last night and feel something? I'm a fool. That was never going to happen.

"Thank you for letting me sleep in your bed," I say meekly. "I had the best sleep. I didn't move all night."

It's a lie, but I see instant relief flood his features. He replaces it quickly and nods his head harshly before leaning down and taking hold of a black shirt. Then he turns and storms out the door, slamming it loudly. Well, that went well. I lean back against the headboard and pull the cuffs. They're not going anywhere, and neither am I. Sighing, I close my eyes and lean my head back.

I just want answers. I need to know what happened to my dad that day. I need to know why Axel did it, and I need to know what the information on that USB stick is. I can't keep running around in circles, but until Axel is willing to speak to me, I just can't give in. So I'll continue to sit here, cold, starving, and empty while I wait for one of us to break.

It's not going to be me.

It's never me.

CHAPTER 9

MEADOW

Your words won't break me, for you will never take me.

I hear the door creak, and I snap my head up. I blink rapidly, trying to get the sleep blur from my vision. I see Colt step in, and his eyes dart around the room before falling on me. He gives me a sympathetic smile, and slowly walks in, stopping at the end of the bed.

My arm is aching from being cuffed upright, and I want so desperately to move it. I need to stretch.

"Hey, Meadow," he says, leaning his hip against the post.

"Colt," I mutter in an angry tone.

He sighs, and sits on the bed, staring over at me, his eyes pleading to understand. "He's my boss, I had to do it. If he found out I'd employed you and didn't tell him, he would have killed me. You don't know what Axel is like."

"That's where you're wrong, Colt," I growl, my voice seething out through clenched teeth. "I do know what Axel is like."

"Then you understand that…"

I cut him off by sticking my free hand up. "I don't need your apologies, and need for my forgiveness. In the end, I'm here, and there's nothing I can do about that."

"I've tried to talk to him," he says, giving a weak smile. "He won't fuckin' budge."

"He wants something I have, and until I give it to him, he won't let me go."

His eyes harden a little, and he mutters, "Then give him what he wants…"

"It's not that easy," I say, staring at my lap and the one free hand that's moving in tiny circles over my thigh.

"Why?"

I snap my eyes up, and stiffen. "Why is none of your business."

He sighs angrily, and his eyes narrow. "Is there really any need to be like this? Fuck, Meadow, I said I was sorry."

"I thought I'd finally found a friend, Colt," I say, hearing the pitiful cracking in my own voice.

He shuffles closer. "You did, but…this club is all I have. Axel comes first. When all this is sorted, we can be friends again. I like you Meadow, and I don't wanna see any harm come to you."

I turn my eyes away because they're welling with tears, and I want no one to see any weakness from me. "Just leave, Colt," I whisper.

He's silent a moment, and then he slides a power bar toward me. "He doesn't know I gave you this. Give him what he wants Meadow, and free yourself."

Then he gets up and walks out, shutting the door quietly. I blink rapidly, trying to remove the tears so stubbornly welling under my eyelids. I hate that I'm crying. I've been through so much, and I didn't cry, but now I'm breaking, slowly falling to pieces. I pick up the power bar, and my heart swells with gratitude. It overpowers the anger I hold toward Colt.

I unwrap the packet, and I take a bite.

Who knows when I'll get fed again.

~*~*~*~

AXEL

"Where are they?" I bark, slamming my drink down onto the countertop in the bar.

Cobra shrugs, and Jax gives me a skeptical look. "No idea, but they're around."

"They know we've got her, and they're goin' to try and find a way to make sure they get their hands on her before the USB is given."

Cobra turns, staring at me with an intense expression. "Then we need to get that information from her."

"I don't fuckin' know how to get it from her. She's more goddamned stubborn than anyone I've ever met."

"Is there anyone close to her? Someone we can use against her?" Jax asks, lighting a joint and inhaling for a long, dragging moment.

"No, her parents are dead, she has no siblings."

Cobra scratches his chin. "There's gotta be something that'll break her."

And just like that, it hits me.

Fuck.

It's me.

I've been living in some stupid fantasy where I thought I could break her with my cruel acts, but all along, she's been hanging on to the one thing that she needs before she'll hand that information over. She's holding hope that there's something inside me she can save. She's hoping that there's some way she can understand what happened. So, the answer is simple, really.

I have to break her. I have to be the one to send her over the edge.

I have to install a fear so great in her that she can't turn me away.

I have to show her how cold I really am.

MEADOW

I'm starving.

There's just nothing I can focus on right now, I'm so hungry. All I want and need is food. I haven't eaten since Colt gave me a power bar this morning, and I'm beginning to feel the affects of not being fed. My body is weak, my head is pounding, and I'm utterly exhausted, even though I haven't moved. My eyes are heavy, and I feel lethargic. My nose is throbbing, and nothing I do will take the pain away.

This can't go on.

"Decided to change your mind yet?"

I hear Axel's voice, and I lift my head to see him standing in the doorway. He's got a cigarette in his hand, and an empty look on his face.

"No," I croak.

"I will win this battle, Meadow."

I blink, trying to stop my eyes from burning. "I need food, Axel. Please."

He stares down at me, as if he didn't hear me.

"Did you hear me?" I hiss. "I need food."

He crosses his arms, looking at me expectantly. He wants me to give him something in return. The USB. Anger swells in my chest, and desperation takes over. I yank the chains, and I begin screaming as loudly as I can muster. "Just give me some food, goddamn you, just give me some fucking food!"

I thrash my head from side to side, squirming in my chains. Axel is beside me in a split second, clutching my arms tightly. "Enough," he warns.

I don't stop.

I kick out at him, and my foot connects with his thigh, hard. He groans and drops to his knees, and I lash out again, hitting him right in the face. I hear the sound of his nose popping, and his roar of pain as blood spurts out and runs down his face. It's still swollen and tender from when I hit it a week ago. I guess now he most certainly knows how it feels. He launches himself off the floor just as my foot lashes out again, and he tangles his hands into my hair, yanking me close to him.

"So help me God, if you ever fuckin' kick me again I'll make you pay in the worst possible way you can imagine. You think of your worst nightmare, and I'll make that look mild."

"I hate you," I spit. "I cared about you. Once, you were everything to me. I adored you. I trusted you. How can you do this to me?"

I'm hysterical, and I know I'll regret this outburst tomorrow, but right now there's nothing I can do to stop it. I just can't. He needs to know what he's doing to me. He needs to know he's ruining me. He's destroying everything I've fought so hard to create. He's breaking me. Slowly, but surely, he's tearing me to pieces.

"You're nothing to me," he thunders, and I feel the warm drops of his blood drip onto my cheek. "Nothing!"

That hurts. It hurts more than I'm willing to admit. Letting me go, he takes two steps back, and I look up at the monster that was once someone I loved. He's got blood pouring down his face, and his eyes are red and glassy with rage and emotion. His fists are clenched so tightly they're going white. I can see his hate, and it's a hate I don't understand. My father might have hurt him, but I didn't…I was just an innocent child who adored someone that came into her life.

"Why me?" I croak, slumping down. "I didn't do anything to you, Axel. In all this, I was the one constant in your life, the one person who didn't let you down."

"You're wrong," he growls. "You did let me down."

I shake my head, feeling a tear slide down my cheek. "How?"

He turns without answering me, and he walks to the door. When he gets to it, he looks back at me, and in a broken, angry voice, he growls, "You stopped trusting me, and you made me the enemy."

CHAPTER 10

MEADOW

Heroes can only save those who need them. I don't need them.

I'm sitting in that same position he left me in, unable to make my body move. I don't know what there is to say. I stopped trusting him...I made him the enemy. I close my eyes, and I try to think back, to think of everything that went down, and it hits me like a brick to the face. I did make him the enemy, and I stopped trusting him, because I ran. I never stopped to let him explain; I just ran.

I stopped believing in him because my father did.

"Axel said to give you this."

I look up to see a girl standing at the door. She's got blonde hair, big boobs, and a curvaceous body that most women would die for. The tiny skirt she's wearing is riding high up over her backside, and the red top squeezes tightly against her breasts. I wonder who she is? I watch with curiosity as she walks in and places the food on the table beside me.

"Who are you?" I ask, my voice coming out scratchy and pathetically broken.

"April, and you're Meadow," she says, and then I'm sure I here her murmur "his Cricket" under her breath.

"Why did he send you in?"

She gives me a hard look, placing her hands on her hips. "Because he can't stand the sight of you."

My heart feels like someone stabbed it, and I feel sick. How do you pick who is wrong and who is right in a situation such as this? He killed my father, so I should hate him. I gave up on him, so he should hate me.

"Axel isn't the kind of man you want to mess with. I would strongly suggest you give him what he wants, and run as far away as you can."

I stare at her for a long moment. "What would you know about me, Axel, or this situation?" I snap defensively.

How dare she thinks she knows what's best.

"Because I've been fucking Axel for six years now, and he's all kinds of fucked up. You have no idea what lurks in the darkness. None. He doesn't need someone like you in his life; you'd never understand his level of sick. You're just a constant reminder of why he's so fucked up to begin with."

Me? What would I have to do with it?

"You don't know what you're talking about," I say, but my voice wobbles.

"I know more than you think, Cricket," she breathes, and even that sounds like a snarl.

She doesn't give me a chance to answer. She just turns and walks out. I stare at the door for a long moment, mulling over what she said. What would I have to do with any of this? I never did anything to anyone. I was just in the wrong place at the wrong time, and sent on a mission I really didn't deserve.

I turn my eyes to the tray of food she placed down, and, regardless of my anxious stomach, I'm starving. I lift the tray off, and see some sort of stir-fry made with plenty of beef, vegetables and noodles. I lift the fork, and I begin gulping the food down, hardly chewing. I'm so hungry it's embarrassing how I'm eating right now, but there's nothing I can do to stop the way my hands tremble with need, or how my body desperately needs to be fed.

Mid way through, I feel my throat beginning to tickle. I cough, and lift a glass of water and swallow it. Maybe it was too hot. The tickle increases, sending warmth up into my cheeks. What is happening? I take another sip of water, but the warm feeling begins increasing, and my throat starts to itch. I realize what's happening then…I'm having an allergic reaction. I gasp for air, and panic fills me. I stare down at the food. I can't see any seafood in it, but that's the only thing that causes this kind of reaction in me.

"This is your last chance," a voice comes from behind me, and I spin to see Axel walking in, a hard expression on his face. "You tell me, or I will let you die."

"You'd let me die?" I whisper, feeling my throat beginning to swell and close in.

"No point in lettin' you live if you're never goin' to tell me where that USB is, so yeah, I'd let you fuckin' die."

I feel panic begin to swell in my chest as breathing becomes more difficult. I gasp for air, and grip my throat, wrapping my fingers around it and trying to rub. I'm highly allergic to seafood, and Axel knows this. He knows because he helped me when I was ten years old, and I had my first reaction.

"Y-y-y-you put seafood in there, didn't you?" I rasp.

His expression doesn't change. "I had to get it out of you, one way or another."

I begin to wheeze, and I feel my breathing decreasing. I'll die. If he doesn't give me a shot, I'll die. I look up at him with tears in my eyes, and I see a moment of hesitation in his. It's there, a moment where his eyes shifted.

"Why…why would you do this to me? I never did anything to you," I wheeze, rubbing my throat. "I adored you. I loved you. I…you saved my life. Why would you do this? Why?"

"Because there's nothing left inside me. Now give me the location, or I won't give you this shot."

He lifts his shirt and pulls out the shot I know I need. He must have got it from my bag, I always carry one with me. My vision begins to blur, and I begin gasping for air so badly it sounds like I'm having a coughing fit, only with air. I don't want to die. I'm tired of the fight. He'll never let me go, and he'll never tell me what went down that day. It's not worth dying over, and it's not worth this pain.

I drop my head, and I gasp through wheezing breaths. "It's in a bank downtown, in a locker."

Then, my vision swims, and my world begins to turn. I collapse down, and I'm sure in those moments before I pass out that I hear Axel say the same words he said to me when I jumped off that bridge.

"Keep breathing, Cricket. Don't close your eyes."

I know it's only a dream though. The monster inside him is far stronger

99

than the man trapped behind it.

~*~*~*~

MEADOW

"Meadow, where you at, girl?"

I hear Axel's voice, and I skip into the living room to see him standing with a great big grin on his face. "Guess what?"

"What?" I cry, running over and leaping into his arms.

He swings me around, and I laugh loudly, my blonde hair flicking in a circle as we move.

"I got a new bike!"

"For real?" I squeal. "Show me."

He nods his head towards the front door, and I run out into the yard to see the shiny red Harley-Davidson in the driveway. I groan in awe and walk out, running my fingers over the candy-apple paint. "It's a Super Glide."

"Your favorite." He grins, putting his hand on the top of my head and resting it there.

"Are we taking it for a ride?"

He beams. "Hell yeah we are, get your helmet."

I run inside, and in a split second I have a helmet on and my riding boots. Axel gets on the bike, and I climb on behind him. He starts the powerful machine, and we speed off down the road.

He takes me around all the good bends, and up to the local lighthouse before stopping at our favorite lake. I jump off, and run toward the water.

When I reach it, I lean down and run my fingers through the cool liquid.

"So, what'd you think?"

I spin toward him, and grin. "It's amazing!"

He drops down onto the grass, and pats it. I slump down beside him.

"You know, you're the only one I wanted to share it with," he says, smiling down at me.

I bump my shoulder into his. "That's because I'm your number-one girl, right?"

He laughs, and wraps an arm around my shoulder. "You'll always be my number-one girl, Cricket. I'll always be here for you."

"Meadow, wake up."

I hear Axel's voice, and I feel my body coming to. Everything hurts, and my head is pounding. I swallow. My throat is so dry that I can't get enough saliva to coat it, so it burns.

I flutter my eyelids open, and see Axel staring at me. He's got a needle in one hand, and a glass of water in another. I realize then I'm soaking wet. He must have been splashing me with it to try and bring me around.

I look up at him, and any sympathy I had for him is now gone.

I hate him.

"Get away from me," I croak, shifting into a sitting position.

He doesn't say anything. He just stares down at me.

"Get out...just get out of here...."

"I need that location, Meadow," he orders.

I lift my scathing eyes to meet his, and he flinches. "You're a no good piece of shit. I hate you. I hate everything about you. Go and die, Axel. You're nothing to me anymore. Now...GET THE FUCK OUT!"

He stares at me for the longest moment, and so much passes between us. Then he turns, and he walks out of the room without another word.

And I put a brick wall around my heart.

I can't feel like this any more.

It's time to end this.

CHAPTER 11

AXEL

Hatred be my friend, stay with me 'till the end.

I take another shot, but the burn doesn't help any. It only adds to the fucking fire in my chest. I tried to kill her. I put her life at risk just to get information. I went over the limit of crazy, and became a fucking psycho. And there was a moment there, just one fucking moment, when I thought she was dead…and something happened…inside me.

I was scared.

For a brief second, I felt fear.

I lift the glass, and I fill it with more of the amber liquid before shooting it back. When the fuck did I end up here? I don't have time to hate myself, and I certainly don't have time to feel a tiny spark of emotion for someone who despises me. I close my eyes, and tighten my grip on the bottle in my hand.

What the fuck am I doing?

~*~*~*~

MEADOW

"I have to go with you," I say in a monotone voice.

I don't look at Axel as he stands in front of me with Cobra and Jax by his side.

"Then let's go," he says, no emotion in his voice. He leans down, and uncuffs me. "I don't need to warn you about not running."

"I don't have any need to run. I just want this over with, so I never have to hear your name again. Better yet, so I never have to see your pathetic, cruel face," I spit, walking toward the door.

I don't see his reaction. I don't want to. I just want this over with.

I'm done imagining there's something good left in his cold heart. I hear Axel following me as I navigate my way down the halls and outside. The sun hits my face, and I immediately breathe it in. I've missed it. Axel takes my arm, and leads me to a big SUV. I climb in the back without a word.

Axel gets in the driver's side, and I catch him glancing at me in the mirror. I turn my face toward the window, and I don't look back until we pull up at the bank I gave him the name of. I get out of the car, and I walk inside. Axel is on my tail. I wait for ten minutes for a free person, and when a young lady calls me over, I walk with numb legs.

"I'm here to get the contents out of my safety box."

"Of course," she says, and begins the process.

Twenty minutes later, I have a tiny USB drive in my hand. I turn to Axel as soon as we get outside, and I shove it at his chest, hitting him with a thump.

"I hope this is everything you ever wanted, Axel. I'm done. I never want to see your face again."

I turn, and I take only one step when the shot rings out. I feel a thump against my leg, and I feel my body going down in slow motion, my body buckling beneath me. A burning pain radiates up my leg, and a ragged scream leaves my throat. Someone has shot me. Axel pulls out a gun, and suddenly Jax and Cobra are out of the SUV.

"Put her in the SUV," Axel orders.

Jax runs over to me, tucking his arms under my legs and lifting me up. He places me in the back of the SUV, and surprises me by pulling off his shirt and pressing it to my leg. He slides in beside me, keeping up the pressure. I scream, and wrap my fingers around my thigh, squeezing, as if it will take away the pain. It feels like someone has put a hot poker through my leg.

I hear guns exploding outside.

A moment later, Axel and Cobra leap into the car. Axel plants it, and the car lunges forward. The tires skid, and the car fishtails across the road. I hear another shot ring out, and the loud sound of a bullet hitting metal fills the car. My screaming has turned into sobbing, and I'm trying desperately to breathe through the pain.

"Who the fuck was that?" Jax asks, still pressing his hand to my leg.

"It was fuckin' Beast."

Who the hell is Beast?

"The fuck is he doin', shootin' her in the middle of the street?"

Axel growls, and slams his hand against the steering wheel. "It's a fuckin' warning. He wants that USB, and he'll do whatever he can to get it."

Cobra spins around in his seat. "How bad is it, Jax?"

"She's bleeding real good," Jax grunts.

Axel glances at me in the mirror. "You good?"

He's asking if I'm good?

I nod my head, not wanting to open my mouth. If I do, I'm afraid I'll start screaming again.

"Did it go right way through?" he asks Jax.

Jax lifts the shirt off my leg, and I wail loudly.

"No boss, it's just a graze, but he got her good and proper."

"Shit," Axel growls. "Let's get back, we can sort it there."

Sort it?

Sort what?

My head spins, and I feel my fingers slide out and take hold of the only thing close by: Jax's leg. He stares down at me in horror, but his eyes soften after a moment, and he places his hand over mine. I pant through my teeth, keeping them clenched tightly for as long as I can to stop myself from screaming. The car moves quickly, and I can hear Axel frantically talking to Cobra in the front of the car. The last thing I hear before darkness takes over, is Axel stating, "She needs a hospital."

~*~*~*~

MEADOW

My eyes open slowly, and I hear the constant sound of beeping beside me. I blink a few times, and as my vision clears I see the pale cream walls and the bright fluorescent lights above me. I'm in a hospital. That much I know.

I move my body slowly, and a dull thudding pain radiates through my thigh. I got shot. Someone shot me. I shake my head, trying to clear the dizziness that has settled there, and I open my eyes to see a nurse fluttering around with a machine beside me.

"Hi." She smiles when she sees my eyes open. "How are you feeling?"

"I…" I croak, with a dry, scratchy throat. "I'm okay."

"How's the pain?"

I shift again, and shake my head. "It's not too bad."

"You were very lucky. The doctors stitched you up, but they had to repair some damage done to your skin. It was quite messy."

God.

I nod. It's all I can do. I'm still in a mild state of shock. The nurse walks over and places a small device on my finger.

"There's a man waiting outside for you. He's not left."

My heart speeds up. Axel?

"A-A-Axel?" I whisper.

She nods. "Yes, that's him. He's been barking orders around, and not letting anyone but us in. He's quite an over-protective boyfriend, isn't he?"

"He's not my boyfriend," I say, shaking my head furiously.

"Oh, I just thought…"

"Why wasn't I informed she was awake?"

I hear the loud, dominating voice, and turn my head to see Axel standing at the doorway, wearing the same clothes he'd been wearing when all this went down. He'd really stayed with me? I chastise myself inside. Of course he isn't here because he cares, he's here because he doesn't want any bikers finding me before he can make sense of the situation.

But if he didn't care, just a little, he would have just let me go. He's got what he wants. Right?

Axel walks in and stops by the bed, staring down at me. His aqua eyes look tired and he's staring at me with a blank look that gives nothing away. "The pain?" he asks, his voice monotone.

"It's okay," I say in the same tone.

He nods, then lifts his head and looks at the nurse. "When can she go?"

She looks confused. "Well, we'd like to see her in for a few days so we can check the wound, and…"

"Is there antibiotics she can take away?"

She stammers. "Well yes."

"And are there instructions on cleaning the wound?"

"Yes, but…"

"Then we are going. You can't hold us here."

I gape at him. "Are you serious?" I snap. "Just leave me here, Axel. We both know you don't really want to take me."

He shoots daggers down at me, and I quickly close my mouth. "Don't tell me what I do and do not want, Cricket."

I turn my eyes away from him, and watch as he argues with the nurse. She finally gives in, and gets a doctor, whom he also argues with. In the end he gets his way, and I find myself dressed after a few hours and hobbling down the hall. Axel has a hand full of medications, and a hard, angry look on his face.

The minute we get outside, I turn to him. "Tell me one thing; why are you keeping me around when we both know you've got what you want?"

He doesn't answer. He just unlocks his car and shoves the door open, looking at me expectantly.

"Goddammit, Axel, can you at least do one thing for me, and answer my question?" I cry, crossing my arms.

He leans down, so we're nearly nose-to-nose. I can smell him, and something inside my body sparks to life. "I'm not going to let you get shot, no matter what I feel for you. Now, get in the fuckin' car."

I narrow my eyes at him, and I know he can see challenge in them. With a low rumble in his chest, he leans down and scoops me up, putting me in the car before slamming the door and turning away, walking around to the other side. When he climbs in, we sit quietly, neither of us saying anything for majority of the trip.

Finally, I get up the courage to be the first to break the ice.

"Who were they?"

He glances at me, and then stares at the road again. "The enemy."

"Really? That's all you're going to give me?"

He sighs with frustration. "They're someone who wants the information on that drive as much as I do. They're someone who has been chasing you for as long as I have, but I've constantly been saving your ass by stopping them. They want you as leverage now, and they'll do whatever they can to get to you."

He's been saving me?

I don't understand.

"You've…been saving me?"

His face hardens, and he doesn't answer me.

"Axel?" I push.

"What I did doesn't matter. All that matters is what we do now."

I growl, and turn and stare out the window. He refuses to budge. It doesn't matter what I do or say. Nothing will break down that wall he's built so high.

Nothing.

CHAPTER 12

AXEL

Don't try to break me, unless you're willing to take me.

"Put her back in the room, don't lock her up. If she runs, she's signing her own death certificate," I snarl, pushing Meadow toward Jax the minute we step inside the clubhouse. "Put everyone on full alert. We're on lockdown."

Jax nods, and Meadow glares at me. She got my point, and she got it loud and clear. She runs—she dies. It's that simple. I turn my eyes away from hers, and walk into my office where Cobra and Colt are waiting. "What do we know?" I ask, kicking a stool back and sitting down on it.

"We know they've been keeping track of her, my guess is through something that's person of hers, likely her phone. They knew we would be at that bank," Cobra says.

"Get her shit and burn it, destroy her phone. Lock this place down. I want no fuckers gettin' information in and out. No one leaves until I deal with this shit once and for all."

Cobra gives me a hesitant glance. "You sure you wanna do this, boss? You and Beast don't have a good history…"

"That's exactly why I need to fuckin' end him."

Cobra nods, and Colt stands. "What about Meadow? Is she in danger?"

"She ain't your concern, boy," I growl.

"Don't get on the defense, boss. You don't even fuckin' like her. I, however, do. And I don't want to see her shot down, because you can't pull your stubborn fuckin' head out of your ass."

I stand, lunging toward him and wrapping my fingers around his throat. He gasps, and struggles. "Who has the authority around here, boy?"

"You," he snarls.

"Then you know if you ever fuckin' speak to me like that again, I'll put you six feet under."

His jaw tightens, and he jerks himself from my grip. The boy has balls of steel; it's why I added him to my club. I got the world of respect for him, but that doesn't mean I won't put him in his place. He turns, and walks out of the room, slamming the door. I turn to Cobra, and he puts his hands up. "Don't look at me, boss. I want nothin' to do with what goes down between you and that girl, but whatever is there, it's fuckin' explosive."

"There ain't nothing between her and me except a whole world of hate."

Cobra doesn't look like he believes me, but he lifts his head in a nod and turns and leaves the room. Fuckin' hell. This is all going to a place I never wanted it to go.

Nothing is ever easy.

~*~*~*~

MEADOW

I groan in pain, and roll to my side. Axel let me sleep in his bed, God only knows why. I guess he felt sort of sorry for me. He's not in the bed, but it doesn't matter, I wouldn't be able to sleep even if he was. The ache in my leg is beyond anything I've ever felt, and nothing I can do seems to ease the pain. I just swallowed two pills, and I can only hope they kick in soon.

"If you're gonna fuckin' roll like that, then you really need to move from my bed," Axel says in a deep, husky voice, walking into the room and kicking off his shoes.

"Excuse me for getting shot," I snap.

"Doctor gave you drugs. Take em'."

"They don't fucking work," I bark, using my good leg to kick the sheets off. I shift and sit up, getting off the bed. "Is there somewhere else I can sleep?"

Axel snorts, gripping his shirt and lifting it over his head. "Sure, plenty of rooms. If you like sharing, and being fucked senseless."

Asshole.

I shake my head, and mumble a curse under my breath, followed by a, "Maybe I do."

"What's that?" he says, walking past me and into the bathroom.

I try to keep my eyes off his ass in those black jeans, but I can't turn my eyes away, I can't stop looking.

"I didn't say anything," I mutter, lying back down.

A moment later, I feel the bed dip beside me as Axel slides in. He turns and faces me, staring at me with that hard expression.

"What?" I ask.

"Do I need to cuff you?"

"Fuck you, Axel," I spit, rolling to my side, and taking the pressure off my leg.

He says nothing, and we lay there in silence. This is more than a little weird for me. The man hates me, yet he's letting me sleep in his bed. Why? I don't understand. If he hates me so much, why am I not on the floor? I sigh loudly, and close my eyes. I hate to admit it to myself, but something about having Axel beside me brings me great comfort.

~*~*~*~

MEADOW

"Fuck!"

I slowly come to, and the agonized cries that fill my ears bring me around quicker than usual. I turn my head to see Axel tossing in his sleep. His back is arched, and his body is rigid. His hand is in his boxers, and he's tugging angrily again. I feel my hands forming fists over and over again as I contemplate whether or not to touch him again. Will he shove me away? Or will he welcome me?

Something inside me screams that this is so wrong, but my body refuses to accept that. It begins to ache in places I didn't expect it to ache. The idea of him allowing me to touch him again has everything inside me clenching with a need I can't fully grasp. I feel guilt swell in my chest, and I know there's something so wrong with what I'm about to do, yet I can't stop myself from doing it.

I reach over, and I place my hand on his belly.

"Yes," he rasps, rolling to the side. "Yes."

His eyes are clenched shut, and his shoulders are so tight that tiny veins have broken out over his smooth, olive skin. I run my fingers up his bulging arm, and stop when I reach his neck. After a moment of hesitation, I slowly slide up, and stop when I reach the stubble on his cheek. I close my eyes, enjoying the feeling of having my hands on him. I slide my fingers down over his lips, and a throaty growl leaves them.

Then his hand lashes out, and he tangles his fingers in my hair. I cry out, and he pulls me closer. Pain shoots up my leg.

"Axel," I beg. "Stop."

Then his lips crash down over mine, and all my fight dissipates into nothing. The kiss begins rough, and the stubble on his jaw scrapes against my flesh, causing a whole new level of burn. A ragged moan leaves my lips, and I open to him, accepting his tongue as it invades my mouth, consuming me.

I've never felt something so amazing in my life.

His lips move with force for the longest moment, leaving me with a bruising feeling, but then they soften, and his kiss becomes gentle, almost affectionate. His tongue dances with mine, and his hand loosens in my hair. A pathetic little whimper leaves my throat, and I forget about the pain in my leg. All I can feel is him, and the way his hand moves against my belly.

He's still stroking his cock.

I groan desperately when his lips detach from mine, but instead they move down my neck and over my shoulder. Is he awake? Is this real? Or is this a dream?

His hand leaves his swollen, rigid cock and finds my hip. He jerks me closer until the hot flesh presses against my stomach. My pussy clenches, and I close my eyes, hating myself for wanting this with someone who's been so cruel.

This isn't how it's meant to go.

So why aren't I stopping it?

Am I so desperate? Have I got some sort of syndrome?

Axel's fingers slide over my panties, and I can't stop the whimper that escapes my slightly parted lips. He makes a rumbling sound, and I feel it vibrating from his chest through to mine. His fingers move again, running up the soft silk that's now damp with arousal. His cock is still lying heavily against my belly, and I'm still wondering if this is all really happening.

He presses his fingers firmly against my panties, right where my clit is, and I feel pleasure shoot through my pelvis and up my spine. I clench my teeth, despising myself for wanting him like this. His fingers move again, and more pleasure fills my body. Then he begins to rub, making small circles. It's a skilled move, too skilled, and I know he's awake. He's with me on this; no one is that talented while sleeping.

Now it's my choice to keep going, or to stop.

If I keep going, I'm giving him a part of myself that I'm not sure I'm willing to give. He confuses me. By day he's a monster, cold and deadly. I see nothing but darkness when I look into his eyes. But by night, he's just a man desperately seeking something to fix the hurts that haunt him. When he's lying against me like this, I know a part of him has found that something to fix the pain. But I know if I give myself to him, there's no going back for me.

I won't be able to let him go.

But for myself, and for everything I've fought for, I know the choice is already made. I can't give Axel that part of me until he's willing to give me a part of him. Something, anything to show me there's a piece of the man I once adored still there. Until he can give that to me, then I can't give him what it seems he's so desperately seeking. I reach down, and take hold of the hand that's gently massaging my clit through my panties.

He stills.

I turn my head away, and roll as quickly as possible away from him.

"I'm sorry, Axel," I whisper into the darkness. "But I can't give you what you want, because you won't give me what I want."

Then I get out of the bed, and I walk out, leaving him there.

Alone.

Again.

~*~*~*~

AXEL

This can't be fuckin' happening right now. It can't be going through my mind the way it is. She's not meant to be consuming me, she's not meant to fucking matter…so what's this aching feeling in my chest that won't leave whenever she's around? I close my eyes, and clench my fists by my side. What the fuck was I thinking, letting her in my bed?

I'm giving away everything I've fought hard to build.

I get out of the bed. It's been more nearly two hours, and I haven't moved since she walked out, spewing some bullshit about me not giving her what she wants. What the fuck does she want? She can't stand me, she's made that very clear, and she sure as shit doesn't trust me. What the fuck could she possibly want from me?

I aint' got nothing to give anyone, except a damned good time.

I get up from the bed, and I hear the music pounding from the living room. Fuckin' bastards never sleep. I get out, and don't bother to put a shirt on, then I tuck my gun in my jeans. I do nothing without it. I walk out and head down the hall. I catch a glimpse of two of the guys fucking the bartender against the pool table in the main dining area, and I roll my eyes. Those fuckers couldn't keep it in their pants if they tried.

When I step into the living room, the music is roaring, and the men are all laughing, smoking pot, and drinking some serious amounts of beer. They go a bit crazy during lockdown. The only thing they can do is get high, and fuck.

I move through the room, scanning them for Meadow. Unless she's hiding out somewhere, then she'll be in here.

Then I see her. She's on Colt's lap in the corner of the room, laughing hysterically at God knows what.

I see red.

And I don't know why.

My fists clench, and I feel my breathing quicken. What the fuck is she doin' on his lap, and what the fuck is he doin' with his hand up her fuckin' dress? I don't recognize my actions, because all I can see is his hand where it shouldn't be, and all I can hear is my heart thudding in my head. I pull out my gun and I lift it into the air, pulling the trigger. A loud, piercing boom fills the room, and everyone falls dead silent. The

118

only sound to be heard is the music.

Colt sees me, and his eyes widen. His hand moves quickly from Meadow's dress, and he grips her hips, lifting her and moving her off his lap. She's still giggling, and her eyes are glassy. She looks high. No one gets eyes like that off just alcohol. I turn to the room, and through clenched teeth, I snarl, "Who fuckin' gave her drugs?"

No one speaks.

"You fuckers. You filthy fuckin' scumbags. If I find out which of you fuckers gave her drugs, I'll put you in the motherfuckin' earth where you belong."

No one moves.

"Didn't give her nothin' boss, you know we don't run anymore more than weed through the club, and she didn't have any. I've been watching her," Cobra says, finally speaking.

I turn to Meadow. "Get the fuck over here, now."

"I didn't take drugs," she says, grinning.

"You're fuckin' lying."

She shakes her head. "I've never had alcohol before, this is my first time," she almost sings. "But I don't do drugs."

"Just get the fuck up."

She rolls her eyes, and gets to her feet, hobbling toward me. "Bossy," she mutters, leaning against a table.

"You fuckin' stupid? You don't know any of these guys!" I growl, gripping her shoulder, and pulling her out of the room.

"Probably. According to you I'm stupid, a waste of space, a loser…"

"Shut the fuck up, Meadow."

She snorts, but she moves, and lets me lead her into my room. I slam the door behind us, and turn to her. "What the hell is wrong with you?"

"Me?" she says, throwing her hands on her hips and pinning me with a determined gaze. "What the hell is wrong with you?"

"Why the fuck did you go out there and get drunk when your leg is the way it is?"

She shrugs. "Why did you put your hand on my pussy when you apparently hate me so much?"

I smirk at her. "Maybe I just needed to fuck."

She lashes out, taking hold of the lamp beside her, and yanking it harshly, hurling it at my head. I duck and snarl as it smashes into tiny pieces on my floor.

"What the fuck!"

"You're a piece of shit, Axel. Why do you have to treat me like this? Like I don't matter? Like none of this matters? Why come in there, and pull Colt away from me? I'm not yours. I don't belong to you. I'm nothing to you, isn't that what you've reminded me of so constantly?"

I walk over to her, taking hold of her shoulders and shaking her. "What do you want from me, Meadow?"

"I don't fucking know," she cries. "I just want something. I want to be let in, just a tiny bit. I want to know why you hate me so much. I want to know what I did wrong. I want to know how I can fix what's broken. I want to know what the fuck happened to you to make you this monster? I just want to understand, just a tiny bit. I want so much, I don't even know where to start, but for some sick, strange reason, more than anything, I want you, Axel."

I let go of her, and reel backwards.

What did she just say? She wants...me?

No fucking way.

I shake my head, and back up toward the door. "You're way out of your depth Meadow. You can't fix something as broken as me, and you sure as shit can't love it. I'm the meaning of damaged, and you're not going to put me back together, so stop fuckin' tryin'. Just stop."

Then I turn and charge out the door, slamming it so loudly I hear the wood crack.

~*~*~*

MEADOW

He doesn't speak to me for four days after that. He finds a way to avoid me. Even though I'm still sleeping in his room, I've not seen him. He's been sleeping somewhere else. He's avoiding me, and I hate him for that. If all this meant nothing, he'd have no reason to avoid me, but he is. I brood on it for too long, and finally I break. It's on the night of day four, and I've had a few drinks with Jax and Colt out at the main bar. I decide I'm tired of being ignored, and I head off to seek him out.

I know he's here.

My head spins as I walk down the halls, and my judgment is way off. I shouldn't be having a conversation with Axel when I can't control what comes out of my mouth. My mind isn't where it should be, and I know it, yet here I am, walking around like a desperate woman. I plant my hands against the wall as I navigate through the halls looking for him. I'm a little tipsy.

I know Axel well enough to know he won't be in his room, he'll be hiding in his office. I stumble as I move toward the end room, the one that has the glow of light underneath the door. I wrap my fingers around the handle when I reach it, and I gently open it. What I see inside that room changes something inside of me, and yet it puts a piece of the puzzle together for me, too.

Axel is standing against the wall. His eyes are closed and his jaw is tight. April is on her knees in front of him, her hands tied behind her back, her mouth moving over his cock. His hands are fisted in her hair, and she's crying out as he forces her mouth to slide up and down his shaft. She sobs as if she doesn't want to be doing it, but something tells me that's not the case.

I stare in fascination at the scene before me. Axel looks traumatized, like the very idea of this bothers him, yet he's doing it, he's tied her, and is enjoying her fight. Is that what he dreams about? Tying girls up and forcing them? A sick feeling swells in my stomach, and I begin to tremble. My foggy brain tries to process what I'm seeing in front of me. I step into the room before I can stop myself.

"Is this what you are now?" I whisper, feeling my voice trembling. "A rapist?"

His eyes snap open, and widen when they see me standing there, watching him in horror. He lets April's hair go, and he shoves her backward. She looks over at me, and her lips are swollen. She smirks, and I feel my own eyes widen. She likes it. She…likes it. I gasp, and

122

cover my mouth, shaking my head from side to side.

"What sort of twisted shit...oh, God..."

Axel takes hold of his jeans, yanking them up before leaning down and untying April's hands. "Leave," he orders her.

"You going to let this bitch finish you off? To be honest," she says, giving me a once over, "I don't think she's got it in her to please a man like you."

"Fuck off, April," Axel barks.

"Whatever," she mutters, shoving past me as she leaves the room.

"What is wrong with you?" I cry as soon as the door slams behind me.

"You wanted the real me," he growls, stalking across the room, and pulling a cigarette from the packet on a desk. "This is it."

"You rape women!"

He spins towards me, his eyes wild. He looks like heaven and hell all mixed in one perfect package right now. His eyes are blazing with rage, and his entire body is stiff and hard, but his lips are moist and soft, and his eyes are so blue with rage, they're breathtaking. He's everything that's perfect, and everything that's fucked up.

"What did you say?" he breathes.

"I said, you rape women?"

"I don't fucking rape anyone," he roars, slamming his fist down on the desk.

"Then you like the idea of raping them?"

He storms over toward me, but I take a wobbly step back.

"Don't you touch me, Axel. Don't you lay your hands upon me, not until you tell me what the hell I just saw."

"I don't need to explain anything to you. When are you going to get that?"

I reach out, and I shove at his chest, hard. "You do need to explain things to me. You owe me that."

"I owe you nothing," he roars.

"You killed my father. You owe me a goddamned explanation. You owe me the chance to move on without all this baggage."

"Your fucking father was a scum bag, and he deserved what he got."

I slap him, hard. He reels backward, and then gathers his footing and lunges towards me. His body hits mine with force, and sends me flying back into the nearby wall. Then he's pressed against me, one hand flat on my chest, holding me there, and the other above my head, pressing to the wall.

"So help me God, Meadow, you're walking a fine line."

"So hurt me, Axel," I yell. "Hurt me. Make me pay. Do whatever it is you feel the need to do. You're not going to answer me. You're not going to give me what I want. So go ahead. I don't care. Show me what you are. Show me what demons eat you inside. Nothing you do will bother me. You want to be sucked off by a girl who doesn't want it, huh? Is that what you need to make you feel good inside? Is that what I have to do to get some sort of emotion from you?"

I shove at his chest, and he takes a few steps back. Then I drop to my knees in front of him. I lash out, taking hold of his jeans and yanking them down. He grabs my hair, pulling my head back harshly. "Don't," he rasps.

"Try and stop me, Axel."

He keeps a firm grip in my hair, but I fight him. I take hold of his jeans, and I pull hard, bringing his hips towards me. Then I yank them down. A pained cry leaves his lips when I wrap one hand around his cock, and I tear the condom off before beginning to stroke. The piercings graze my fingers as I move my hands with hard, determined strokes.

"Stop..." he pants.

"But you want this," I cry, feeling tears well in my eyes. "You won't let me have you any other way. You want me to fight. You want my mouth on your cock, and you want me to hate it, isn't that right? Isn't that how this works? Well, I hate it, Axel, I fucking hate it."

Then I lower my head, and I wrap my lips around his cock, taking him deep with one movement. His pained hiss fills the room, and his hips buck, filling my mouth even further. Salty tears run down my face, and I can taste them as my head bobs up and down, swallowing him deep into the back of my throat. I choke on a sob as I wrap my fingers around the base of his cock, and begin stroking.

This is so fucked up.

So beautifully fucked up.

And I feel like I belong here, on the ground...like this...broken.

"Meadow," he practically chokes. "Stop."

"No," I cry, taking him deeper, sliding my hands down to cup his firm, warm balls.

I look up, and he's shaking his head from side to side, agony in his features. He's hurting. This is a situation he's been in before, and the idea of that has a mortified sob wrenching from my throat. I slide my hand back further, until I feel the soft flesh between his balls and his ass. I press in there, and his ragged cries grow louder.

"Fuck, please," he begs, tugging my head back.

I fight against him, and keep my mouth closed over his cock while pressing my finger into that soft skin. I feel his cock swell in my mouth, and with one final press he comes, with a gush that shoots into the back of my throat. Warm salty liquid fills my mouth, and his pained bellows fill the room. Tears burn my eyes as I take all of him, and then I let him go, slumping down onto the floor.

He doesn't look at me as he turns, and charges out of the room.

What the fuck did I just do?

Did I just break something that was already so broken?

CHAPTER 13

MEADOW

Jump my sweet, accept defeat.

My fingers tremble as I take hold of the door handle. I shove it open, and blink through the blurring in my vision. I need to find Axel. What I did back there...it was so cold...so heartless. I walk down the halls, and my head is spinning from the drugs that were clearly put in my drink earlier. I run into Jax in the hall, and his eyes are frantic. When he sees me, he storms over and grips my shoulders.

"Where the fuck is he?"

What.

"I don't..."

"Where the fuck is Axel?"

Oh God, he's gone.

"I don't...know..."

"He's gone, we're on lockdown, and he's gone. What the fuck happened?"

I ignore him as I step past his body, feeling everything in mine shaking. Where would Axel go? I move through the halls past people like a zombie, keeping my eyes fixed on the door. The minute I step out of it, I hear Colt's voice thunder through the night. "Meadow just left. Get her back, now!"

Even though my leg is still achy, I pick up into a run, heading for the gate. The moment I reach it, I launch upward, tangling my fingers through the wire. I haul my body up and over, scratching myself on broken bits of wire. I land with a thump on the other side, and I cry out, but I don't stop. I get to my feet and I begin to run along side of the road, heading for the bridge and the trees that lie beside it.

I need to find Axel.

I reach the bridge within five minutes, and I begin to cross it but skid to a halt when I see the shadowy form standing over the other side of the railings. Axel. My heart leaps into my throat. Is he going to kill himself? I force my legs to move, even though all they want to do is stay glued to the ground. I reach the railings, and wind begins whipping my hair across my face. I stare at him, and I see the pain in his features, but I know he's not going to hurt himself.

I can see it in his eyes.

So, I do the only thing I can think of. I climb over the railings, and stand beside him.

He turns, and his eyes widen slightly, but he says nothing.

"You know, jumping off… it helps. It gives you a sense of power, a sense of freedom. It used to scare me, but now, somehow, it soothes me. Jump with me, Axel."

I reach my hand out, and he turns, staring down at it with confusion in his gaze. I swallow as I peer down at the water below us. My entire body begins to tingle, and a feeling of fear fills my chest. It's terrifying being up here, but the moment you let go, that fear is replaced with relief. For a moment, just a moment, you feel free. I stare at my blank hand, wondering if he'll take it.

"You can trust me," I whisper. "I know I let you down once, but I won't do it again."

Just as I'm about to give up and pull it away, he reaches out, and his large fingers curl through mine.

We don't look at each other. We just step over the side.

Together.

~*~*~*~

MEADOW

The minute we begin to fall, I feel my heart leap into my throat, and fear course through my veins. It's an addictive feeling, one I'm growing accustomed to. The minute our bodies hit the water, and that all familiar sting radiates over my skin. I feel my heart begin to calm, and a sense of peace washes over me. I surface before Axel, but when he comes up, I hear his rough coughing.

I can see him beneath the moonlight, and I watch with need as his hair falls across his forehead, making him look so ridiculously perfect. He meets my gaze, and I'm really not sure what is going to come next. I hurt him. I pushed all his limits. I expect, more than anything, that he will open his mouth and spit curses at me, making me regret every second of what I did earlier.

Like I don't already regret it enough.

But he doesn't yell at me, or spit curses. No...he lunges towards me in the water, and his fingers curl around the back of my head. I gasp, but he smothers it quickly, by pressing his lips over mine. My entire body sinks

129

into him, and a contented sigh leaves my lips. He crushes his lips harder against mine, turning our kiss from demanding to desperate. I reach up and tangle my fingers into his hair, tugging him closer to me.

He begins pulling our bodies backward until we reach the bank. Wrenching his mouth from mine, he lifts me, and places my body on the soft grass. Moments later, he's beside me, laying me down, pressing his lips to my cool, wet cheeks. He snakes his tongue out, sliding it across and over my flesh before pressing his lips back against mine and kissing me once more. His free hand slides down my side, finding the hem of my shirt.

The moment I feel his fingers slide up underneath it, I groan. His fingers tickle my flesh as he moves them higher, finding the curve of my breasts. With a groan, he cups them, massaging them in his big palms. I whimper, and arch my back, not getting enough of what I need from him. What I've needed for so long. He is my undoing, and nothing I tell myself will change that.

I reach up, and slip my own hands under his shirt, finding his hard, wet flesh. I gently press my nails into his skin, and a ragged groan leaves his lips. He takes hold of my pants, and he yanks at them, pulling them down as he pulls his body away from mine. I moan as he moves lower, taking hold of my panties and tearing them off in one quick swipe. Then his hands are on my hips, and he's using his face to spread my legs, before his mouth finds my pussy.

I drop my head back into the grass, and I arch into him, mewling his name as he slides his tongue up my slit, and then circles it around my sensitive clit. I feel him nip at it with his teeth before removing a hand from my hip, and gently sliding a finger inside my damp opening. Oh,

God. Oh, yes. I cry out, and writhe beneath him as he moves his tongue faster in perfect rhythm with his finger.

I'm on the edge.

"Axel," I breathe. "Oh God."

He grunts against my flesh, and then his teeth close over my clit, and I come so hard I see white. My entire world is taken away from me for a second, and all I can hear are my own screams of pleasure. Before I've even come down from my orgasm, before my body has stopped shaking, he's over me, his hips between my legs, the rough material of his jeans pressing against my exposed clit.

"Fuck me," I beg, needing him inside me, needing to feel him pounding into my flesh.

"Fuck," he growls, reaching down between us, and yanking his jeans down. I feel the moment his cock is freed because the head spears against my opening, giving me a taste of what's to come.

"Now, Axel," I breathe. "Fuck. Me."

He reaches down by my side, and takes my hands, lifting them above my head. I squirm beneath him, loving that he's restraining me. His chest rumbles with want, and I know he likes it when I fight. So, I continue squirming. I continue tugging my hands in his. He moans, and then he jerks his hips forward, filling my pussy with his sweet, hard cock in one swift movement.

I scream. I can feel every inch of him inside me, and the burning pain that's shooting into my pelvis is exquisite. Axel hisses through clenched teeth, and he rotates his hips, not pulling out of me, but letting me feel all of him. Oh. Fuck. Yes.

He slowly slides his cock out, and then he plunges back in again, causing my body to slide up the grass just a little. God, I want to touch him, I want to put my hands on those bulging arms, I want to put my lips on his skin, I want to taste him, and feel every part of him.

"Let my hands go," I beg. "I want to touch you."

"No," he grunts, jerking his hips again, and driving his cock deeper.

"Please," I whimper, tugging my hands again.

"God," he growls, and I realize my fight is turning him on.

I decide, in that heated moment, it's turning me on too.

"Let me go," I plead, squirming beneath him.

"Stop movin', God, you know I fuckin' love it."

I tug hard, and one of my hands comes free. I reach up, and I shove my fingers into his hair, tugging his head back. "Let. Me. Go."

He lets off a ragged groan, and I watch the muscles in his neck work while his head is on this angle. I lift my head, and press my lips to the bulge in his throat, and he groans. His hips work faster, and I can feel his piercings rubbing every part inside my body. God, I want to come, I need to come. I haven't had a man fuck me like this before; so raw, so brutal, so completely fucked up.

"Axel," I murmur, "I need to come."

"Then come," he grunts, thrusting his hips harder. "Cricket, come for me."

Oh God, when he calls me Cricket...it tugs something deep inside. He rotates his hips again, and his jaw is tight and straining. He wants to come, too, but he's holding back. I feel myself tightening around him, and it seems, in the throes of passion, that I need something to take me over too. "R-r-restrain me," I rasp.

"What?" he chokes.

"Restrain me!" I cry out, arching into him.

He moves quickly, taking my hands again and shoving them painfully behind my back, which means they're under my and squashed against the grass. His lips crush down on mine, and like this, I can't move.

It's all I need. I come, and I come with force. My screams fill the night, and my body shakes uncontrollably.

Then Axel is pulling out of me, and jerking my body up.

His cock is in my mouth, and I can taste myself, and him, all mixed in one. I groan raggedly, and I take him as deep as I can.

"Fuck, Cricket," he bellows, as the first warm spurt of come hits my tongue.

I take all of him, relishing the taste of our arousal. He jerks his hips, fingers tangled in my hair, until there's nothing left. Then slowly, he slides his cock from my mouth, and presses my face against his belly. I can feel his muscles bulging against my cheeks. I take the moment that's been given to me, and I wrap my arms around him, holding him to me.

"Well, well, well, how fuckin' sweet."

I jerk back at the voice that has come from behind us in the darkness. Axel's entire body stiffens, and he's on his feet in a split second, jeans up, gun drawn. I scurry about for my pants, and I jerk them on before getting to my feet beside him. He takes my arm, and pulls me behind his

133

body.

"Fuckin' the daughter of the man you killed? That's low even for you, Axel. I bet she likes it when you make her fight, doesn't she?"

Axel growls, and his hand goes to his gun. "What the fuck are you doin' here, Beast?"

"I'm here to get what's mine. I believe she's right behind you."

"She's not yours, she's mine, and if you so much as take a step toward her, I'll blow your fuckin' brains out."

I peer around Axel to see a large man standing with a massive shotgun in his hands. He's huge, with a bald head, a long beard, and tattoos covering all of his skin. My eyes widen, and I step closer to Axel, suddenly needing to feel safe.

"I wonder what she'll look like on her knees with her hands tied behind her back, sucking a poor victim's cock. You'd like that, wouldn't you, Axel? Tell me, does she know all your dirty little secrets? Does she know what you did to them?"

Them?

"I did nothing," Axel roars, "you piece of shit."

"Now, now, Axel, don't lose your temper. We're just old friends talking."

"Three seconds, Beast," Axel warns.

I hear the cocking of a gun, and I stare around again to see Beast pointing the gun at Axel. My heart leaps into my throat, and I gasp.

"Step around him, girl, and come to me. Even if he shoots me, I'll make sure I blow his brains out before I go down. Come to me, and I won't hurt him."

I take a step around Axel.

"Don't fuckin' move, Meadow," he warns.

"Three seconds, and he's bloody chunks on the ground," Beast snarls. "One..."

I take another step.

"Meadow!" Axel growls.

"Two."

I rush toward Beast, just as he raises his gun. It takes me only a second to realize he's going to shoot Axel anyway, there's something in his eyes. I lift my fist, and I punch him hard in the throat. He makes a gagging sound, and stumbles backward. I hit him again, cutting off his air supply. He falls to the ground, and wheezes, panting for air. Axel turns his gun on him, and shoots him in the leg.

"Why don't you just kill me here and now?" Beast roars through heavy pants.

Axel takes my arm, and begins pulling me away. "Because you're going to suffer first. I'll be back for you, you fucking bastard."

Axel pulls me again, and we run up the bank and towards the road. The wind whips against my skin, and I feel my body trembling with cold. We don't say anything the entire way back to the compound; I don't even know why Axel left Beast there. It just gives me more confirmation that he needs to make Beast pay, and shooting him like that, with no fight, isn't the way he wants this to end.

That frightens me.

As soon as we step back into the compound, Axel turns to me, his eyes scanning my face.

"Where the hell did you learn to throat-punch?"

I meet his eyes dead on. "I've learned a lot. I've had a badass biker chasing me for over a year."

For the first time in the years since darkness consumed Axel's life, I see him smile.

And it's beautiful.

~*~*~*~

MEADOW

I sleep for two solid days after that, exhausted both physically and mentally. I can't function without rest, and Axel has given me what I need for showers, so I finally feel refreshed.

I wake on the morning of day three to the sun shining through and into my eyes. I groan and stretch, noticing that the pain in my leg has finally faded to nearly nothing. I peer around the empty room, and see the space beside me hasn't been slept in.

Which means Axel hasn't come back in here.

He's been avoiding me once again, and I won't lie and say I'm not frustrated by that. After what happened at the bridge the other night, I thought we might have broken some ice, but it turns out nothing has changed. He's still as angry as he was before, but I will give it to him—he's not snapping at me...as much. I close my eyes for a moment, knowing I should just leave, but also knowing that my heart isn't going to allow that.

I can't turn my back on him again.

I get out of the bed, stretching with a loud yawn. I ruffle about until I find a dress and some panties, and then I head out into the halls. It's quiet, which is unusual. I don't know where the guys are.

I run into April when I step into the kitchen. She's making herself some coffee. When she sees me, her eyes narrow and a scowl forms on her face.

"Well, well, I can't believe you're still hanging around."

I put a hand on my hip, and lean against the counter. "What would you have me do? Go out and get shot?"

She shrugs, and chews on a fingernail. "I really don't care what happens to you."

"Look," I say, walking over and taking a coffee cup. "I get it. I wouldn't like me, either. You're what he's had for many years, and I've come in, and suddenly he's not looking at you the same. That's not my fault. I didn't ask to be here any more than you want me here."

She narrows her eyes, and studies me. Then, she sighs. "I've always known I came second to you. Not even I'm that stupid."

"Axel doesn't like me, April."

"Do you honestly believe that?"

I turn to her, my eyes wide. "Do you have any idea how he's treated me in the past week?"

"Do you have any idea how he would have treated you if you were anyone else? Do you not think that if you weren't important, that he wouldn't have just shot you, instead of chasing you for over a year?"

I'd never thought of it like that. My heart flutters.

"He didn't kill me because he's known me since I was a young girl. It's got nothing to do with caring, or anything else."

She snorts. "If you say so, but I can tell you now, Axel looks at you like you're something different."

I shake my head. I can't believe it…not after everything Axel has said and done.

"So you're telling me he hasn't fucked you then?"

I feel my cheeks heat, and she snorts. "Exactly."

"That means nothing. Axel probably fucks half the women in this compound."

"No," she says, her eyes growing a touch sad. "I'm the only one."

Really? She's the only one?

"Why?"

She glances at the door for a second, before saying, "Because I let him fuck me the only way he knows how."

"Restrained?" I say in a small, timid voice.

"Restrained, and fighting. It was good…for a while…I thought it was just a fetish, but I quickly realized that it ran far deeper. I started digging, I overheard things, and I figured it out. Axel was abused. I don't know how, exactly, but when Beast took him for all those months, something bad happened. It fucked him up. Now, he needs to fuck women in a certain way to get off, it's imbedded in his head. He won't change who he is. I tried...I thought maybe I could be the one to save him, but then I heard him dreaming, and I knew there was only one person who could save Axel Wraithe."

"And that is?" I say, feeling my eyes grow wide.

"You."

I shake my head again. "Me?"

"You're something to him, even if he won't admit it. Don't give up on him. I'm a lot of things, hell, I'm probably what you'd call a whore, but I see something in Axel that can't be put back together by just anyone. It takes a special person, someone who knew what he was before all this. Don't walk away, not if you don't have to...I think he needs you."

She gives me a weak smile, and walks out of the room, leaving me standing there...confused. I thought April was just a cheap fuck for Axel, but I can see she actually cares about him, and I feel bad for her. Sometimes you just know you're not enough for someone, no matter how desperately you want to be.

I take my coffee cup, and I walk out, staring down the empty halls. My guess, from experience, is that they're at church, a bikers' weekly meeting that no one is allowed to be involved in, except them.

I tred slowly toward Axel's office, and I peer through the door when I open it. It's surprisingly neat, for a biker's office. I walk in, shutting the door quietly behind me. I walk over to his desk, and begin lifting papers and snooping. Don't judge; I'm a woman, and let's face it, we'd all think it, and most of us would do it. I open his top drawer, and the first thing I see there is a badge. A policeman's badge.

I lift the golden, heavy piece into my hand, and stare down at it. I don't really know a lot about Axel's family, but maybe his granddad or someone close to him was a cop? It would make sense.

I place the badge down, and I catch a glimpse of my USB right at the back of the drawer. Seriously? He just left it in a drawer. Okay, granted, most of his men would never dare enter this office the way I have...but still.

I lift the device, and stare down at it. This caused so much pain for me, yet it brought me here, and sometimes I wonder if that happened for a reason. I hear the door knob turn, and I spin around, gaping. Axel walks in, and when he sees me, his eyes widen. His mighty arms cross over his chest. "The fuck are you doin' in here?"

I could do one of two things in this situation: I could lie and stammer, and rush out of the room, or I could take April's advice, and I could push Axel, to see if there really is a chance for something between us. Seeing him standing at the door, his dark jeans hanging low on his hips, a tight black singlet stretched across his chest, makes me so damned wet I find myself squirming just looking at him.

I know what I want to do. I lift the USB into the air, and his eyes widen.

"You little...give me that, Meadow. Don't fuckin' start that bullshit with me. I refuse to chase you across the country again."

I can't help the smile that creeps across my face. Axel's eyes narrow with confusion, and I keep my eyes locked on his as I bite my lip, and move my hand around to my back, holding it tight. I see the moment when he catches on, because his eyes sparkle, and then his expression turns hungry. He begins walking toward me, and I walk backward, quickly.

He lunges when he gets around behind the desk, but I quickly dodge him. With a smirk and a growl, he stalks toward me until my back is against the nearest wall. He presses his hard, large body against mine, and I quickly tuck the USB deep down into my panties, placing it right between my butt cheeks. Axel grips my shoulders, and runs his hands down over my shoulders and down my arms, until he reaches my ass.

"You want it, biker? You gotta get it."

His eyes blaze, and he makes a throaty sound as his hand cups my ass cheeks, and he squeezes, lifting me off the ground before gyrating against me. I can feel the hard, firm denim rubbing against my pussy, and I whimper, pressing myself harder against the wall. Axel jerks my ass, and begins rotating me, moving his hips so the friction causes bolts of pleasure to shoot though my body.

"God," I whisper, dropping my head back.

"You want to be searched for that, Cricket? I'll fuckin' search you."

He spins my body around quickly, and slams me against the wall, pressing my cheek to the cool wood. His body presses against my ass, and his cock rides between my ass cheeks. I can feel his solid body moving over me, and I want to push myself against him, but the idea of letting him have all this control is doing crazy things to my sex drive.

"Hands above your head," he directs, taking my hands and lifting them high above my head.

"Now," he rumbles against my ear. "Spread your legs."

Biting my lip, I slowly spread my legs. Axel starts with his hands up near mine, and slowly he moves them down over my arms, making my skin break out into tiny goosebumps. When he reaches my shoulders, he squeezes them, before moving his hands around to my breasts. He cups them, and gently massages them, pinching my nipples through my soft, flimsy bra.

"Are you concealing anything in here?" he rasps into my ear.

"No, sir," I whisper.

He moves his hands down my sides, stopping to slide them over my stomach. He flattens his hand just over my belly button, and uses it to push me gently backwards, so he can take the opportunity to grind his cock against my ass once more. I let off a little squeak of pleasure, before he begins moving his hands down to my panties. He slides his fingers down my legs, until he reaches the hem of my dress. He lifts it up, and then proceeds to hooks his fingers through my panties.

"What about in here?"

"No…sir." I breathe, closing my eyes.

"You understand I have to check. It's the law."

"Yes sir."

He slips his fingers inside my panties, and runs one right down my damp slit, skimming my clit as he ventures lower.

"Spread your legs further," he orders in a husky tone.

I do as he asks, spreading them until they're a solid meter apart. He slides his finger down to my entrance, and then slips a finger inside. I cry out, slapping my hand against the wall. He thrusts his finger, and I feel my eyes roll. God, it feels so damned good.

"Are you gaining pleasure out of this?" he chastises.

"No sir," I croak.

"So you won't come if I continue this inspection?"

"No sir."

"If you do, I'm going to spank you, and then I'm going to cuff you."

I whimper as he thrusts his fingers again. I can feel how wet I am, and I know his fingers will be coated in my arousal. I'm on the edge, biting my lip so hard, trying desperately to stop the warm feeling that's rushing into my pussy. I need to come. Axel reaches his other hand around, and flicks my clit, and the flood gates open. I come all around him, whimpering his name and arching into him.

"Bad girl," he murmurs into my ear.

He slides his fingers from my damp depths, and raises them up, pressing them against my lips.

"Open," he orders.

I do as he asks, and he slips two fingers into my mouth. His fingers are big, and rough, and they taste like me. I suck on them, wrenching a ragged groan from his lips. He slips them from my lips, and I hear him shift about, then he takes my hands and lowers them, pulling them behind my back.

"I don't believe you're not concealing something. We need to continue this search while you're detained."

"I don't have anything," I protest.

"We'll see about that."

He takes me over to his desk, and he pushes my front down. My hands are cuffed behind my back. I feel his boots edge between my legs, and kick my feet apart, so I'm spread-eagled with my ass in the air. My heart picks up. The idea of playing a game like this with him excites me. I feel my throat constrict as I try to smother my moans of pleasure. I feel his hand run down my back, stopping at my ass. He cups it again, his fingers biting into my flesh.

"What about in here?"

Oh God.

No one has ever gone there.

"Answer me, girl," he orders, his voice hard, rough, and sexy as hell.

"No...no, there's nothing in there."

"You ever had someone touch you here?"

I squirm, and he chuckles softly. "A sweet virgin ass. Do you know what I want to do to you now?"

I shake my head, biting my lip. He leans down, putting his lips beside my ear. "I want to fuck you there. I want to slide my cock deep inside you until you scream my name."

I gasp, and turn my head, meeting his eyes.

"You want that, Cricket? Do you want me to put my cock in your sweet ass?"

"I do-do-don't..."

Smack!

His hand comes down over my ass cheek, and I squeal loudly.

"Answer me properly," he breathes. "Do you want my cock in your ass?"

I shake my head, confused. I don't know if I want him there. I've never had anyone there before, and the idea of having him fuck me there, kind of scares me.

"Is that a no?"

"That's a no…for now," I whisper.

He leans down again, and I can feel his warm breath against my ear. "You scared to say no to me, baby?"

I shake my head quickly.

"I think that's a lie."

Smack!

His hand slaps my bottom again. I mewl loudly, and push my ass back into his jeans. I feel his cock graze against me.

"Do I scare you, Cricket?"

"No, Axel," I say in a small, meek voice.

"Do you trust me?"

"No…Axel."

He stiffens behind me, and the room falls silent for a moment. I don't want to lie to him, because the truth is that I don't entirely trust him. After the things he did to me, I can't fully believe he won't do more. If I let go, if I believe that this is all perfect and dandy after one session, then I am an idiot. Axel has problems that run far too deep for a few good sex sessions to cure.

"Well," he says, his voice barely above a whisper, "you will."

I make a mmm sound with my lips, and he's silent a moment. I hear the sound of his belt buckle being undone, and then I hear his zipper. My body tightens in anticipation. I want him to fuck me like this. Restrained. A captive to him. He slowly removes my panties, and I hear the USB drop onto the floor. He doesn't move for it, instead he takes hold of the cuffs and pulls them, jerking my body up and into his.

"How do you want this? Rough and hard, or soft and slow?"

"Both," I purr, thrusting my ass back into his groin.

"I like a challenge."

He pushes me back down onto the desk, and then I feel him behind me, his cock pressing against my damp entrance. He takes hold of my hands and pulls them, all while slowly sliding his cock deep inside me. I make a strangled, pleasured sound as he buries himself to the hilt. Then he sits there, not moving, just letting me feel the fullness that is overwhelming my body right now.

"Do you like my dick rings, Cricket?" he growls.

"Y-y-yes," I moan. "Please, Axel, move..."

He laughs, and it's a deep, throaty sound. He slides his cock out of my eager depths, and then he plunges back in, quick and nasty. I cry out, throwing my head back and bucking against him. He drives into me like that three or four times, pulling out and plunging back in, then he slows, and begins lazily dragging his cock in and out. Then he stops.

I hiss, and squirm. "Why are you stopping?"

"You wanted both. I'm giving you both."

"Goddammit, Axel," I grind out between clenched teeth. "Fuck me, hard, fast, deep...make me come."

"That's more like it."

He pumps his hips, starting off with a slow, but firm rhythm, and then he picks up his pace until his balls are slapping against my ass, and the sounds coming from both of us sound more like animals in heat then two people fucking. He's grunting, and every now and then, my name slides from his lips. I'm screaming, and moaning, and squirming. Pleasure is swirling in my core, ready to erupt.

"Come on," he moans, his voice tight. "Come on, Cricket..."

It takes a few more thrusts, and I'm sent over that blissful edge. I scream his name as my body jerks with rush after rush of intense pleasure. Axel works me until I stop trembling, then he pulls out, repeating the same process as yesterday. He spins me around, lowering me, and then he thrusts his cock into my mouth.

"Fuck, suck it," he bellows. "Suck my dick."

God, hearing a man talk so dirty has my entire body warming for him again. I take all of him, swallowing him down, and relishing in the feeling of his cock swelling, before he spurts his release into my mouth. His groans fill the room, and I realize his fingers are tangled painfully in my hair as he uses my head to drive his thrusts. When he's done, he slowly pulls out, and stares down at me, his eyes wild.

"You look so fuckin' perfect down there, on your knees, lookin' up at me with those innocent-as-fuck eyes."

"I'm not innocent, Axel," I mumble, not taking my eyes from his.

"You are, Cricket. If you fucked me the way I need to be fucked, it'd break you."

I shake my head. "You don't know what would break me. Not even I know that."

He shakes his head, and pulls his jeans up, before leaning down and taking my arms, pulling me up. He turns me around, and uncuffs me. While his chest is pressed against my back, I think about how our sex continues to end...without him coming inside me. He has to come with his cock in my mouth, and curiosity has me blurting out, "Why don't you come in me, Axel?"

He stops moving behind me, and he's silent for a long moment.

"Because, Cricket, that's the kind of fucked up I am. I have never, nor will I ever, come inside a woman. I don't trust them enough. I refuse to give them that part of me."

He thinks coming inside me is a weakness.

My heart hurts just that much more for him.

~*~*~*~

AXEL

I stare down at her, sleeping, her brown hair fanning out against the pillow as she breathes softly. I lift my hand, and run my fingers through my hair, feeling like a weight is sitting heavily on my chest. I shouldn't be doing this. I'm playing with fire. A girl like her, she doesn't deserve scum like me. She deserves only the best, but I'm letting her get in, and that shouldn't be happening.

This isn't how this is meant to go down.

She'll never understand what kind of shit runs through my head. She'll never understand that the reason I don't come in her sweet depths is because I can't. Me showing that kind of weakness isn't something I've ever wanted to let myself do. I've never wanted to give a woman a moment where she sees I've lost my control. The only way I can find release is in her mouth. Seeing her kneel before me, it gives me a feeling of dominance, like I'm not weak, like I'm not completely fucked up.

I turn and walk from the room. I head back to my office, and slam the door behind me when I get in. I slump down in the chair, and stare at the desk. There's paper everywhere, because I bent her over it, and fucked her…hard. Damned hard. She liked it. She's got a dark side, and I don't want to delve into it, because then I'll let myself believe that maybe something can happen between us.

But it can't.

It won't.

"Yo, Pres," Cobra says, walking into the room. "How's things?"

I lift my eyes, and give him an intense expression. "Fuckin' great."

"Yeah, somehow I think you're pullin' my chain, boss. What's goin' on?"

"Nothin'," I grunt.

"Has it got something to do with how hard you just fucked Meadow in here?"

I snap my head up, and shoot daggers at him. "What the fuck did you say?"

149

"No offense meant, boss, but the entire club heard her screamin' your name."

Fuck.

Shit.

I put my head in my hands, and growl loudly. "This is fucked up."

"You two...a thing now?"

I jerk at his words, and begin shaking my head. "Fuck. No. I can't be...we can't be. Shit, I've gotten myself in deep, man, fuckin' deep."

"You care about her, boss?"

I can't answer that, because the answer is pointless. It makes no difference to how this has to end. Caring, or not caring, either way she has to go. She can't be here in all this fucked-up bullshit. It's not where a girl like her is meant to be. She's spent her life around lies, and she doesn't even know it. She lost her mom at an early age, and she lost her dad pretty soon after. She's been running since then, trying to protect something she doesn't even fully understand.

Hell, I bet the girl has never even been to a party.

And that shit is partly my fault. I can't keep holding her back. As soon as Beast has been dealt with, I'm letting her go. Hell, if there was a way I could let her go sooner, I would...

I stare down at my hands. There is one person who could take care of her until all this is sorted, but I don't know if she's willing to do it. I look up just as the door opens, and Colt comes in. I meet his gaze.

"Colt, I got somethin' for you to do."

He narrows his eyes, and crosses his big arms across his chest. "What's that? If it's got somethin' to do with hurtin' Meadow, you can forget it."

"Stop your bullshit, and listen to me. I need you to go into my office, and get my phone, scroll through until you find a number with the title Lady Matilda. Get it, dial it, tell her I'm bringing someone to see her tonight."

Colt raises his brows. "Lady Matilda?"

"Yeah," I grunt, turning and meeting Cobra's confused expression. "Lady Matilda."

~*~*~*~

MEADOW

My entire body is on fire. Everything I touch is sensitive. My lips are swollen, my breasts are full and achy, and my pussy is still damp from having Axel deep inside me. I feel my body shiver as I step underneath the shower, feeling the cool water wash down over my overheated body. If you asked me what the hell just went down in there, I'd tell you I have no idea, but it was fucking hot.

So damned hot.

I fill my palm with soap, rubbing my hands together before pressing my palms over my breasts, lathering them up. I keep thinking about Axel and why he won't allow himself to show that kind of pleasure to a woman. It's like he's keeping it so alpha, so male. Maybe he's afraid of getting one pregnant, and not being in the right place to deal with it—not that he even asked to use a condom. Thinking of that has my heart picking up a few paces. I hope he's clean...I mean...what if he's not?

God, what the hell was I thinking, just letting him screw me like that?

I push the thought from my mind, adding it to the many things I have to ask him while I'm here. I close my eyes, lathering my hair up, and I am taken back to the feeling of having his hands on me, his cock deep inside me, his lips on mine. My pussy clenches, and I find myself sliding my fingers down and over my sensitive nipples. A small moan escapes my lips as I pinch the hard buds, and then slip my fingers down lower, gently spreading my folds.

"If you're gonna put your fingers inside that sweet pussy, I'm watching, darlin'."

I jerk my head up, and see Axel standing at the bathroom door, wearing only a pair of faded black jeans. I move my fingers from my throbbing sex, and turn my eyes away quickly. "I was just...ah...washing..."

"That was some pretty fuckin' seductive washing. If you wash yourself like that every night, I'm not gettin' out of this shower."

I flush, and press my arm over my chest, hiding the fact that my nipples went from hard to so stiff they ache. A grin appears on his devastating face, and I want nothing more than to go over and wrap my arms around his neck, kissing him until we both can't breathe. But Axel doesn't just kiss. He doesn't peck. He doesn't hug. He fucks, and he fucks good, but that's where the connection lies. There is no affection.

My heart aches at that realization.

"Get outta there, and come and eat with me. We gotta talk, Cricket."

I feel my body tense, just slightly. Something is lying in his gaze, something like...sadness? No, Axel Wraithe doesn't get sad, so what could it be? Has something happened? Did they catch Beast? Am I able to go home? Do I even want to go home? My heart, which was before only filling my body with a dull ache, is now thudding.

I don't know if I can walk away.

"O-o-okay," I whisper.

His eyes search my face before he turns and walks out, leaving me standing there, confused. I quickly get out of the shower and dry myself, before throwing on a pair of shorts and a tank.

Then I walk out into his room. Axel is sitting at the office desk in the corner, and when I walk in, he looks up at me. He's got two sandwiches, and he slides one toward me. I take a seat next to him, and stare down at the food with no interest.

"So," he begins, his voice not giving away any emotion, "you know I got shit to deal with, and I can't keep my club on lockdown. I need to get out, and I need to finish this with Beast. I can't have you here while that shit goes down. It's club business, and it ain't safe for you here. I can't just let you go home, either, because you're in too much danger. Until I've sorted this, I'm sending you to stay with a very good friend of mine."

"What?" I say meekly, shaking my head. "I don't want to go and stay with someone I don't know, Axel."

His expression hardens just slightly, enough to push his authority. "You're not getting a choice, Cricket."

I skid my chair back, still shaking my head. "You can't choose how I live my life, Axel. I don't even have to be here. If you're done with me, then just send me home, but I'm not going to stay with someone I don't know. I do get a choice, because it's MY life. So if we're finished whatever the fuck it is we're doing here, I'll be on my way."

Axel is out of his chair before I can take one step toward the door. His fingers curl around my arm, and he spins me around. I stop, nearly nose to nose with him, and his eyes are telling me he's not happy with me deciding how this is going to go. Well, fuck him, he can't choose what I do with my life. If he wants to chase that no-good son-of-a-bitch across the countryside, that's up to him.

"Whatever the fuck we're doin' here," he breathes, "ain't done yet. And you'll do as you're told, because you're the one who made a choice to run with information that was never for you."

"To be clear, Axel, it was never for you, either. It was for Raide, and because of you I never got to get it to…"

"Raide is dead, Cricket," Axel snarls, cutting me off. "There is no Raide."

"What?" I squeak, perplexed.

"He's dead. Beast killed him. I'm the best option you have right now, because while that man is alive, you're not safe. If you're goin' to run again, and give me hell, then give me some warning, yeah? So I can make sure to give Lady Matilda a good set of chains."

"I hate you," I whisper, in a pained, broken voice.

"No darlin'," he murmurs, taking the back of my head in his large hand, and pulling me close. "You just hate that you can't walk away."

"You're wrong," I breathe. "I could walk away. You're just not giving me the chance."

His body flinches at my words, and he lets me go, stepping back. His stony expression returns, and he crosses his arms. "No, you're right, I'm not. I won't have your death on my hands. I don't need any more shit in my life. So you're goin', whether you like it or not. We clear?"

"Crystal," I spit.

"Good. Pack your things, we leave in an hour."

With that, he turns and walks out of the room. And I push the burning sensation forming under my eyelids back.

If this is what he wants…so be it.

CHAPTER 14

MEADOW

Your monsters excite me, let them ignite me.

The ride to this "Lady Matilda's" house is long, and draining. I sit on the back of Axel's bike, leaning up against the backrest and trying to take my mind off the fact that all this has gone downhill so quickly. One minute I'm beginning to feel like Axel and I are connecting, the next he's got me on the back of his bike, riding to the house of a woman I don't even know.

I was worried about safety, being that the club was on lockdown, but Cobra and Jax had managed to secure Beast's location before we went so we slipped away. It's now late afternoon, and the sun is dropping down over the horizon. We've been on the road for two hours, and my backside is numb from the lack of movement. Axel hasn't stopped, and something about his rigid position tells me he's not going to.

So I suck it up.

We ride for another half an hour before he finally turns down and old, well-worn driveway. We ride through thick trees, until we come into a clearing, with a large, wooden, two-story home sitting right in the middle. It's a faded white, with blue shutters, and a balcony running the entire length of the bottom. Out front is an old car, and a motorbike. Great. Is Lady Matilda someone's Old Lady?

Axel comes to a stop outside the large home, and I slide off the bike, groaning at the sudden rush of blood to my ass. I unbuckle my helmet, and put it on the back of the bike before taking my backpack, and slinging it over my shoulder. I stare at Axel as he looks up at the old house as if he's not seen it in a long time. Maybe this is his aunt? Or mother? I don't know.

"Come on," he says, walking toward the front steps without turning back to me.

I follow him with a grumble, and when we reach the front door, it swings open, revealing…oh…my…God. My mouth drops open, but I quickly close it, not wanting to seem rude. There in front of me…is the biggest…maybe even the prettiest…drag queen I've ever seen.

Lady Matilda is a drag queen.

Of course she is…or he…?

"Axel, sugar, well look at you," Lady Matilda purrs, placing her hands on Axel's cheeks, and looking at him with a soft expression.

"It's been a long time, Lady." He smiles.

"Too long, honeypot, too long. God, I've missed you. Come inside, tell me how you've been."

Axel turns to me, and I step out from beside him and stare up at Lady Matilda. She's tall, with thick yet elegant legs and a long, lean body. She has this golden hair that sits around her shoulders so perfectly I ponder for a moment how she does it. Her clothes are elegant and defined, and they make her look so…womanly. She's wearing what could likely be the nicest pair of flats I've ever seen, and her toenails are so perfectly manicured I'm in awe. Her make up is utterly amazing, like she's had it done professionally, only I have no doubt she did it herself.

"Well, I'll say," she breathes. "Isn't she gorgeous?"

Axel stares at me for a long moment before turning back to her. "Yeah, she is. Can we come in?"

"Of course you can, sugar." She smiles, and then stretches her hand out to me. "I'm Lady Matilda, but you can call me Lady. What's your name, sweet thing?"

"It's Meadow," I say, in a small, timid voice.

"Well, that's a darling name. Come in, let me get y'all something to eat."

I step inside her huge home after Axel, and peer around. Everything is decorated brightly. She has pale blue walls, with a dark blue lounge. Her kitchen is stark white, but she's got numerous pot plants, and pretty, colorful paintings filling the room to make it seem like someone threw up paint all through it. She leads us past the living area, and into a large dining hall with a long, wooden table. Again, with accessories that really do make you want to gag.

"Take a seat. I'll bring some iced tea."

Axel and I both sit, and I watch as she walks out of the room. Damn, she's huge but in such a feminine kind of way. I turn to Axel, and he gives me a weak smile.

"You're making me live with a drag queen?" I whisper.

He leans close. "That woman...she's the damned best thing that'll ever come into your life, Cricket. You need to trust me on that."

"How do you know her?" I ask.

His eyes go vacant, and he murmurs, "She helped me through some shit, a long time ago."

"Oh," I say, sitting back.

"Here we are," Lady says, walking back into the room with a bunch of glasses on a tray. I can hear the jingling of ice as she moves.

She places the tray down, then tucks a long, blonde strand of hair behind her ear. She sits down, and smiles at Axel. Her expression is warm toward him, her eyes are filled with love, and I can clearly see she adores him. Not in a sexual kind of way, but in the way a mother adores her child. She reaches over, and takes his hand, staring down at his thick rings.

"I heard you were the president now."

It's not a question, and the look she gives him is one of concern, as if she doesn't like to hear this kind of news. Almost as though...she's disappointed in him. He closes his hand over hers, and smiles at her. God, he's breathtaking when he smiles.

"I am, and it's all fine, Lady. Don't worry."

"You're so much better than all that, Axel."

"They're my family," he says stiffly.

"They're also the reason you don't smile right up to your eyes anymore."

I narrow my eyes, and stare at them. I know what she means by that, of course. Even when Axel smiles, it never reaches his eyes, nor is it ever a true smile. I wonder what happened? Why would she say something like that? Axel obviously gives her a look, because her eyes turn to me.

"And the girl knows nothing of your past," she says softly. "Where are

159

you from, sweetheart?"

"Nowhere important," I say, forcing a smile.

"How do you know Axel?"

I stare over at Axel, who's watching me with a curious expression.

"We were friends when I was younger. Well, he was my father's friend."

Lady Matilda's eyes narrow, and she turns to Axel. A moment of silence falls between them, and I can see she forces a smile on her face, but there's concern etched there, I can see it.

"Well then," she says. "I'm going to get us some of these delicious cookies I baked earlier, and you two can tell me what's going on. Axel, come and help your old friend."

I'm not stupid. She's calling him out of the room because she wants to chastise him. He gets up, and murmurs a "stay here" to me before following her out. Curiosity far outweighs my need to obey his orders, so I get to my feet and creep over to the doorway. I can hear their hushed whispers on the other side.

"She has no idea, does she?" Lady whispers.

"No, and she don't need to know yet. I'll tell her everything that needs to be told when the time is right."

"You can't keep lying to the girl. She's been through enough."

"Look, Lady, I just need you to take care of her for me. She's...she..."

"She what, sugar?" she pushes. "She means something to you?"

"No," he says quickly. "She means nothing to me! I'm just makin' sure she doesn't get killed, then she's goin' her own way."

I hear Lady tut at him, but I turn quickly, rushing back to my seat. My heart throbs as I lower myself down. I stare at the iced tea in front of me, and try to focus so I don't end up crying and making myself look weak. Of course I mean nothing to him. I should know that by now. The man tried to kill me to get information, for God's sake.

I hear the door creak, but I don't lift my eyes.

"Here we are," Lady says. "I made these fresh."

I lift my eyes to meet hers. She studies my face, and a knowing look crosses her features. I turn my eyes away quickly, and mumble a thank you before taking a cookie. Axel doesn't sit back down.

"I gotta run," he says, and I know his eyes are on me. "Lady, I'll come back as much as I can to check on her. If you have any problems at all, you call me. Meadow, walk outside with me."

It's not a question; it's an order. I get to my feet, and I follow him outside. As soon as we're on the front porch, he hands me a cell phone.

"I took yours. It's not safe to use. I put my number in here, along with Jax's, Colt's and Cobra's. If you can't get me, got to Cobra second. If you need somethin', just text or call. Lady will take care of you, and as soon as I've dealt with Beast, I'll come back and get you."

"And then you can send me on my way," I whisper, lifting my eyes and meeting his. "Don't pretend that I mean anything to you Axel, just go, do what you have to do. I don't care. I'll be fine here, and when you're done, I'll leave, and you'll never have to put up with me interfering in your life again."

I turn and walk toward the door.

"What the fuck is this about?"

I turn, and look at him. Then I repeat his words. "She means nothing to me. I'm just making sure she doesn't get killed, then I'm sending her on her way."

His eyes widen, but I don't give him the chance to say anything.

"Goodbye, Axel."

I step inside and slam the door, not waiting around to see if he has anything to say.

I hear his bike start up a minute later, and then it disappears down the road.

And my heart breaks just a little more.

CHAPTER 15

MEADOW

Take me, my sweet, let our two hearts meet.

"Are you hungry, sweetheart?" Lady says as I walk back into the house.

I look up at her, barely registering what she's saying. All I can think about is Axel. My heart aches, and I hate that I've let him get in so deep. When did I lose what I was fighting for? Lady Matilda walks over, placing a hand on my shoulder. Even with all her strange make-up, and her more-than-interesting look, she's gentle, and I need gentle right now.

"I don't know how I ended up here," I say in a small, timid voice.

"Sometimes we end up where we're meant to."

I shake my head, and let her lead me into the living area. I sit on one of her odd colored couches, and she takes a seat across from me. "You know, Axel is a hard man, but he's got something inside him that a lot of men don't have. He's got fierce loyalty to those he loves."

"He doesn't love me. He doesn't even like me," I say, staring down at my hands.

"But he does, love. He wouldn't have ridden all the way out here to keep you safe, if he didn't care what happened to you."

I look up, and meet her eyes. "I appreciate what you're doing here, Lady, I really do. But Axel and me...there's nothing there."

She smiles knowingly. "Love, don't give up on those that are broken. Because when put back together, they can be the most faithful lovers, but more, they can be the best and loyal friends."

I give her a weak smile. "So you've known Axel a while, then?"

She leans back against the chair, and her eyes soften again. "I have known him a solid five years. I have a soft spot for him. He's like my own son."

I feel my smile turn from weak to warm. She cares a lot about Axel, and I'm glad to know he has someone in his life who adores him the way she clearly does.

"So, you're not hungry then?" she says, snapping out of her moment.

"No, thank you, though."

"I imagine you just want to shower and rest?"

I nod, eagerly. "It's been a long few weeks."

"Of course. Come on up, I'll show you to the guestroom."

I follow her up a long, curved stairwell to a wide hall. We walk down, and stop at the second room on the right. She opens it, and I step in. It's got pale green walls, and a bed in the middle that's old and rustic, with dark green covers. There's a cream rug on the wooden floor, and a small, light pine desk in the corner on the left.

"It's very nice," I say gratefully.

"Make yourself at home. Anything you need, just help yourself. There's food downstairs, and I'm usually always around. The shower is down the hall to the left. I've put fresh towels in the cupboard for you. There's plenty of shampoo and soaps, so please use them."

I smile gratefully. "Thank you, Lady. I mean it."

She walks over, pulling me in for a hug. It's in that moment, that I'm reminded that she…is actually a he. But, that doesn't matter, the comfort she's giving me warms my heart. She is all woman, there's nothing masculine about her, and that gives me a sense of comfort. She pulls back, and smiles warmly down at me. "Get some rest. Goodnight, sugar."

"Goodnight, Lady."

AXEL

"Another," I growl to the bartender, and he slides me another shot.

I throw it back, slamming the shot glass down.

"Another."

"You sure, boss?" he asks, hesitantly pouring.

"You own this joint?" I hiss.

"No, boss."

"Then shut the fuck up."

He slides the drink over, and I shoot it back. The burn eases the aching in my chest. I hate that it aches—I fuckin' hate that she's gotten to me. The way she looked at me when I left, I felt like a dog. A fuckin' no good piece-of-shit.

"How's it going, Axel?"

I hear April's voice, and I lift my head and turn to see her slide onto the stool beside me.

"How does it look like it's goin'?"

"Bad day, then?" she mumbles.

"Somethin' like that."

She's silent a moment, and then she says, "Why don't you go back for her, if you're so hung up over it?"

I turn, and shoot daggers at her. "What did you say?"

She narrows her eyes, and her expression hardens. "Don't pretend with me, Axel. I've been around you long enough to know what sort of shit goes down in your head. You want her, you're just too fucking stupid to admit it. Quit being so pigheaded, and go back for her. I know she's waiting for you."

"You don't know shit," I growl, skidding the stool back. "And don't speak to me like that in my club again, or I'll toss you out on your ass."

I spin, and walk out of the room. I can't deal with these children tonight. I can't think of anything but her.

I start walking outside, and the minute the cool night air hits my face I breathe it in, and then ruin that by lighting a cigarette. My head is spinning, and I can feel my keys jingling in my pockets. I begin walking toward my bike, knowing what I'm going to do even before it fully registers.

I get to my bike, and throw my leg over it.

Then I start it, and pull out of the parking lot of the compound. I shouldn't be riding, I already know that, but I can't stop myself. I need to see her. I need to feel her surrounding me. I need all of her, and I can't deny that shit any longer.

I pick up the speed. She needs to know...she just needs to know that she's not nothing. If that's all I can give her, then I'll give it with all I am.

I ride until I reach Lady Matilda's driveway. I park the bike in the trees and get off, walking down. If she hears me pull up, I'll never be able to get in like I need to. My boots crunch on the gravel as I move.

When I reach the old home, I peer up at the only window with the light on. I know it's the guest room, and I know Meadow will be in there. I walk to the side of the house, and I take hold of the drain-pipe.

And I begin to climb.

CHAPTER 16

MEADOW

Sticks and stones may break my bones, but your love completes me.

I can't sleep. It doesn't matter what I do. I've tried a shower, I've tried to have a glass of warm milk, but nothing is working. All I can think about is Axel. Tonight he's haunting my mind, my thoughts, and nothing I can do is going to push him out. So I've decided to read as much as I can, trying to take my mind off it. I'm midway through a sappy romance that has me snorting more than it has me intrigued when I hear my window rattle.

I stiffen, and fear washes up my spine.

Is someone breaking in?

My lamp is only dull now, but my eyes are locked on the window trying to see what's outside. I should call out to Lady, but I can't make myself move. Fear is funny like that. You know you should run, but your body refuses to acknowledge that need, and freezes.

I'm sure for the longest moment I don't breathe, and when the window slides up, I let out a scream. I scurry off the bed, and crash into the nearby bedside table.

"Whoa, Cricket, it's just me."

Axel?

My heart is beating so loudly I can hardly hear anything else. I slowly lift myself off the floor to see Axel standing in front of the window. His eyes are slightly bloodshot, and I realize he's been drinking. What the hell did he ride out here drunk this late at night for? I open my mouth, but he shakes his head. Something in his eyes tells me he doesn't want me to speak and ruin whatever he's come out here for. So I don't.

He walks around the bed, and over to the door. He locks it before turning to me. I feel my body become aware of him. He looks gorgeous—not that there's ever a time he doesn't. His hair is messy from being in his helmet, and he's got a good few days worth of stubble on his jaw. He's the beautiful side of darkness. I feel my lip slip into my mouth, and I clamp down on it, feeling my body becoming anxious.

When he reaches me, he stretches his hand out, tucking a strand of dark hair behind my ear. Then he steps forward, wrapping a hand around my hip, and pulling me close.

His mouth closes over mine before I get the chance to think or protest. His lips move softly, claiming mine, bringing me to new heights. He slowly pushes us back toward the bed, and, gently, he lays me down.

I don't understand what he's doing, and I don't really want to. I just want him.

I'm sick of feeling like that's such a bad thing.

His body moves over mine, and I can smell the leather of his jacket. It's a smell I've always loved, even back when my father used to wear his colors. I reach up, curl my fingers around the tough material, and I tug him closer. With a groan, he complies, and his hand runs down my thigh, lifting it up and over his hip. A whimper escapes my mouth, and

169

he takes the chance to bite my lower lip softly.

"Axel," I breathe. "Please."

He slips his fingers underneath my nighty, and finds my panties. He circles around them for a minute, before slipping his hand inside and finding my damp sex. He makes an appreciative sound in his throat, before taking hold of my panties and moving off me, taking them as he goes. I lift myself up onto my elbows and watch as he rocks backward and tosses them onto the floor.

Then I watch with full female appreciation as he grips his belt buckle, and undoes it, before sliding it completely off. He undoes the top button of his jeans, and jerks them down, freeing his cock. I lick my lips. I can't help it, he looks so fuckable like this. He wraps his hand around his length and begins stroking as he slowly moves back over me. He doesn't take his jacket off, or even pull his jeans further down—he just slides over me like that.

It's so brutal. So raw. So dirty.

I love it.

He takes my thigh again, and then he guides himself into my already waiting pussy. I arch into him, smothering my groan into his shoulder as he slowly fills me. I love the feeling I get as I stretch to accommodate him. It's a feeling of pure satisfaction. He takes my hip in his hand, and he begins to thrust, slowly, driving into me just perfectly.

"Oh God, Axel," I whimper, trying to keep as quiet as I can.

"Fuck," he murmurs into my shoulder as he drops his head, and keeps up the steady, perfect pace.

He's not being rough, and he's not being gentle. He's giving me the perfect amount of both. I reach up, and tangle my fingers into his hair, and I lift his head from my shoulder to seek out his lips. He lets me take them, and I kiss him softly, moving my lips over his, and occasionally sliding my tongue out and running it across his bottom lip. My entire body is wound up, and I know I'm ready to come, but I don't want this moment between us to end.

"You need to come," he rasps into my ear. "Now, darlin'."

I squirm beneath him, trying to hold back, but it's pointless. He's just got me at that point. With one last thrust, I come. My teeth close down on his shoulder to smother my moans, and I hear his almost pained growl as his body stiffens. I prepare myself for the moment where he'll pull out and find his release in my mouth, but he doesn't stop thrusting.

His entire body is stiff, and his eyes are tightly shut, like it pains him to keep going, like it's going against everything he's ever known. He thrusts his hips harder, and our skin slaps together. I don't know what to do. My heart aches for him. I reach up, and I cup his cheek. This seems to soothe him just slightly, and his thrusting becomes a little less desperate.

"It's okay," I whisper.

He buries his head into my shoulder, and with a ragged, almost feral cry, I feel his cock pulsing deep inside me. His body jerks, and his fists are tight up beside my head as he milks every last drop from his body.

We lay for a long moment, with him still inside me. I don't know what to say; I don't even know if he wants me to say anything. After a moment, he pulls out of me, and rolls off the bed. I watch with a look of confusion as he pulls his jeans up, and runs a hand through his hair. He looks disorientated, but more than that, he looks completely shaken.

His eyes fall on mine, and I give him a weak, wobbly smile. He leans down, taking the back of my head and bringing me close, pressing a soft kiss to my lips. Then he pulls back and turns toward the window.

Just as he reaches it, he turns, and stares at me once more. "You're not nothin', Cricket, and you never will be," he says, his voice barley above a whisper.

Then he climbs out my window.

And I can't help the small smile that creeps across my face. Axel just gave me a part of himself. Albeit tiny, it was still a part of him.

He let me, for just a second, see the broken man hiding behind the monster.

CHAPTER 17

MEADOW

Cherish what you love, hold onto it with all you have.

I've been with Lady for a week now, and I'm staring to feel a little more comfortable around her. She really is a fun person to be around. We've spent a lot of time getting to know each other, and I've enjoyed the female company. I don't see her as anything but female, because that's what she is to me now. On day six of my time with her, I'm sitting up in my room, staring out the window at the beautiful garden she's created, when my phone buzzes with a text message. I drag my eyes away from the garden, and stare down at the phone.

It's Axel.

I hurriedly lift the phone into my hand, opening the message.

A – Coming 2 c u 2nite. Be ready.

My heart flutters. He's coming to see me? I've hardly heard from him since the night he came through my window, and now he's letting me know he's going to be here tonight. I quickly reply.

M – Be ready for what?

A moment later he responds.

A – To take my cock.

Such a male response, I roll my eyes.

M – What if I have my period?

A – There's always the back door.

M – You're an ass.

A – Are you saying no, darlin?

M – No, because I'm horny. And BTW, I don't have my period.

A – Doesn't mean I won't try the back door.

M – Eat me Axel.

A – Oh baby, I plan to.

With a flush and a nervous giggle, I close my phone. I slide from my position at the window, and head out of my room in search for Lady, just to let her know Axel will be coming. I find her in her room, applying make up. Her hair is up in rollers. I guess she's got a show tonight. She sees me in the mirror, and gives me a warm smile.

"Hello love, is something wrong?"

I walk in, stopping at her bed. I stare down at all her makeup, hair products, clothes and shoes, and my heart aches a little. I never had any of that. I never had a mom to teach me how to do my hair, or paint my nails. Hell, I've never even had my nails painted. I must have a sad look on my face, because Lady stops what she's doing and turns to me, touching my arm.

"You lost your mom very young, didn't you honey?"

I nod. "Yeah, I just guess I never had any of this."

Her eyes widen. "You've never had your nails painted or your makeup done?"

174

I shake my head, and reach up, tugging my hair. "This is the only thing I've ever had in my hair, and it's fading and ugly."

She taps her finger on her chin, and her eyes lighten. "Then we're going to do something about that. Sit down, right here," she points to a stool.

I look hesitantly at her. "Oh no, it's ok. Axel is coming later and..."

"Even better, don't argue with me sugar, just sit."

I do as she asks, sitting on the stool and staring at myself in the mirror. I scrunch my nose up, not entirely happy with how I look. I just feel so...plain. Lady lifts some strands of my hair into her fingers, and inspects them. "You're not naturally dark, are you?"

"No," I admit.

"Is there a reason you are now?"

I shake my head. "Not really anymore."

"Then lets get this out, shall we?"

I beam. "We can?"

She grins, big and beautiful. "Oh honey, leave it to Lady. We'll get that out and have you shining in no time. Now tell me, what sort of underwear have you got?"

I feel my eyes widen, and she laughs. "Honey, if you don't love yourself enough to wear good underwear, then we have a problem. You have to love *being* beautiful. You have to love *feeling* beautiful. Let me tell you," she says, tapping a brush in her palm. "A man can find you divine, and then go below only to see you've got granny panties on."

I giggle. "I don't have grannie panties."

"There better not be any cotton ones either."

I flush. She shakes her head, and rushes to her phone, lifting it to her ear after she's dialed a number. "Petra, yes, it's Lady. I need you to do something quite urgently for me. Go into town, get me the sexiest underwear, dresses, shoes and clothes you can find for a young girl, blonde hair, simply gorgeous."

I gape, and shake my head, but she puts up a hand.

"Use my card. Yes, bring it here when you're done."

She continues to rattle off my size as if she's lived in my body, which only makes me gape further. Then she hangs up the phone and turns to me with a devilish smile. "We're going to make him drool."

~*~*~*~

MEADOW

Lady fills my hair with some interesting smelling product that has all the brown just rinsing right out. Then she massages some beautiful creams and conditioners in, tucking it all up in a towel while she works on my face. She cleans my skin, tweezes my eyebrows, and applies a light amount of make up. Then she sits beside me, and takes my hand, panting my nails. My chest swells with happiness, and a warmth I've never felt.

"Thank you, Lady," I say, staring at the pretty light pink she so perfectly applies to my now immaculately trimmed nails.

"Anytime sweetie, all girls deserve to feel beautiful."

"I certainly feel beautiful now."

She looks up at me, her warm gaze pinning mine. "And so you should, you're a very gorgeous girl."

I smile, and we continue to chat for hours about boys, dresses, shoes and anything we can think of. By the time she's had my new clothes delivered, and has dressed me in a stunning pink, halter neck dress, I'm feeling like a whole new person. When I look into the mirror, I see the girl I once was. My long hair is now back to it's honey blonde, dropping softly down my back in loose curls. My face is clean, and my cheeks are rosy. My eyes shine with happiness. My dress is perfectly fitting for my body type, and the underwear I'm wearing is the reason for my rosy cheeks.

I hear the low rumbling of a Harley Davidson outside, and my heart picks up. I feel nervous, like I'm about to go on a first date. Lady smiles down at me, her eyes filling with unshed tears. "He's going to have a fit when he sees you, a fit!"

I swallow nervously, as I hear the front door slam. Lady shoves me towards the top of the stairs. "Go, make him stop breathing."

I quickly hug her, thanking her once again, before heading to the stairs. Axel is half way up when I take my first step down. He skids to a halt, and his eyes widen when he lays them on me. I smile nervously, and tuck a strand of hair behind my ear. His breathing deepens, and there's something powerful in his eyes. He's looking at me like it's the first time he's seen me. His mouth opens slightly, like he's about to say something, but it closes quickly.

He takes another step up.

He stops in front of me and looks up into my eyes. I feel my cheeks heating, and I try to keep my gaze from running down his body, and over that tight black shirt and those ass-hugging jeans. Instead, I keep them on the aqua orbs staring right at me. He reaches up, stroking his fingers through my blonde hair. He's staring so intensely at me, my heart is hammering. He swallows, and before I can say anything, he leans down and scoops me into his arms, walking us to my bedroom and kicking the door closed.

The moment he sets me on my feet, his lips come down over mine. I smile and press my body against his, letting my fingers run down over his hard body and back up to tangle in his gorgeous hair. He groans, and turns us, pushing me towards the bed. I go down with one shove, and my dress flies up. I don't stop it. Axel's eyes move to my panties, and a sexy grin spreads across his face before he crawls over and positions himself above me.

"I feel like I've stepped back to the last time I saw you, standin' on that bridge," he murmurs. "Your beautiful hair flicking around in the breeze."

I shiver at the memory. "Am I better like this?"

His eyes search my face. "You're fuckin' beautiful like this."

Then he lowers his hands and takes hold of my satin thong, and tugs it. "And fuck, these…"

I giggle softly. "Lady got them for me."

He grins, and gently lowers them down over my legs. "Better not tear them off then."

He starts kissing his way up my thigh, until he reaches the middle. He blows a hot puff of air of my clit, and then his tongue snakes out and slides up my slit, causing me to cry out with pleasure. "Oh, God, Axel," I moan. "I've missed you."

He consumes my pussy, plunging his tongue into my depths and swirling it over my clit until I'm coming beneath him, little desperate whimpers slipping from my lips. Then he's standing, taking his clothes off and shoving them to the floor. When he's standing in front of me, so perfectly naked, I feel my body spark to life. He crawls onto the bed, and sits against the headboard, and then he reaches for me.

"Ride me, baby. Let me see your god damned gorgeous face while you do."

His words have warmth shooting through me, so I quickly unzip my dress and remove my bra before crawling over and onto his lap. He wraps his arms around my waist, and his lips find my throat as I gently lower myself onto his hard cock. He groans as I slide down his length, and he makes little sucking sounds with his mouth as he continues his assault on my neck. I gasp, and wrap my fingers around his arms, gently lifting myself back up before lowering myself again.

"Fuck baby," he murmurs. "You're so fuckin' tight."

He lifts his head from my neck, and looks over my shoulder. Then a growl escapes his throat. "Turn around."

Huh? I lift my head and look down at him, and his eyes are wild with need. He lifts me off his cock, and spins me around, so my back is pressed against his chest, but I'm still riding him. I realize the moment I lift my head why he's done it. There's a mirror in front of us, and like this, we can both see...everything. He takes my hips in his hands, and he lifts me, and I feel my heart begin to pound.

I can see his cock slide out of my pussy, and when he lowers me down again, I can see it slip back in. Bolts of need shoot through my body, and I watch as my own nipples harden. Seeing myself like this would usually horrify me, but seeing Axel wrapped around me, his big arms encasing me, his mouth on my shoulder as he kisses me, makes it all so much more...*beautiful.*

"Watch with me," I breathe, as I lift myself up again, watching his cock slide from my depths, before dropping back down.

Axel lifts his eyes, and his hands come around to cup my breasts. I can see his gaze like this, and it's wild with lust and want. We stare at each other in the mirror, as I continue to lift myself up and down. His jaw is tight and his hands are rough on my breasts, but I don't care. I love it. I love every second of it. I can feel my orgasm building, and right when I'm on the edge, Axel rasps, "Watch me when you come, watch me, Cricket."

I fix my gaze on him, and I come so hard my body jerks in his lap. He groans, almost in delight, and keeps his eyes on me as he too, begins to come. Watching him lose control, watching the way his eyes almost haze over, and the way his mouth drops open with a groan, has everything inside me wanting more. Needing more of this. *Of him.* I whimper just from the sight of him releasing alone.

He's so perfect.

Even when he doesn't see it.

CHAPTER 18

MEADOW

If you love me you'll see, I'm everything you're meant to be.

Lady is having a party tonight. It's been four days since Axel came and visited, but since then I've heard a little more each day from him. Tonight, I'm hanging out with Lady and her friends. I'm quite used to it now, most nights she has had friends over—three in particular. Trigg, Lisa and Coby. Lisa is a drag queen, too, and Trigg and Coby are bad boys, without fail. They seem like they're her projects, in a sense. She looks after them like a mother would.

"There you are, dove."

I hear Trigg's voice, and I turn and see him standing in the doorway with two beers. I'm in the kitchen chopping some cheese for Lady's platters. Trigg is tall, with blonde hair, and big brown eyes. He has tattoos all over him, running right up his neck, and even down over his fingers. He's got piercings in his lips, and his ears, and he kind of reminds me of a gothic biker. Tonight, he's wearing a leather jacket over a gray T-shirt with a set of old, faded denim jeans.

I won't lie: there's something about Trigg that has me uneasy, but he's been really friendly to me this past week, and I can't deny that it's nice to have the idea of a friend right now. I give him a smile, and walk over, taking the beer from his hands. He leans against the doorframe, taking me in, letting his eyes roam over my body before looking back up at me.

"What's happening tonight, dove?"

I shrug. "Just helping Lady prepare for her party."

"She sent me in to help you out," he smiles.

I don't quite believe him. "I'll go and out check on her, make sure we're doing what she needs then."

I squeeze past him, taking a sip of the beer as I go. I don't entirely like being alone with him. I walk through the living area, and smile and wave at Lisa, who is talking on her phone. She blows me a kiss, and I can't help the silly smile that spreads across my face. She's lovely, and funny. I step out front, and run into Coby. He grins down at me. He's far nicer than Trigg, though I know he's had a pretty rough life.

Coby has a massive scar that's disfigured half of his face. Lady told me he got into a really bad knife fight, and went to jail for a few years. No one ever took care of that wound properly, and it ended up healing really bad. He's got gentle eyes, though. He's got dark, olive skin, and blue eyes so light the sky has nothing on them. His hair is surfer blonde, and even with the scar, he's a very attractive man.

"Looks like Lady is having quite a party," I say.

"'Fraid so, little lady," he groans, rolling his eyes.

I giggle. "Well, if it gets out of hand, I'm sure we can escape."

He chuckles. "I'll hold you to that."

I flash him a smile, and slip past him onto the well-lit front lawn. It's evening now, the only time Lady comes to life. I spot her right away, talking to two older gentleman, and when I approach, she smiles at me and wraps an arm around my shoulder. "Glenn, Marcus, this is my friend, Meadow."

I smile at the two men quickly, and then look up at Lady. "Is there anything else I can help with?"

She shakes her head. "You just enjoy some food and drink, and mingle. Don't worry about the rest of the food preparation in the kitchen, I've sent someone in to finish it."

"Not Trigg, I hope," I grin.

She laughs. "No sugar, not Trigg."

I smile, and nod. I turn back to the house, and continue sipping my beer. I decide to take a walk through Lady's extensive gardens. I haven't yet had the chance.

I walk down the worn rock path until I reach a massive gazebo. I can hear the faint music from the party, and I guess this is quite a distance away. I take a seat, and finish the rest of my beer. I pull out my phone, hesitating. I want to talk to Axel, but I don't want to come across as needy either.

I blink my eyes as I try to focus on the screen. My mind whirls a little, and I shake my head. Jesus, I only had one damned beer. Okay, it's been a while and all, but seriously? I rub my eyes, and blink again. This is weird. I tuck my phone back into my pocket, and stand, only to see Trigg coming into the gazebo.

"Oh, I was just going for a walk. What are you doing in here?" he asks.

I shake my head, still trying to control my vision. "I was just," I blink rapidly, "taking a walk."

"You okay, dove?" he says, but something in his voice isn't genuine.

He walks over and takes my hand, forcing me to sit back down. I shake my head. "I think I just need to lie down."

"You shouldn't walk back there. It's dangerous."

I turn and look at him, and he's staring down at my breasts. My heart begins to hammer, because something doesn't feel right about this situation. There's just something screaming at me to get up and run, but my body is tingling all over, and my legs feel numb. Like they're no longer attached to my body. I open my mouth to speak, but my lips feel heavy and full. I don't understand. Have I been drugged?

"You're so beautiful, Meadow," Trigg begins, taking my hand. I try to pull it back, but my body won't work. "You're so fucking perfect. When I was in jail, I missed women so bad. I just wanted the feeling of being inside a woman again, you know?"

I shake my head, feeling my world beginning to spin.

"And then I came here, and like sunshine, you were there. I want you, Meadow."

I feel his finger run down the curve of my breast, and bile rises in my throat. I push off the chair, only to land in a heap on the floor. My legs won't work. I try to stretch my hands out in front of me, but I can't pull myself along. *God, no.* Trigg leans down, and takes my body, lifting me up. My back is pressed to his chest, and he's got his hands over my breasts. I try to squirm.

"You're so fucking beautiful. God, I want you."

His hands squeeze my breasts again, and I let out a little yelp, which was meant to be a scream. Everything in my body seems to have stopped working, and terror fills my veins. Tears leak out of the corner of my eyes, and I feel helpless. My insides are screaming at me to fight, but I can't fight, my body won't work. Trigg slides his hands down my belly, and I want to vomit.

"So perfect," he murmurs. "I'm going to fuck you, but I promise you'll like it, Meadow. I promise."

No.

No.

My tears get heavier, and the only sounds coming out of my mouth are little squeaks of desperation. His fingers slip under my shorts, and skim my panties, and I feel sick. I want to throw up. How the hell did he get me here? He drugged me. He must have put something in that beer. God, all along, he'd probably been planning this. He's sick. Lady should have known he was sick. He was in prison...God, probably for rape.

His fingers slide under my panties, and I feel one of them slip inside me. I desperately try to scream again, but my mouth won't even open. I'm panting, and I can taste my own tears dripping into my mouth, but I can't stop him. He's going to rape me, and I can't even fight. I move my hand, but the movement is too slow. He takes it, and pulls it around behind me. Pain shoots up my arm.

His fingers keep thrusting.

No, oh God, *no.* I make a strangled sound, and manage to rasp out a please, but he doesn't stop. "No, dove, you'll like it. I swear."

Sick fuck. I'd *never* like it.

He pushes two fingers inside me, and I can feel his erection against my ass. Vomit comes up in my throat, and I'm sobbing. He slips his fingers out of my dry flesh, and lays me on the floor in front of him. He takes my pants, and pulls them down, before discarding my panties. I'm naked from the bottom down. I try to shuffle backward, but my vision is beginning to blur. I'm only catching glimpses of him now.

I feel the moment when he presses against me, ready to thrust inside me. I can hear his little mumbles, trying to convince himself that I'll like it. I hiccup loudly, and find myself praying. Praying that something will happen. Just as he starts pushing inside me, I hear a distant voice. I don't know how far away that voice is, but suddenly Trigg is off me, and he's pulling his pants up.

"I'm coming, I was just taking a walk!" he yells.

Through my haze, I see him looking down at me. "You'll not remember this, and if you do, and you tell Lady, I'll slit her throat, then yours."

Then he leans down, rolling my body underneath the chair so no one can see me, and he kicks my pants in too. Then he turns and walks off, whistling. I desperately try to move. I need to get out of here. He could come back later; he could finish what he started. I slowly stretch my hand out, taking the phone that fell out of my pants when Trigg kicked them. It takes me a solid ten minutes to find Axel's number, and by the time I press ring, my head is spinning and I'm starting to drop off into darkness.

"Yeah?" he answers.

"A-a-axel," I slur.

"Cricket?" he asks. "That you?"

"H-h-help."

186

"Meadow," he says, more frantically now. "Where are you? Are you with Lady?"

"I...he...I..."

"Meadow, speak to me," he bellows.

"At...L-l-l-lady's. H-h-he...drugged...help."

"Who drugged you? Did someone hurt you? Where are you, Meadow?" he yells frantically.

"I..." I begin to sob hysterically.

"Shit, baby, talk to me." His voice comes across with more concern than I've ever heard before.

"He tried to r-r-rape..."

"What?" he says, and his voice is suddenly dripping with venom.

"I need...h-h-help."

"I'm coming, tell me where you are, Meadow?"

"L-l-lady's," I murmur, before the phone slips from my hand and smashes onto the ground.

Then everything goes black.

MEADOW

"Where the fuck is she?"

I hear the angry roar, and I blink my eyes open. It's so dark out now, and there are tiny bugs flying around my face. I hear the sound of music, and people chattering. I blink a few more times, realizing I'm alone, and freezing. My teeth begin to chatter together, as I force myself out from underneath the chair, and up into a sitting position. My head spins, and I'm disorientated for a second.

Until I remember why I'm lying here.

Cold fear shoots through my body, and I stare down to see that I'm not wearing any panties. Oh God, Trigg. He tried to…oh…bile rises in my throat, and I begin to panic, trying to move toward my clothes as tears trickle down my cheeks. Cool air whips through the gazebo, and I'm still struggling to fight past the cold taking over my body.

"Meadow?"

I hear Axel's bellow, and I snap my head up. He's here?

"A-a-axel?" I cry out as loudly as I can. Even then, it's a pathetic whimper.

"I don't know where she is," Lady cries. "I thought she was in the house."

"She's in trouble," Axel roars at her. "She's hurt."

I try to reach out for my panties, but my hands are shaking so badly I can't wrap my fingers around them. My sobbing is loud and crackly, and my heart is thumping. I feel ill, knowing what nearly happened out here tonight. I hear the crunching sound of boots, and I lift my head to see Axel step into the gazebo. The moment his eyes fall on me, anger washes over them, but he drops to his knees in front of me anyway.

"Shit, Cricket, I got you," he murmurs, reaching out for me.

"Oh God, Axel," I hear Lady breathe from behind him.

I sob harder, and reach for Axel. He shrugs off his jacket, and wraps it

188

around me before scooping me up into his arms. My bottom half is still bare, and Lady quickly takes off her shawl and drapes it over me.

"She's fuckin' freezing. We need to get her warm."

"I…I'm sorry Axel," Lady says, her eyes wide in horror. "I didn't…"

"We'll talk about this as soon as we find out who did this to her."

Axel walks with me around the back of the house, and he enters through the back entrance. He takes the steps, two at a time, until he reaches the top.

The moment we're in the spare room, he lays me down onto the bed, and takes the blanket, rolling it over me. My teeth are chattering together, and I feel sick to my stomach. I lift my eyes, and through my tears I see Axel looking down at me. He's angry—no he's wild—but he's trying to keep calm.

"What. Happened?" he bites out.

"I…"

He turns away quickly, getting a glass of water from the beside table. "Drink this, Cricket. You need to flush whatever drugs are in your body out."

"He must have d-d-drugged me," I whisper, sipping the water. "I…he gave me a beer and I w-w-went for a walk. He came in, and…"

"And what?" Axel growls, clenching his fists.

"H-h-he touched me."

Axel leans down, meeting my eyes dead on. "You need to tell me, girl, straight down the line. Did he fuckin' rape you?"

I shake my head weakly. "He…used his f-f-fingers. Someone called out just as he…as he…" I close my eyes, and tears leak down my face.

"It's all right," Axel says, trying to soothe me, but his voice is coming out like gravel.

"He just started to r-r-rape me when someone called out," I croak. "He r-r-ran off and told me if I told anyone, he would k-k-kill me."

Axel's fists tighten. "He put his dick in you?"

I nod weakly. "Only for a s-s-second."

Axel stands, spinning around, and smashing a nearby lamp. Then he whirls back to me, and the look on his face is murderous. "What's his name?"

"T-t-t-trigg."

Axel spins, and charges towards the door.

"Axel…" I squeak out.

He turns, his face ripped with rage. He must see fear in my eyes, because his expression softens a touch. He walks over, leaning down, and pressing a warm, soothing kiss to my forehead. His hand is wrapped around the back of my head, and he stays there like that for a long moment with his lips pressed against me. He pulls back, and strokes my cheek softly.

"I'm goin' to sort this, you know I gotta. You need to rest. You've got drugs in your system. You want me to shower you first, before I go?"

I shake my head, knowing that he needs to deal with this. I want him to deal with this.

"I'll come back, okay?" he says. "You rest."

I nod, and he tucks the blankets tighter around me before storming out of the room.

I close my eyes. God help Trigg.

CHAPTER 19

AXEL

To show weakness is a sin, I'll never let you in.

I storm down the stairs, trying to control the burning anger inside my chest. My fists are shaking. I want to get hold of this fucker and tear his fucking head off. Lady comes rushing in, just as I hit the bottom step. Her eyes are wide, and she looks devastated.

"Axel," she says. "I'm so sorry."

"You were meant to be watching her," I roar. "I trusted you with her safety."

"I didn't think...I didn't expect something like this would happen. I thought I could trust them all, and..."

I step toward her, grinding my teeth. "He fuckin' raped her, Lady. He put his dick inside her, he drugged her, and he tried to fuck her."

"W-w-w-who?" she says, with a trembling lip.

"Trigg."

Her eyes widen, and she shakes her head from side to side. "No, he wouldn't..."

"You want me to take you up there and see that broken girl?" I roar.

"Axel, please, this has to be some sort of misunderstanding..."

"It's not."

I hear a voice coming from behind me, and I spin to see another man with blonde hair holding a tall, squirming guy in his grips.

"Coby, what are you doing?" Lady gasps.

"I saw him running from the gazebo earlier, but I didn't know Meadow was in there. He was fumbling with his pants. I figured he was just pissing, but when I heard what went down, I found him trying to fuckin' leave, and I found these in his pockets."

Coby lifts a hand full of drugs, and my rage gets the better of me. I charge over, ripping the scumbag from Coby's hands and slamming him so hard against the wall his head busts open. He bellows in pain, and begins to plead. "She wanted it, she said she wanted it," he yells in a high-pitched, squeaky voice.

I lift my fist and I drive it into his face, busting his nose. Blood spurts out, but I don't stop. I drive another fist into his eye, relishing in the feeling of his bones crunching.

"Axel, stop!" Lady cries.

I spin around panting. "This is my business now, Lady. I'm takin' him."

"We will call the police, and…"

I step toward her, letting the scumbag drop to the ground. Coby reaches out, putting his boot down on him, stopping him from crawling away.

"Meadow is club property, and he fucked with club property. This is my business now, and if you call the police, you're only goin' to get questioned. I'm goin' to deal with him, and you're goin' to stay out of it."

"Axel," she whispers. "I'm sorry. I didn't know…I didn't know he would do that, and if I had…I would have never…"

I can see the genuine pain in her eyes. She really believed this guy wasn't bad. I walk over, controlling my rage for long enough to put my hands on her shoulders. "I know, Lady. It wasn't your fault. I'm goin' to deal with this now, but what you can do is go and look after my girl until I get back."

She nods. "I will, I swear."

She stares down at Trigg on the floor, groaning in pain. "I trusted you," she whispers, shaking her head sadly. "I hope he makes it hurt."

When she disappears up the stairs, I turn to Coby. He's glaring down at Trigg, and his foot is planted firmly on his ribs.

"You fancy a ride?" I growl.

He looks up at me. "You're gonna let me in on this?"

I stare down at the worthless piece of shit on the floor, then back up at him. "I figure he wouldn't be here if it wasn't for you, so yeah, I'm lettin' you in."

Coby leans down, hurling Trigg up. "Then let's do this."

AXEL

"*Please,*" Trigg bellows, thrashing in the chains.

I'm standing in front of him. Coby and Cobra are to my left, and Colt and Jax are to my right. They were all too eager to be in on this when they found out what the scumbag did.

"You think it's okay to fuck women that don't want it?" I growl.

"I…I…" he stammers.

"You think it's okay to drug them so they don't get a choice?"

"I just…I just…"

"You fuckin' answer me, boy," I roar.

"No!" he cries. "No!"

I take step toward him, and the knife in my hand shimmers in the dull light. "Did it turn you on to see that she couldn't move?"

His eyes are frantic, and he begins babbling again.

"I wonder how it'll feel when I cut your dick off, and you can't do anything to stop me."

"Please," he cries. "Please, I won't do it again. Don't hurt me. I fucked up. I swear I won't do it again."

I take another step forward, yanking his pants down. I glare at his flaccid cock with a rage that is uncontrollable.

"That was my girl you fucked," I spit. "No one fucks with my girl."

"Please!" he screams.

I stare at his dick, and turn to Cobra. "Hold it up."

His face scrunches up. "Fuck that, I ain't touchin' that shit."

"Don't be such a fuckin' pussy, hold it."

Jax snorts from behind me, and I glare at him.

"Boss, seriously, you want us to touch his fuckin' dick."

"Someone needs to so I can make sure I get it right off."

195

"No!" Trigg screams, twisting and turning.

"Shut the fuck up," I bark at him. "Come on you pussies, hold his fuckin' dick."

"You hold it then," Colt says, walking over. "I'll cut it."

"Fuck that, I need this satisfaction."

They shake their heads, putting their hands up. "Then you hold it, boss."

"Bunch of girls!" I mutter staring down at Trigg. "I'm not touchin' his cock."

"I have a better idea," Coby says.

I turn in time to see him pull a blowtorch off the wall, and light it. My grin is wide.

"Good choice, boy."

CHAPTER 20

MEADOW

There's enough room in my heart for you, come in, I'll welcome two.

That night, after Lady comes in and helps me shower, I cry myself into exhaustion. She tried to give me some food, but my stomach couldn't handle it, so with a kiss to the head and whispered sorry, she left. I know she's blaming herself, and maybe when my emotions aren't so shaken I'll tell her it wasn't her fault. It was no one's fault, except maybe mine, for accepting the drink so easily.

I clutch Axel's jacket to my chest, breathing in the smell of leather mixed with that smell that is all Axel's. I haven't heard from him. It's been more than five hours, and I've not heard anything. It's early hours, now, and I'm still listening for that rumble of his Harley-Davidson. I can't hear it. Is he hurt? Or worse? My heart pounds angrily in my chest, and I try to do anything to take my mind off it.

My phone vibrates beside me, and I peer down at it. The number on the screen is Cobra's. My heart nearly leaps out of my throat, and my entire body stiffens. Why would Cobra be texting me? He would never text me…unless…with trembling hands, I open the message and read what he's written.

C - Boss is on his way. He's in bad shape. I know you're fucked

right now, but he needs you. Take care of him. Yeah?

I feel sudden relief flood my system, and I quickly reply.

M - I promise.

A moment later my phone beeps again.

C - You doin' ok?

My heart swells that one of these guys, one of these brothers, would even ask me such a thing.

M - I'm doin' ok.

I smile at the response I get, because I can imagine Cobra saying it.

C - Well, alrighty then.

I listen for Axel's bike for a long, long time. Three hours later, I hear the rumble as it comes to a stop outside of Lady's house. I get out of my bed, and with shaky legs I walk out of my door and to the top of the steps. I hear the front door slam, and when I see Axel, I gasp. Lady walks out, and she does the same, stopping in her tracks.

He's got blood all over him.

I mean...all over him.

His hair is messy, his face is gritty, and there's blood on his cheeks, on his hands, on his arms, on his shirt, and on his jeans. Lady covers her mouth, and he gives her a sad expression, then he turns and looks up at me. The pain and utter exhaustion I see in his eyes makes my heart ache. He takes a step toward me, and then doesn't stop until he's a step down.

Looking up at me, I can see something I've never seen in Axel's eyes before.

It's need.

He needs me.

He drops his head forward into my belly, and I react by wrapping my arms around it, holding him to me. I try to ignore the smell of burned flesh on his clothing because I know Axel doesn't cuddle, but this is his way of showing me that he just needs me with him, and I need to be there. I stroke his hair, ignoring the blood there, and when he lifts his head, I reach out and take his hand, walking us to the shower.

The moment we get in, I turn and take hold of his shirt, slowly lifting it over his head. He works with me, lifting his arms when I need. I move to his jeans next, trying to ignore the mass amounts of blood on them. I unbuckle his belt, and then I slide it out of the loops before unbuttoning him and lowering his jeans. When he's naked before me, I quickly strip out of my own clothes.

I don't take my eyes off his.

I take his hand, and pull him into the shower the moment I'm naked. The first thing I do is fill my palms with soap and begin lathering it over his skin, taking extra long on the bits coated in dried blood. The bubbles foam red, and I feel my stomach turn, but I don't stop. I rub until there's nothing left, and all the blood has washed down the drain. Then, I reach up with a palm full of shampoo, and I begin to lather his head. He puts his palms on the wall in front of him, and drops his head, closing his eyes.

I finish up, and then I slowly turn him around, and tuck myself into his chest. He doesn't put his arms around me, because Axel doesn't hug. It doesn't matter, though; he's letting me hold onto him, which I know we both need. He lowers his mouth to my ear, and in a crackly voice, he rasps, "He bled for you, and anyone who ever hurts you again will bleed for you."

~*~*~*~

MEADOW

I stare down at Axel as he sleeps, knowing he's exhausted. He's on his back, with his hands up near the pillows. He's breathing deeply, and I know he needs this rest.

I slip out of the bed, and I tiptoe out of the room. I walk down the stairs, and into the lounge. I peer around, looking for Lady, and I see her outside with a phone pressed into her hand. I step out, and she spins around when she sees me.

"What are you doing, Lady?" I ask.

She looks at me sadly. "I just called Coby, I needed to make sure he was okay…"

"Is he?" I say, walking over, and leaning against the railing.

"He is. He said Axel was ruthless."

I swallow. "I don't imagine he would have made it easy on Trigg."

She looks out over the yard. "Trigg deserved what he got. I just…I feel like I failed somehow."

I take her hand, and she looks down at me. "You didn't fail, Lady. Some people can't be helped—or, worse, they don't want to be. Sometimes you can give a person everything you are, but it won't mean they're going to give it back. He didn't want to accept a better path. That's not your fault."

"You know, when Axel came to me, I thought I'd never be able to help him. He was so broken. So angry. But then, with time, something happened, and he found a way back, even just a little. With love, and understanding, and space, he found his way. I made it my life's mission to help people after him, and I've had a few go through. Coby and Trigg were my most recent, and Coby has come so far, but Trigg...I just...I'm so sorry, Meadow."

I squeeze her hand. "This isn't your fault. Sometimes these things...happen."

"You're a brave girl. What you just did in there, for him...you don't know how much strength that took."

"He's everything to me," I say, looking away. "If I didn't do it, then who would have?"

She cups my cheek. "He's lucky to have you. You're going to be the reason he keeps fighting. Promise me that no matter what happens you won't let him push you away. He'll try, it's how Axel works, but promise me you'll fight for him."

"I promise," I say with determination in my voice.

"How's he holding up now?"

I shrug. "I'm not sure. I imagine Axel has seen worse in his life—hell, I'm sure he's even done worse, but it rattles him all the same."

"It can never be easy to take a life, no matter how many times you do it," she says sadly.

"No, I don't suppose so."

"I'm going to get some rest. You wake me if you need."

I nod, and let go of her hand. She leaves me alone on the balcony, and I watch as the sun begins to rise. My eyes are heavy, and I'm tired, but I know sleep won't come to me right now. There's no point in trying. I sit on an old porch swing, and I stare out at the rising sun. My mind is struggling to comprehend how this has all gone down. Only a month ago I was running from Axel, and now he's here…in my bed.

I wonder how much my father would despise me if he knew I'd betrayed him so.

My heart clenches at that thought, and I tuck my legs up to my chest. I never had it easy—not really. I never got the chance to have a good go at things. My father was always working with the club, and my mother killed herself long before I could get a decent memory of her. I often try to think about her, but I just don't remember. My father said she had a problem with drugs, and overdosed one day. That's all I know.

I imagine now, it's all I'll ever know.

I feel the chair shift beside me, and I turn to see Axel sitting beside me, fully dressed. I narrow my eyes, and my skin prickles. "You're leaving."

He turns his eyes away from mine, and stares out toward the trees. "I have to."

"And you're going to leave me here?"

He doesn't look at me, but I know he's fighting against himself. "I have to, it's too dangerous. I haven't dealt with Beast yet, and…"

"And what?" I cry. "I'm no safer here, Axel…or have you forgotten already what went down?"

"Meadow," he begins, but I cut him off.

I stand, and stare down at him. "When are we going to stop doing this? You can't keep hiding yourself from me. You can't keep pretending there is nothing here between us. I...I...care for you, Axel, more then you know. Why won't you let me in? Why do you keep pushing me away?"

He sighs deeply. "I can't give you what you want, Meadow. Even if I want this...I can't...I just can't give it to you."

"You haven't even tried," I snap.

"You won't like the man that's in here," he growls, thumping his chest.

"You haven't let me see him. Not really. How do you know I won't like him?"

"I just fuckin' do!" he growls, clenching his fists. "I'm not good enough for you, Meadow. I'm not what you want."

"How do you know what I want?" I cry, feeling my lip tremble. "How would you know?"

He storms toward me, and grips my shoulder. "You're so adamant you want to see this part of me. I've given you what you think it is you want. I've put my cock deep inside you and come. I've held you to me, I've opened the part that you've been seeking, but what about the other part, Meadow? The part you haven't accepted?"

I feel my lip tremble. "I'd accept all of you, Axel. You just won't let me."

"No," he roars. "You think you'd accept me. You think that me needing to control women is a problem you can fix. You think that this hard side is something you're slowly cracking into, but it's not. You're not even scratching the surface of the fucked-up shit in my head."

He turns and walks down the front stairs, not letting me answer.

In a small, timid voice, I say, "You can't make me stay here, Axel."

He stiffens, and turns, staring back up at me.

"Then go, Meadow. If that's what you want."

With that, he disappears into the trees.

MEADOW

I stand in the room, debating for a solid two hours. I know this is my moment to make my choice. I've been coming backward and forward with Axel now for too long, and I'm tired of it. He walked away from me, leaving the door open. He told me I can't accept what he is, and then he left. Now it's my turn to decide if I can deal with what he's got to give, or if I'm going to walk away.

Since Axel came into my life, there have been so many things pulling me toward him, and an equal amount pushing me away. He's the kind of damaged most people would run a mile from, but for me, he's the reason I breathe. I don't want to let him go, not without knowing what it is he hides behind the shadows. The only way I'll know is to go to him, and let him show me.

I'm being unfair if I deny him the chance to be himself.

Only when I've seen all of it can I make an informed decision.

I turn and walk toward the door, shoving past it and heading downstairs. Lady is standing in the living area, staring blankly at the television. I know it's still bothering her, and I can't say I blame her. I would hate to be in the position she's in. I walk over, placing a hand on her arm. She jerks and turns to me, forcing a smile.

"What's the matter, love?"

"I need you to take me to Axel."

She stares at me. "What for?"

"I have things to sort out, and I need to do it now."

She sighs. "Sweet, I have direct orders not to let you go. I can't take you, you know that."

Dammit.

"Please, Lady, this is important to me."

She looks sorry. "I'm afraid I can't, I'm sorry."

She's not going to take me, which means I need to find another way. I plant a fake smile on my face, and nod. "I understand, I'm sorry. I'll just call him."

"Give him a little time. He'll come to you."

She's wrong, but I don't tell her that. "I hope so," I say in a timid voice.

"You should get some rest. You must be exhausted."

At her words, my body tingles with warmth. I know I need to rest, and I know the better time to go to Axel is at night. I'm safer if I go at night. So, I hug her, and head back up the stairs. When I reach my room, I close and lock the door behind me. I change into a pair of panties and a long shirt, and then I climb into bed, feeling my body ache with exhaustion.

Within minutes, I'm out.

~*~*~*~

MEADOW

When the sun begins to set that night, I decide it's time to find a way to get out of here and to Axel. Lady is resting right now, but I know I can't walk past her, or she'll hear me. I remember Axel climbing through my window, and decide it may be the only way I can get out without raising alarm. I walk over, staring down. It's only one story, and if I do it right, she shouldn't hear me.

Deciding this is my only option, I pull on some jeans and a tank, then I throw my hoodie on, and my best pair of sneakers. I have to prep myself to get the guts to climb out that window, but I think of Axel, and I know it's something that has to be done.

It takes me a solid ten minutes to get down without making noise, and I come close to slipping at least four times. By the time I reach the bottom, my heart is pounding, and a fine trickle of sweat is running down my face.

God.

I turn and quickly rush down the driveway. It's getting darker by the minute, and a cool air is whipping across my skin. I wrap my hoodie around myself, and keep running. When I reach the road, I head the right direction back into town.

It takes me forty-five minutes to flag down a car. It's an old woman that pulls over, and she seems to take pity on me because she goes out of her way to turn around and take me where I need to go.

"What's a girl like you doing out on your own?" she asks, just as we get into the city.

"I got a bit lost after a party," I lie.

"Young girls these days." She shakes her head. "I never went to parties when I was young."

I smile, but it's forced.

"Where do you need to go, love?"

I give her that address and her eyes widen. "Isn't that a biker lot?"

"My…father is there."

"You shouldn't be hanging around with them. They're scoundrels, the lot of them."

I don't bother arguing with her.

"I just need to get my dad, that's all."

The minute we arrive at the Angels compound, I jump out of the car, quickly thanking the woman before she has a chance to argue with me, then I run through the open gates. I'm surprised they're open, but it makes sense as soon as I get to the front door of the clubhouse, and I hear the pounding music coming through the door. They're having a party.

I open the front door, and step inside. The scene before me has my head spinning. There are men and women everywhere, and the brothers are all up in the women. Some of them are having lap dances, others have their women bent over the bar, driving into them like mad men. Well then, I guess this is the real side to an MC club. I shake my head, and push my way through the people, looking for Axel.

"Meadow?"

I hear Colt's voice, and turn. He smiles down at me, taking my shoulders. "What are you doin' here?"

"I came to see Axel."

He frowns. "Aren't you meant to be with Lady Matilda?"

"It's a long story. Is he here?"

His eyes grow a little hard. "He's...busy."

"Busy?" I say loudly, so he can hear me over he music.

"Meadow...he's...ah...got someone with him."

My blood turns to ice, and I feel my fists clench. "He what?"

"Look, I don't think tonight is the right time for you to be here..."

I roll my eyes. "Do you think this shit shocks me?" I mutter, waving my hands around, indicating the room in general.

He looks confused. "I thought..."

"Look, just tell me where he is...please Colt?"

He sighs loudly, and rubs his forehead with the palm of his hand. "He's in his office."

I shove past him, and rush toward the hall. I don't know what I'm going to find when I go into Axel's office, but I have to go in. I push past a couple fucking against a wall, and only once I'm past do I recognize that it was Jax, and one of the whores. Nice. I get to Axel's door, and I don't wait, I just swing it open. The first thing I see is the blonde-headed girl on his lap. She's got hair halfway down her back, and she's wearing nothing but a thong.

She's grinding against him, shoving her big fakies in his face. He's got his hands on her hips, but I can't see his face. My heart beats wildly, and I want to be sick, but I step in further, slamming the door loudly behind me. Axel jerks, and his head whips around the girl. His eyes lock directly onto mine. His entire body stiffens, and we hold eye contact for the longest moment. I see a challenge in his eyes, and I imagine he can also see it in mine.

The girl doesn't stop giving him a lap dance. She doesn't even notice I'm there.

She's probably off her face.

"You said I didn't want to know what you are, that I wouldn't like it, but you haven't given me the chance to find out. So, here I am. I want to know, Axel," I say, my voice stern and determined.

I spot the handcuffs on his desk, and I lean over, taking them, and holding them up. I keep my eyes locked on his as I snap them on my wrists, binding my own hands in front of me. "Show me."

His body stiffens, and his eyes fill with lust and need. He searches my face, to see if I'm for real about this.

"I'm not walking out of here, so you either throw that whore off your lap, and give me what I want, or I'll walk out, and I'll never come back. You choose, Axel."

His jaw ticks, and he growls to the girl. "Get the fuck out."

She frowns, turns her head, and shoots me an icy glare. "But Pres..."

"You heard me," he snarls at her, not taking his eyes from mine. "Get the fuck out."

She gets off his lap and without putting her shirt on she walks past me, and out the door, slamming it loudly behind her. Axel doesn't move from his chair, but his eyes are filled with something deadly, something terrifying that has my body spiking with need.

"You want to give me what I want?" he says in a gravelly tone.

"Yes," I whisper.

"You fuckin' sure about that?"

"We've been dancing around this for long enough. Show me what you are, and I can decide if it's something I want in my life."

The room fills with silence for a long moment, then his eyes narrow, and a deadly look appears on his face.

"Run," he says, his tone husky and laced with dominance.

I don't need him to say anything else, because I know what it is he's asking me to do. He wants me to run, and he wants me to give in to the dark side of myself. He wants to catch me, he wants to put me on my knees, and fuck me with brutal force. The idea of that has my blood pumping. I turn, without giving it a second thought, and I run.

I fly through the door and down the hall, and I hear his chair skid back. I don't even think about the fact that my hands are still cuffed. I shove through the people in the main living area, and I get a few whistles from the boys, and a few "Atta girl, Meadow!" I guess they know what Axel likes. I stumble through the front door, and I take a quick left, heading past the bikes and into the trees to the left of the house.

I hear Axel's boots crunching through the dirt, and I know he's close behind me. The idea of being chased, the idea of having him catch me and fuck me, has everything inside me throbbing with need. I duck behind an old shed, and I try to catch my breath. It's dark out, except for a few faint streetlights. I peer around the shed, and I see Axel jogging towards me. God, he looks so fucking dangerous.

It does great things to me.

I tiptoe out from the side of the shed, and bolt toward the bikes lined up at the front of the lot. I hear Axel's pleased growl, and his husky, "You keep runnin' baby, but when I get you, I'm goin' to fuck you so hard you won't be able to scream my name."

My skin tingles, and I run harder towards the bikes. My entire body is aware of him, and adrenaline courses through my veins. I want him to catch me, yet at the same time, I want to keep running, and feeling this overwhelming urge that's washing through my body. Sweat trickles down my face as I stop beside the front gate. I drop my cuffed hands to my knees, taking a breath, but it's too long.

Axel's body slams against mine.

I start to scream, and I kick back, hitting him lightly in the shins. He groans, and presses my body against the wire fence. My face smooshes against it, and I cry out, feeling the bite of pain as I bite my own lip. Blood trickles into my mouth, and I find myself reacting, even though it's so incredibly wrong. I'm turned on. I want him to hurt me. I want this rough.

"Fight me, don't you stop," Axel breathes into my ear. "I won't hurt you, Cricket," he murmurs, running his finger down the side of my face. "But I need you to fight."

So, that's what I do.

I start by squirming, trying to twist my body around. He presses his body against mine, and reaches up, tangling his fingers into the fence. He thrusts his hips, ramming both out bodies harder into the wire. I groan, and throw my head back, hitting him in the face. He snarls, and takes my hands, quickly uncuffing me before pulling them harshly behind my back and jerking my body back into his.

I hear the cuffs drop onto the ground.

I guess he's letting me play this fairly.

"Stop that," he rasps into my ear. "I'll make it hurt if you do that again."

"Maybe I want it to hurt," I hiss, fisting my hands together and shoving them backward into his stomach.

He stumbles off me with a grunt, and I spin around, ducking to the left and attempting to run. I don't get two steps before Axel lashes out, taking my ankle and pulling me so hard I go down into the dirt. My face just misses being smashed into it by mere centimeters. Axel flattens his body over mine, and takes my head in his hands, jerking my head back by my hair and breathing down on me. "You're being a bad girl," he husks, running a finger down the side of my face.

"You're not letting me play fair," I whisper. "I was cuffed before, it wasn't a fair chase."

I feel his weight lift off me, and he jerks me up, pulling me into a standing position.

"Run, then. I'll give you five seconds, and if I catch you again, Meadow, I'm going to fuck you," he murmurs, and then his eyes grow lusty. "Hard."

I turn without answering, and I run into the trees at the back of the lot. I hear Axel counting loudly, and my body shivers. I am sweating now, and my breathing is hard and ragged, but the chase is so worth it. I hear Axel take off after me, and I squeal with delight as I weave through the trees. It's dark, but I can see enough because of the lights surrounding the clubhouse.

"The minute I get hold of you," Axel yell, "I'm goin' to rip your panties down, and put my dick so deep inside you, you're goin' to scream."

I shiver, and swallow. I make my way to the fence line again, and I press myself against it for a second, letting my eyes scan the trees.

"Then I'm goin' to kiss you so hard your lips will bleed."

Oh, my.

I take off, using the fence line as a guide to get back to the other end of the lot. I can hear Axel to my left, and I know he's gaining on me, but if I run, it'll make a lot of noise, and he'll figure out where I am.

"Come out, come out, wherever you are," he sings. "You know I'll make you come so much your legs will give way."

I feel a smile on my face as I keep moving along the fence, keeping my body plastered against it. I can feel my own arousal dampening my panties, and now I'm eager for him to get his hands on me. I want to know what he's got to give.

"You can run, Cricket, but you can't hide."

I stop moving and catch my breath, staring to the left of me, waiting for him to lunge out of the trees. He's clever, because he's managed to get ahead of me, and come around from my right.

I'm not looking, but the moment I hear his boots crunch the other side of me, I know I'm done for. I squeal and launch off the fence, but he has me, my face smashed to the fence in a split second. I squirm in his grip, crying out.

"Let me go!" I scream, playing the perfect part.

The part that has my heart thudding.

The part that has my panties dripping.

Axel uses one hand to hold me against the fence, while the other goes to my jeans, yanking them down so hard the entire lot goes. My bare ass is now on display, and I can feel the cool trickle of air against my skin. I shove backwards, but Axel slams me forwards. "Uh-uh-uh," he croons. "Time to get fucked."

I hear his zipper go, and then he's inside me. Deep. Brutal. I throw my head back and scream as he crushes my body against the fence, and thrusts deeper, harder, faster. His fingers go up and tangle in the wire beside my head, and my screaming intensifies. I shove back again, trying to get away, wanting to keep playing. Axel growls, and his hand comes down and whacks my backside. A painful sting radiates through my body.

"Oh God," I whimper.

"You like it," he snarls into my ear. "You fuckin' love my cock deep inside you."

"No I don't," I spit. "You fucking pig."

He chuckles, and pulls out of me, spinning me around. I stumble because of the jeans that are around my ankles. I land on my knees, and his cock shoves into my face.

"I have something for my girl with her sassy mouth."

He tangles his fingers in my hair, and gently pulls my head back, before plunging his cock into my mouth. I groan and reach up, wrapping my hand around his shaft. He moans, and begins using my hair to drive his thrusts. Getting a cheeky idea, I move my hand from his shaft, and I cup his balls. His cock swells in my mouth, and with a grin, I squeeze. He roars, and takes two steps backward. I shove to my feet, yanking up my jeans as best I can while darting off into the trees.

"You little shit," he bellows after me.

A giggle erupts from my throat as I dodge the trees. Axel catches up to me quickly, and I relish in the feeling of his arms wrapping around me, spinning my body and throwing me over his shoulder. He carries me to a clearing, and lowers me onto the soft grass. When he's over me, I look up into his eyes. A smile tugs at his lips, and it makes him look so incredibly flawless.

"My dick is so hard for you right now, so tell me, Cricket. You want it hard, or you want it slow?"

I stare up into his eyes, and I see a softness there I've never seen before. A huge part of me wants him to fuck me hard on this grass after our little chase in there, but a bigger part wants him to fuck me slow, making me come over and over again.

"Slow," I mumble. "Fuck me slow, Axel."

His smile widens, and he leans back, taking my jeans and discarding them. Then he's back over me, cock in hand, shoving it toward my entrance. I inhale deeply as he slides in, and my eyes grow heavy. He leans down, taking my leg and bringing it up over his hip as he begins to rock against me, gently sinking his length in and out of me.

"Axel," I tremble. "God, it's so good."

"So fuckin' sweet," he murmurs, leaning down and pressing his lips to mine.

I let him take me in a deep, hungry kiss. He kisses me like it's the last time he'll ever do so. His hands cup the side of my head, and his hips work my pussy, driving that beautiful cock in and out, hitting the perfect spots.

"Oh, God," I cry out. "I'm going to come."

"Mmm," he murmurs against my skin.

He moves one hand from my face, and reaches between us, stroking a finger over my clit. I erupt beneath him, shaking and shrieking out his name. He rumbles against me, and his hips work faster. Just before he comes, he pulls out of me and squeezes his cock, holding his release back.

"Roll over onto your hands and knees," he orders.

I can see the desperation in his eyes. He's so close. I do as he asks, rolling onto my knees and putting my ass into the air. He takes my hips, and sinks into me quickly. I throw my head back, and arch my body as he thrusts toward his release.

"You want it on your ass, darlin'?" he groans.

"Yes, oh, yes."

He thrusts three more times, before pulling out. I hear his raspy cry, and then I feel the hot spurts of come hit my ass and begin to slide down.

"So fuckin' beautiful," he murmurs between groans.

I lower my body onto the soft grass, exhaling.

Well, that wasn't so bad. In fact, if I'm being honest with myself, it was quite thrilling. Axel uses his shirt to clean me off, and then he flops down beside me. I roll to face him, propping myself up on my elbow.

"I survived," I whisper.

He meets my gaze. "There's more."

Oh?

He sees my expression become curious, and elaborates. "Those shackles in my room? Next time you suck my cock, you're going to be chained to them."

My pussy pulses and I bite my bottom lip.

He grins.

"Looks like that's going to be sooner rather than later."

~*~*~*~

AXEL

I grin, watching her sitting on the bar talking to Jax and Cobra. The two men were wary of Meadow when she first came into the picture, but now they're warming to her. She's between them both, laughing, throwing her head back, and letting those gorgeous locks tumble down her back. Her laughter is like a melody flowing through the room, making it light and warm. I shake my head, horrified that I'm thinking such…pussy thoughts.

"Pres, we need a word."

I turn to see Colt standing beside me, his eyes hard. I nod, and following him down the hall. We get to my office, and he closes the door once we're inside.

"What's up?" I ask, leaning against the desk and crossing my arms.

"Just got a call. There was some trouble in town."

I narrow my eyes. "Trouble?"

"Bunch of girls were...raped. Some club members."

I feel my neck prickle. "Club members? Have you motherfuckers been out, and if I so much as find out you've put your cocks in someone that doesn't want it I'll..."

"It's Beast, Pres."

I feel anger swell in my chest. "Beast?"

"He's fuckin' with us. The cops know the only MC in town is us, and Beast has made a run for it. You know what's goin' to happen if they pull us up? We got that gun shipment in last night. We haven't moved it on yet. If the cops show up here..."

"That smart motherfucker," I snarl. "We can't move that shit right now, it's not due to be delivered until Thursday. Fuck, we need to get into town and sort out this mess. Now."

"Most of the brothers are drunk."

I clench my fists. "You find the ones that can ride, and you gather them. We need to get in and sort this situation. Who rang you?"

"Jake, he's at the bar down the road. He heard the commotion and asked around. There were three girls raped in an alley about an hour ago. They came into the bar, and the bar attendant is trying to convince them to call the cops. He said there was talk of the local MC's doing it. People assume it's us. The cops will be onto it, if they're not already. We can be expecting a visit if we don't wrap this shit up."

"Scrap the fuckin' bikes, we'll take the trucks. They'll be lookin' out for us. Let's move."

Colt nods, and leaves the room. I turn, taking the keys for the trucks from my desk. I shove them in my pockets, and head back out. Colt has six mostly sober guys lined up. Meadow is staring at me, her eyes narrowed. I walk over, putting my hands on her knees. She's still sitting on the bar.

"Stay here; don't go. I've got shit to deal with, but I'll be back in a few hours. Go sleep, if you need."

She nods. "Okay."

I press a kiss to her lips, and then turn, gathering the men and shoving them outside. I give them a run down on what's happening as we drive.

Fuck, this is the last thing I need.

~*~*~*~

AXEL

"He still got them out there?" I ask Jake, as my men move around the bar, checking things out.

"Yeah, so far no cops have showed. They're not really talking, and one is refusing to allow him to call the cops. She copped it real bad. She's all fucked up and battered."

219

"Right," I grunt, and then turn to Colt. "Let's get out the back and talk to this guy before he calls the cops."

We walk as a group through the bar, shoving the girl out of the way when she tries to stop us. We step out back, and see a familiar face soothing three girls. We've known Max for a long enough time, that he's familiar with us and how we roll. Colt's bar is just up the road, and we've always had good communication.

Upon hearing our entrance, Max turns and stares over at us, then he gets to his feet.

"You fuckers come any closer, and I'll call the cops, but not before I put a fuckin' bullet in your heads."

"Pipe down, Max," I say, my tone bored. "You know we didn't do this shit."

"Funny that, because you're the only bikers that run this town, and these girls know what they saw."

I turn my eyes to the girls, and I study them. Two of the girls are wide-eyed and confused, and I can tell just by glancing at them, that they're off their trees. Beast gave them something to confuse them. They're both blonde, busty, and pretty enough. They're not beat up.

The third girl, she's staring at her hands, but I can see her battered face. She's trembling, and her entire body is rigid. When she finally lifts her eyes, I feel mine widen.

She's got jet-black hair, long and curly, half way down her back. Her eyes, through, they're cat yellow. I shake my head, never having seen anything like it. She's a strange, yet oddly attractive-looking girl, but she's been through the ringer. Her eyes are puffy and dark, and she has

220

blood dripping from her lip.

"It wasn't us," I finally say, turning to Max. "It was Beast and his gang. They're in town causing shit. Ask your girls here, go on."

Max turns to the girls. "Were these the men who hurt you?"

The dark-haired girl shakes her head frantically. "N-n-n-no."

Max narrows his eyes, and glares at me. "Then why are you here?"

"I'm here to clean up the fuckin' mess that prick left behind. I'm takin' the girls, Max. I need to sort this out, and keep it away from the cops."

Max storms over to me, getting up in my face. "They were gang-raped," he hisses. "You can't not call the cops."

I lean in closer, gripping his shirt. "You involve the cops, and a whole new world of trouble starts. You know how that shit goes down, Max. I'll take 'em, help 'em, and then let them go when Beast has been sorted."

"You know I don't fuckin' agree with this."

"And you also know you get no choice."

I step past him, and over to the girls. I kneel down in front of the dark-haired girl.

"My name is Axel, and I'm here to take care of you. Me and my boys, we won't lay a hand on you, but you gotta trust us. We're gonna take you back. We got some real nice old ladies in our club, and they'll let you stay with them."

The dark-haired girl shakes her head, her eyes wide. "No, please."

"Listen to me," I say gently, but firmly. "My men and I won't lay a hand on you or your friends, but we can't leave you here. You're not safe, but I promise once you are, we'll let you go."

She studies my face, and her eyes glisten with unshed tears.

Then she croaks out, "I don't get a choice, do I?"

"No, darlin'."

CHAPTER 21

MEADOW

Let me fix your broken soul, let me make your world whole.

I'm just dozing off on the old couch in the dining area of the clubhouse when I hear the trucks pull up. I lift my head, but I'm still hazy. I hear doors slam, and a moment later, Axel and the guys come through the door, only they're not alone. They have three girls with them. Two of those girls look like they're meant to be models, with their blonde hair and busty bodies, but the last girl looks completely broken. She's got her dark hair falling partly over her face, and her eyes are haunted. Not only are they haunted, but also they're the most incredible eyes I've ever seen. They're a stark yellow, and against her creamy, pale skin, they are piercing.

I get off the couch and walk over to them.

"What's happening?" I whisper to Axel.

He looks at the girls. "Colt, take them to the bunks in the back room. Keep two watches on them. We don't want them running."

"You stole them?" I say, feeling my eyes widen.

Axel studies me for a moment, and then he murmurs, "We need to talk."

He barks a few more orders, and then he takes my hand and leads me down the hall. We go to his office, and he shuts and locks the door behind us.

"What's going on?" I ask, getting a little worried.

He walks over and drops down onto his chair, and I take the seat beside it. He turns to me, and I see his fingers are biting into his knees.

"Those girls were gang-raped by Beast's club tonight."

"What?" I cry, throwing my hand over my mouth.

"We took them, because we don't want the cops getting involved. I'm not discussing club business with you, but you need to know we'll be keeping them here until we can sort out something safe for them."

"You're helping them?"

He nods, lifting his eyes to meet mine. "Yeah, but listen…that's not all I wanted to talk to you about. For years now, we've been jumping back and forth about why you even had to begin running in the first place. You want to know about the USB, your dad, and the rest of it, and it's about time I gave you the fuckin' truth."

My hands begin to tremble. He's going to tell me…oh, God.

"O-okay," I say.

"You gave yourself a part of me tonight. It's only fair I give it back."

He jerks his drawer open, and pulls out a flask. He unscrews it and swallows a shot down, then offers it to me.

"Is it that bad?" I say, my voice wavering.

"Well, it ain't good."

I take the flask, and shoot it back. Axel doesn't waste any time; he starts talking right away.

"Basically, to understand this story, you need to know your dad wasn't a biker."

I shake my head. "What? He created a club, and…"

"The club was fake, Meadow. Your dad was a cop, and he went undercover in a project that was meant to bring down numerous biker clubs in the area. He created his own club, and he got himself a name. It took years, but he did it. I found out what he did. I overheard him talking one day when I showed up at your house. I confronted him, and we got into it. Things went bad after that, and I constantly threatened to expose him. One day, he set me up. He knew my club was going to be involved in a big shipment coming into town—he had his sources everywhere. He gave Beast's club an anonymous tip off, knowing they'd show up before us. He knew we were sworn enemies."

"Why would he do that?" I gasp, unable to process this kind of information.

"He was angry at me, at himself, and he was tired of doing undercover work, and he wanted it over. He figured if two clubs showed up, a war would break out, and he could get what he needed to close us down. Chances were that we'd stuff up, and he could take us over that edge, bringing us down. He had enough evidence against us. He just needed us to fuck up."

I try to mull this over, trying to process it in my own head. So, my dad set Axel up, and threatened his club. It's slowly starting to make sense to me now. Slowly.

"So you killed my dad for revenge?" I ask, needing to know more.

His eyes harden, and I know the memory pains him. "It wasn't just about revenge. It was about him trying to destroy the only family I had. He lied; he let me develop a bond with him, and he fucked me and my boys over. He was going to take us all down. When I got wind that he was headed in to deliver information that would take the clubs down, I knew I had to interfere. Turns out Beast heard about it, too. That's the way it rolls when you're dealing with the shit we deal with. Your business is everyone's. Bikers had begun to hear about your dad, and word leaked about his undercover behavior. He was taking you that day...he was taking you to a different city so you would be safe. He was going to drop you off, then he was going to turn the information in, and go into witness protection."

I feel my stomach lurch, and tears fill my eyes.

I have so many questions, like how does Axel know all this? He couldn't possibly know so much just by word of mouth, but I can't focus on that right now. I just can't stop feeling the thudding pain in my heart about the news that's just been delivered to me.

"I went after him," Axel continues. "And I shot him. I didn't know you were in the car. I thought I'd had it planned out. I thought he'd dropped you off already, and that you were safe. I saw the car, and I shot him. I thought I'd missed anything vital, and he managed to get into the alley. I didn't know until a few hours after that you weren't in a different city, but instead, running with the information that could destroy my entire club."

"How did you know that I hadn't been dropped off?" I croak.

He shrugs. "Your dad had a shirt pressed to his wound. He couldn't have done that himself, because it wasn't his shirt—it was yours. The information was missing. I made some calls, found out you hadn't left the city, and I came after you."

"So what you're saying, basically, is that my father was a cop, going undercover as a biker, and he set you up to start a war. It went bad, you got hurt, you came back, and you killed him out of both revenge and to protect your club?"

He nods, letting his eyes scan my face for my reaction.

"And he was going to leave me behind?"

My voice cracks, and I turn my eyes down. My father was all I'd had. My mother I couldn't remember, and there were no other family members in my life. He was all I'd had. He knew he was all I had, and yet he was going to drop me off to a strange city alone, and go into witness protection, never coming back for me. The reality of it makes my heart burn, and tears trickle down my cheeks.

"I'm real sorry, darlin'."

I shake my head, standing. "I just...I need to go for a walk."

I turn before he can answer, and I rush out of the room.

"Meadow," Axel calls, but I don't stop.

The minute I get outside, I fall to my knees and I cry.

CHAPTER 22

MEADOW

When will you break, how much more can I take?

I see the flashing blue and red lights long before it registers. The minute it does register, though, I am scrambling to my feet and running inside the clubhouse. I'm not stupid; I know cops are never a good thing. I skid into the main area, and shove past people, running down to Axel's office. The minute I swing the door open, I see him. He gets up, his eyes fierce as they search my expression. Then he grates out, "What's wrong?"

"Cops."

"Fuck!"

He tears past me, and runs out into the hall. "Boys in blue, make sure nothin' can be found. Move!" he roars.

The men kick into gear, suddenly sobering, and running down the halls. They're moving things quickly, barking orders at each other. I've never seen anything like it in my life. One moment, they're men fucking women against counters; the next, they're up and running, fully alert, ready for action. Axel disappears down the hall, and comes back a moment later with something clutched in his hands. He takes my arm, pulling me into a nearby room.

"Need you to do somethin' for me. It ain't real nice, darlin', but I need you to do it all the same."

"What?" I ask, feeling my eyes darting around frantically.

He opens his hand to reveal the USB and a condom. What the hell?

"Need you to put this…"

His voice trails off, and his eyes flash with desperation. It clicks to me then, and I gasp. "You want me to insert that into myself."

"If they search us, Cricket, they'll search this entire place, including me."

"They can't just search you," I protest.

"They're cops—they do whatever the fuck they want to the club. They've been out to get a warrant for long enough that they've probably got one. But to you…you have rights. They can't touch you without permission, and if they come looking in here…for this…they won't be able to find it if it's on you."

I shake my head, trying to process what he's just said. I lift my eyes, and nod quickly. I don't really have time to argue. I don't want just anyone to get hold of that USB. I've not finished piecing the story together yet, and until I do, I don't want it taken. I'll do it, no matter how awkward. Axel nods his head toward a bed, and I scurry over.

"You want me to?" he asks.

"Um, yeah."

I take my shorts off, and heat floods into my cheeks. I lay back, trying to think of anything else. I feel like a drug smuggler, and it takes a lot to lie still while Axel unwraps the condom, and puts the USB inside it. Then he kneels in front of me. His eyes connect with mine for a moment, reassuring me, and then he gently parts my folds. "You ok baby?" he asks.

"Just do it, Axel."

He slips the USB inside me, just enough that it sits much like a tampon would. Part of the condom hangs from my depths, and I feel sick that I'm here, smuggling information in my goddamned private areas. It's not easy to process, and it's certainly not easy to lie through. I'm hiding something, just in case the club gets raided. That's basically what's happening, only I'm hiding it in a part of my body that is really not awesome.

"I'm real sorry…"

"Just don't," I whisper, putting my hand up as I pull myself up and yank my shorts up. I can feel a pressure down below, and I want to scream.

"Meadow, I know a lot of shit has happened today, and you're tryin' to deal with it all, but after this…I wanna finish it. Once and for all."

I meet his gaze. He's staring at me with a firm expression.

"Can we just deal with what's happening right now?" I ask.

He nods, and we walk out of the room. Cobra stops in front of Axel the minute we reach the front door.

"Bud, I don't know if you're gonna like this…"

I hear the skid of tires, and the distinct sound of doors slamming outside.

"Don't have time," Axel mutters to Colt. "You got that girl secured?"

"She's secured. Ain't gonna talk."

"Right, then let's deal with this shit."

We walk out front, and I see three cops standing in front of the car, all decked out in blue, hands on their guns as if they're expecting to get shot at. I narrow my eyes, and stare at the one in the middle. He's tall, and extremely handsome. I mean, the kind of handsome that takes your breath away. He's got emerald-green eyes, and dark, messy hair. He's bigger in build, with wide shoulders and long, sinewy arms. I drag my eyes away from him, and notice that Axel has stopped moving.

I turn to stare at him. His mouth is slightly agape and his fists are clenched. I didn't pick Axel to be one that was intimidated by cops, yet something about his stance is saying he's shocked, confused, worried. I look back toward the cop who is walking forward, his eyes pinning Axel. He's scary, and not even in the kind of way that is bad, or dangerous. He's just leaking dominance, like he's the kind of man that could bark one word, and you'd crumble.

"Axel, my boy, how are you?"

I'm confused. Axel knows him?

"The fuck are you doin' here?" Axel breathes, clenching his fists so tightly his knuckles are white. He steps in front of me. I hear shuffling behind me, and imagine the guys are lined up to show their support to their president.

"I got transferred. Thought I'd pay you a visit. Let you know I'm in town."

Axel doesn't say anything.

"What?" the cop says, stepping forward with a grin. "You're not goin' to give your old dad a hug?"

I feel like I'm going to pass out.

Did he just say…dad?

Silence falls behind me, and it sounds almost like the guys have stopped breathing. I guess they didn't know Axel's father is a cop. Oh my God, he's a fucking cop.

"I got nothin' to say to you, but fuck off," Axel hisses. "This is my grounds, and unless you got somethin' you need, old man, then you can get the fuck off my lot."

The man grins, and tilts his head, looking behind Axel and connecting eyes with me. He seems familiar, somehow, but maybe that's just because he looks a little like Axel.

"Meadow, long time no see."

What? My mind is spinning now. I've never met this man before. How the hell does he know my name?

"Step back, and don't you fuckin' speak to her," Axel snarls.

"Don't be like that, boy. I have a right to speak to her. You know you can't stop me."

Why does he want to speak to me?

"Step around here, Meadow. Let me see you."

I look up at Axel when he glances down at me, unsure what I'm supposed to do. He nods, and I step around him, trying to avoid walking funny. I stop in front of the big man, and he smiles warmly down at me, but there's something tricky lying behind that smile. He extends his hand, and I hesitate, staring down at his long fingers for a long moment.

"I don't bite," he assures me.

I reach out, and put my hand in his. He curls his fingers around mine, and shakes my hand. "I know you don't remember me, but I'm Raide."

My head snaps up, and my eyes widen. He chuckles.

"So you have heard of me? I believe you had something for me, though I imagine my son, here, has convinced you not to give it to me."

The USB. This is the Raide my father wanted me to give the information to? Raide is Axel's father...I don't...I don't understand.

"I don't know you," I say in a small voice.

"No, you wouldn't remember me. You were only young. We need to talk, Meadow."

"You can refuse him, Cricket," Axel says from behind me. "You don't owe him nothin'."

Raide looks up at Axel, and his eyes harden. "Now, don't make her mind up for her, boy. This ain't your business."

"It is my fuckin' business. You're on my soil."

Raide chuckles. "I see nothing changes."

I look between the two, confused. I honestly don't know what's going down, but I don't want to be a part of it.

"I'm not going to stick around here pressuring you. But I do need to speak with you, Meadow. I have a lot of answers to your questions. You call me, when you have time," he says, tucking his hand into his pocket and bringing out a card. He hands it to me, and I take it.

"You done?" Axel barks.

Raide lifts his eyes, and for a moment, I see a look of longing. I don't know what went down between the two but whatever it is, it was bad. I look at Axel, and I'm angry he lied to me. He told me Raide was dead. Why would he tell me that? I don't understand it, but right now, I'm trying to process so much information I just can't do it all right now. Raide calls his boys back to their cars, and with one last look at Axel, they drive away.

Axel turns back to the guys, and his eyes harden. "It ain't your fuckin' concern, and I ain't discussing it."

Then he walks inside, not giving anyone the chance to argue.

~*~*~*~

AXEL

"Don't fuckin' start on me, Cobra," I hiss, storming down the hall.

"You knew the boys were goin' to find out eventually, Pres..."

"Yeah, and that cunt showing up wasn't how it was meant to go down."

He grips my shoulder, and I spin around, lashing out at him, and slamming him against the nearest wall. "Don't you fuckin' put your hands on me."

"They're good with it, Pres," he grunts. "They've got your back."

I search his face, and then shove him back, letting him go. He rubs his throat where his shirt pressed against his skin. I shoot him one more glare before retreating to my office, and slamming the door. He doesn't follow me, but the minute I sit down, the door swings open and Meadow walks in. She's staring at me with eyes that are all betrayed and angry.

"You lied to me," she whispers.

I clench my jaw. "Wasn't your business, Meadow."

"You. Lied. To. Me."

I get out of my chair, and charge over, backing her up against the nearest wall. Her lips part, but her eyes hold that same determined glare.

"Don't you fuckin' come in here, throwin' your weight around. I wasn't obligated to tell you shit, but I did. I gave you somethin' earlier. I just left one thing out. And I don't owe you that, 'cause it ain't your concern."

"Not my concern?" she cries, and her eyes fill with tears. "I've been busting my ass trying with you, Axel. And for what? You've given me nothing. Nothing! I let you show me what eats at you, and I accepted it, but you're still holding back. You still don't trust me enough to share it all with me. When are you going to give me a bigger piece of yourself?"

I glare at her, and my anger boils over. "I was goin' to give you a piece of myself, Meadow. Tonight. I was going to patch you in as my old lady, because I want you in my fuckin' life. I want to try. I want to give you somethin' that you can hang on to."

Her eyes widen, and a little gasp escapes her lips. "What?"

"You fuckin' heard me. I'm claimin' you."

She shakes her head, backing up. "You don't get to just claim me, Axel. It's not that easy."

"Do you want me, Meadow?"

She shakes her head, her eyes wide. "What?"

"You fuckin' heard me," I grunt.

"I do, but…"

"Do you want to walk away from me?"

"No, but…"

"Then that makes you mine. I'm claimin' you, because I want you in my bed every fuckin' day, and I'm sick of denying that."

Her mouth forms a tiny O, and she continues walking backward.

"You killed my father," she croaks out. "You chased me across the country for nearly two years. You treated me like a dog, and you hurt me. You lied to me. You kept yourself away from me. Through all of that I still fought for you, hoping there was something left. Now you're going to just tell me I'm yours, and it's all happy days? I don't think so," she whispers.

What?

I narrow my eyes. "You fuckin' rejectin' me, Cricket?"

"I'm no one's property, Axel, especially not yours. I'm never going to give myself to someone who refuses to be honest with me."

"It was one fuckin' thing!"

"You want me to be your old lady?" she growls. "Then open the last door. Tell me what happened to you those months you were away."

My eyes harden, and my skin crawls. She can't ask me that shit. It ain't for her to know. "No."

"Then this," she says, pointing between the two of us, "is fucking done. Don't you follow me."

236

She turns, and runs out the door, not giving me a chance to react. I slam my hands against the table, and pain cascades through my heart.

Fuck it. I can't be back here.

I close my eyes, and drop my head into my hands. It's all been fuckin' too much. Chasin' her across the country, then havin' her in my bed, and opening something I never thought I'd open, then my fuckin' father shows up, and now we're here. I need to end this shit, once and for all. I'm tired of chasing, tired of hiding. I'm getting my girl back, even if she doesn't fuckin' want it.

Then it hits me, hard, like a ton of bricks.

She's still got my USB.

CHAPTER 23

MEADOW

**Promises are made to be broken, that's why the words were
never spoken.**

He doesn't come after me. Not that I expected him to. So, I flag down a
cab and order him to take me to the police station. I need answers. I don't
trust Raide, but I want to hear his side of it. My entire destiny has been
warped. Everything I've looked forward to, everything I've believed in
has been slammed into the dirt, and crushed. I can't begin to process
everything that's been put into my life, but I do know there's always a
reason for it.

Axel has a reason—a purpose—I just don't know what it is.

I know I love him. I've known it for long enough now.

It doesn't change that I can't keep fighting against a soulless man. He
doesn't want to let me in. He's refusing to acknowledge what this really
is. He wants me as an old lady, just a girl that does as she's told. That's
not me. I need him to love me. I need him to want more than just a claim.
He doesn't, though, because he won't open up. That should have been
my answer then, and it's certainly my answer now.

Axel and I are done.

The minute the cab pulls up to the police station, I get out, handing the
driver a twenty. Then I stand out front, staring up at the big building. I

need a toilet before I go in there. I'm fully aware that I still have a USB drive in a place a USB drive shouldn't be. I don't know if that makes me feel more powerful, or if I'll just throw it in the mail and send it back to Axel, cutting all ties forever. He'll want this. His father will want this. I'm tired of being the meat between the sandwich. If he has it, he can deal with it.

I find a public toilet, and my heart aches as a sense of loss washes through me. As much as I hated how Axel and my relationship has been, it was still mine, and because of that, letting it go is like letting go of my home. I felt a certain comfort around Axel and the guys. I can't explain it, because there really was nothing that happened to make me feel at ease, but I did. Now, here I am, in a toilet, about to go in and talk to a man I don't trust.

I don't know why I'm here.

I finish up in the toilet, and dispose of the condom before tucking the USB into my knickers, just to keep it safe. Then I make my way back to the station. I stare at the front doors for a long moment, struggling to breathe. I'm not entirely sure this is a good idea, but I know I have to do it. I need to know how Raide played his part in this, so I can decide for myself how this story is meant to unfold.

I walk inside, and the cool crisp air from the over air-conditioned room hits my face. I shudder. I walk up to the main desk where a lady in a dark gray suit is sitting, typing away. She lifts her eyes to see me standing there, and a small smile breaks out on her perky face. "Well, hi, how can I help you?"

I force a smile. "I'm actually here to see Raide."

Her eyes narrow. "Have you got an appointment to see him?"

"Well, no, but…"

"I'm sorry ma'am, unless you have an appointment I can't let you see him."

"He told me to come and see him, anytime I needed," I croak out, feeling my voice tremble.

"Look, just give me a minute. What's your name?"

"It's Meadow."

She picks up the phone, giving me a snooty expression. I want to reach over the reception and smack her in the face.

"Mr. Wraithe, yes, it's Lisa. I have a girl up the front, insisting on seeing you, I've told her that's not going to happen, but…"

Silence falls.

"Pardon?"

More silence.

"Her name is Meadow."

Her face pales, and she begins nodding her head.

"Yes sir, sorry sir."

She hangs up the phone, and looks up at me, her eyes flaring. "He'll be out in a second."

I nod at her, and wait with my hands bound tightly together. I hear a door slam to my left, and I spin around to see Raide approaching me. He's smiling, and his eyes sparkle as he approaches me. His blue shirt has a few buttons undone, and he looks far more casual now than he did earlier. I don't want to like this man, but...he has something about him. Something familiar. I give him a wobbly smile. He stops in front of me, and extends his hand. I can see the receptionist watching us from the corner of my eye, and I decide then she must be his fuck buddy.

"Meadow, I didn't expect you so soon. Are you okay?"

I hesitate. "Ah, yeah. I just wanted to, um, talk to you."

He nods. "Can I get you something to drink? You look upset."

"No, thank you."

He extends his hand further toward me, and I take it. He leads me down a small hall, and into a large office. He points to a big, comfy gray sofa in the corner of the room, and I sit. He takes the one across from me, sitting down too. I entwine my fingers back into their comfy position, and I lift my eyes to meet his. God, he's like Axel now I'm looking at him, really looking...I can see it.

"You want to tell me why you're here so soon?" he asks, leaning back in the chair.

"I want to know...your story. I've heard Axel's, but I haven't heard yours, and I think...I think I need to."

He stares at me for a long moment, and then he nods. "Yes, I believe you do."

"So are you going to tell me...?" I say, hesitant.

"Tell me what you already know..."

I shake my head. "So you can leave details out? No. You're either going to tell me, Mr. Wraithe, or you're not."

"Raide. And I'll tell you. I've got nothing to hide from you, Meadow."

I stare at him, not answering, just giving him one of those *well, hurry it up* expressions. He sighs, and stares down at his hands.

"I met your dad in our first year training. We hit it off right away. We both got situated at the same place, and things were great. It was great for a long time. He got married, and you were born. I was there through it all. Then Axel came back into town. I love my son, don't get me wrong, but I had him young. I was only fifteen when his momma got pregnant. We were young, and stupid, and he got adopted out. We really didn't get a choice."

He sighs before continuing.

"Axel tracked me down when he was old enough, and came back for me. It didn't go so well. He was angry at me, and when he found out I was a cop, shit hit the fan. I didn't know he was in a club at that point, but when I did, we knew we couldn't associate with each other."

"So, what happened then?" I ask, leaning forward, and resting my hands on my knees.

"Your dad and I got put on an undercover mission together: to create ourselves a biker club, and get as much undercover information as we could to bring down the clubs. At that point, there were a lot of drugs being illegally run, and the cops couldn't get close enough. It took us a solid eight years to earn the respect of the clubs, and get our name out there. Axel hated us. He knew what we were doing, and he chose to cut ties with both of us. He only came back to see you."

"Me?" I ask.

He nods, smiling. "He adored you, and it was the only time we saw him. He'd come and pick you up, taking you out."

I feel myself smiling at the memories. Axel used to take me riding, right up until I was about twelve. Then he distanced himself from me, leaving me heart broken. I don't recall ever seeing Raide, and I narrow my eyes.

"I don't remember you, if you were friends with my father, why don't I remember you?"

"We worked in the same place for a while, but I was always away. You did meet me a few times, but it was with groups of people, so you wouldn't remember. We tried to keep it all away from family, your father didn't want you involved, so he usually kept people from your house."

Makes sense.

Shaking my head, I continue. "So, you and my dad set Axel up?"

He shakes his head. "No, that wasn't exactly how it was meant to go. Axel thinks it is, Meadow, but it wasn't. We were after another club, but unfortunately, Axel's club was involved in the shipments that we were looking at. He thinks we set him up to start a war between the clubs so we could bring them down, but it wasn't the case. We sent Beast in with false information to the docks, to pick up a shipment. We were going to bring him down; we had enough evidence. Axel got wind of it, and he showed up first. By the time we got there, both of them were gone. We didn't see Axel again for nearly six months after that. When he came back, he wasn't the same."

"Beast took Axel?" I gasp, fear coursing through my veins. No, that can't be right.

"Yes, we got there and Beast and Axel were already gone."

"So, how did I come about running with that USB?"

Raide rubs his temples. "Axel came back on a rampage. He wanted revenge. He believed we'd set him up. He started tapping lines, finding out as much information as he could. I'd been transferred at this point, only your dad was left. The case had basically been declared a failure when we lost Axel and Beast, but then your dad started gathering information again. He was getting threatened, and it was becoming too dangerous for you and him to stay in town. A war was brewing, and you couldn't be around."

God, I clench my hands tighter together, trying to steady my pounding heart.

"Your dad had only one choice. The bikers knew what he was, what he'd done. He had to go into witness protection. He didn't want to make you go. You were young and fragile, so he was going to take you out of town, and let you go. He put all the information on the USB, and he was going to drive it to me to continue with the case…then you know what happened after that."

I feel my eyes burn with tears, and I swallow, shaking my head rapidly.

"So…you want the information to take down Axel, too?"

He shakes his head. "I know you don't believe it, but I turn a blind eye to my son's club. It's not easy, but I do it. I've always found a way to protect him, even if he doesn't believe it. I want the information to take down Beast and his club, as well as a chain of other outlaw clubs."

"Taking them down would cause a war, wouldn't it?"

He shrugs. "No, not if we have enough information."

"The information on the USB," I whisper.

"I swear to you, Meadow. I will not bring any harm to my son's club. They're careful; we have nothing on them. They don't have to be involved in this."

"You'll understand that I need time to process this?" I whisper, lifting my eyes and meeting his.

"I understand."

I stand, feeling my knees wobble. "Do you know what happened to Axel?"

Raide shakes his head. "No. I tried to find out, but I could never get a lead."

I nod, walking to the door. "Can I ask you one more thing, Raide?"

He nods, looking exhausted.

"Do you love him?"

He smiles weakly. "I never had a chance to get to know my son, to love him, but every part of me aches every day to try. I want to love him, Meadow. He just won't let me."

"I know the feeling," I mumble under my breath.

Raide stands, walking over. He places a hand on my shoulder. "I'm sorry about Mitchell…"

I swallow the lump that forms in my throat. "My dad didn't deserve to die, but sometimes these things can't be helped."

"No," he says. "They can't. Do you have money to get yourself some accommodation?"

I smile, but it's weak. "With all due respect, sir, but even if I didn't, I wouldn't ask you."

He grins at me. "No, I suppose you wouldn't. Let me at least pay for a cab to get you where you need to go."

I won't argue with that. "Okay, thank you."

"Call me when you decide what to do, Meadow."

I nod, and walk out of the room. My head is spinning.

MEADOW

I go to the only place I can think of. Even though it hurts to go back and face the memories that lay there, I have nowhere else to go. The cab stops, and I smile at the driver and get out. I stare up at the big house, and sigh. I hope Lady will let me stay a few days, because if she doesn't, I don't know where I'll go.

I'm halfway up the drive when my cell buzzes. I stare down at the screen, and I'm surprised to see a text from Axel.

A – Are we goin to be runnin again?

I'm angry at him, but more than that, I want him to know that I'm done playing his little games.

M – I'm not running anywhere. I went to see Raide.

My phone is silent a long moment—too long. I lean against the tree, and wait for it to buzz again. It does, five minutes later.

A – Glad to see I mean so fuckin much to you, Meadow.

Oh, he's not going to use that on me. No fucking way.

246

M – You wouldn't give me answers. I had every right to go to him. Don't make me feel bad about that. I don't have to answer to you any more, remember?

A – No problem.

Ouch.

M – You know, I figured something out today…

A – And that is?

M – That I'm in love with a self-righteous pig who refuses to let me into his heart, even though I've fully accepted the darkness there. I'm tired of playing your games, Axel. We're done here. Come and get your USB. To be honest, I don't care what you do with it. I'm done playing with you, and it's about time I moved on. I'm at Lady's. Send someone to get it, or get it yourself. I no longer care.

I switch the phone off before I can see if he answers or not. A loud crack of thunder fills the sky, and I stare up at the angry gray clouds rolling in. I didn't see them coming. I rush up the stairs of Lady's front porch, and rap on the door. A moment later, it swings open, and Lady stands there, staring at me with shock.

"Sugar, what are you doing here?"

I fumble a little with my words. "Well, uh, it's a long story but, uh…I've got no where else to go, Lady."

She smiles right away. "Come in, love, it's freezing out, and we're about to get rained on."

I step into her house, and I feel a little shiver pass over me. I try not to think about what went down here, because I know it's the only place I have to go right now.

"You look hungry, sugar. Let me give you something to eat."

Lady rushes into the kitchen, and I sit on the couch, trying to think of anything but the fact that I just told Axel I loved him over a text. I mean, come on, seriously? I shake my head, disgusted with myself for losing my temper.

Lady comes out a moment later with a sandwich and a cup of tea. She places them down in front of me, and looks at me sadly.

"This can't be good if you're here, and not with Axel."

I give her a weak smile. "I found out about his dad, and all the things that happened with mine, and when I asked him what happened to him he still refused to tell me. I love him, Lady, but I can't keep coming second to his demons."

She nods, understanding. "Axel is a hard man. I wish there was something I could say to make this better for you."

"It's okay, I'm not here to feel better. I just needed somewhere to go."

She smiles, and taps my hand. "I have to go out now, love. But you're welcome to stay. Go back up to your room, and make yourself at home."

"Thank you, Lady. I can't express just how much this means to me."

She beams. "I'm sure I get it."

I'm sure she does, too.

CHAPTER 24

MEADOW

Come back to me, my love, let me give you all I have.

I flop down onto the bed in Lady's guest room, and contemplate turning my phone on. Part of me wants to know what Axel said; the other really doesn't. I decide that leaving it off is my best option right now. I roll to my side, and stare out the window. The storm is rolling in, crackling in the distance. Rain is thundering against the window, making splatting sounds. Most times I'd love lying here, listening to the rain, but right now it's making me uneasy.

I get up, deciding to go and make myself something to eat. Really, it's just to try and take my mind off all the information Raide gave me, mixed with what Axel gave me. My heart is constantly aching, and it's taking all my strength not to run to Axel and just forget the past and find the future. But that's not so easy to do right now. I just need some time, some space, to figure out how this is going to go down.

I spend the next two hours reading in Lady's library. I've picked up an old Virginia Andrews book, and I'm flicking through the pages.

That's when someone raps on the door, loudly, frantically. I get to my feet, staring at the entryway. I didn't hear a car. I walk slowly toward the door, wondering if it's a good idea to answer it. I mean, what if it's one of Lady's cases, and he or she is on a rampage? I scrunch my nose up in contemplation, and continue toward the front door.

It bangs again, louder, more desperate.

Swallowing, I take the handle, and open it. In front of me stands a very drenched, panting Axel. My eyes widen, and a little squeak leaves my throat. What the hell is Axel doing here? I never expected him to come, I was sure he'd send one of his guys. His eyes are wild, and he must be soaked to the bone. Before I can open my mouth to say something, he rasps out, "Beast took me, and he tortured me."

My mouth snaps closed, and I say nothing.

Axel shoves past me, and I can almost feel the emotion radiating off him. This isn't easy for him; I can tell by the way his shoulders are tensing, and untensing. He's dripping water all over the floor, but I don't bother to say that. I just watch him as he walks over to the window, staring out. His fists are clenched, and when he speaks, his voice comes out ragged and tight.

"He took me the day your father and my father set me up at that dock. I went alone; I didn't expect him to be there. He outnumbered me, and he took me. He was hoping to use me as leverage, but then he just decided he liked the idea of torturing me. And that's what he did."

He pauses, and then continues.

"Every day, for nearly six months, he tortured me. He beat me, he burned me, he starved me—you name it, he did it. Those things weren't what broke my spirit. It was the girls..."

The girls? I swallow, feeling my heart speed up, but I don't say anything. Axel doesn't turn.

"He used to bring them in daily, bound and shackled. He would make them get on their knees, and suck me off until I came. They were there

250

against their will, crying and gagging as they were forced to shove my cock into their mouths and suck until I came." He spins around, panting. "Do you have any fucking idea how hard it is to come when you know you're basically raping a woman?"

I shake my head, and tears tumble down my cheeks.

"The first day, he made the girl suck me for over two hours. My dick didn't want a bar of it. I was so mortified I was gagging, but eventually, after experimenting further, she got me there. It's hard not to come when someone is sucking you. Even if you know they don't want it, it's so fucking hard."

I make a strangled sound, and press my hand to my head. Oh God, the poor thing.

"This continued on, every fucking day. Eventually, I got used to it. I knew the quicker I got it over with, the quicker they would get to leave. They came to trust me, flashing me smiles before they'd leave. They knew I wouldn't hurt them, and we grew an understanding."

"H-h-h-how did you get out?" I whisper.

"One of the girls let me go," he snorts. "Can you believe it? She was forced to suck my dick every day for at least a few weeks, but she managed to get that key and let me go. It wasn't easy to get out, but I did it. So there it is, Cricket. You know all of me now..."

His voice breaks at the end, and I lift my eyes to meet his. His beautiful aqua orbs are glassy and red, and his jaw is tight. He's waiting for me to say something, and probably to run and be disgusted. How can I be? It's no different to a woman being raped. How could I ever find him repulsive? It wasn't his fault. He endured one of the worst things a human can endure.

Slowly, on wobbly legs, I walk toward him, stopping when we're nearly chest to chest.

"It changes nothing for me," I whisper, reaching up, and grazing my fingertips over his cheek. He shudders, and closes his eyes. "I love you, Axel Wraithe. That hasn't changed."

His eyes pop open, and his lips part slightly. "How the fuck can you love me? After everything I've done to you, you should hate me, Cricket."

"Hate and love are powerful emotions, equally the same. If I have to pick one, I'm going to go with love."

He reaches up, and cups my cheek. Then he drops his head and his lips graze over mine. Before I can say a word, he reaches down and scoops me up into his arms, carrying me up the stairs. He takes me into the bathroom, and sets me on my feet.

I stare in full appreciation as he slowly strips out of his drenched clothes. When he's naked before me, I smile. That view will never get old. I remove my clothes quicker than lightning, and then I step forward, placing my hands on his chest.

"Once you go here, Cricket, you can't go back. If you accept this, all of me, then I'm never lettin' you go."

His voice is serious, his tone determined. I smile up at him.

"I say, bring it on."

He grins, and then swings the shower door open and shoves me into it. The moment the water runs over our bodies, and we press ourselves together, I know I don't want to wait. I don't want foreplay, I don't want roaming fingers—I just want him inside me. Hard and fast. Right now. As if reading my mind, Axel spins me around and presses my chest against the shower wall. His hand runs down my back, and around the front to my pussy. He cups it.

I can feel his cock pressing against my ass, and his lips grazing my ear. I make a happy sound, and push my ass back into him. He growls, and lowers his body just slightly, before driving upward and sliding into me with one swift thrust. I cry out, tensing right away at the tiny sting of pain that radiates through my body. That's soon replaced with pleasure as Axel begins to slide in and out of me.

"Always wanted you like this. Pressed against a wall, with nowhere to go," he rasps into my ear.

"Maniac." I giggle, but it's cut off with a moan as he tilts his hips, hitting that sweet spot.

"You're goin' to come for me, at least twice."

"Didn't think you could hold out that long," I grate out between clenched teeth as I try to stop myself from screaming.

He reaches around and pinches my nipple for my comment. "We'll see," he murmurs.

He slides his hand down, still thrusting, and finds my clit. I groan, "That's unfair."

He chuckles into my ear, and nips at my lobe. "Life's unfair, baby. Get used to it."

I whimper, and curl backward as sparks of pleasure find their way to the surface. I want to come already, and there's no holding back.

I scream as Axel pinches my clit, and the first wave of pleasure racks my body. He grunts, and lets me ride it out before spinning me around, and reaching down for my legs. A moment later, I'm jacked up on his body, my legs wrapped firmly around his waist. He gently lowers me, not moving his eyes from mine, and he fills me again.

"Number two is coming right up," he husks, placing a hand on the wall beside my head.

I tilt my head, opening my mouth, and closing it over his bicep. He grumbles, and I bite down, hard. He hisses, and drops his head down to my neck, clamping his own mouth onto my skin.

I cry out, snaking my tongue out, and licking the spot I bit. He chuckles again, and pulls his head back, causing me to turn my head. The minute I do, he closes his lips over mine, and we lock ourselves into a kiss so deep and beautiful, it has my skin prickling.

It's a kiss of love.

He thrusts his hips so gently, so slowly, that my release is hanging on the edge, causing my entire body to tense. I want to go over, but at the same time I just want him to keep fucking me like this, nice and slow. He wrenches his mouth away from mine, and his eyes are filled with lust. "I'm goin' to come, baby, you need to join me," he rasps.

"Fuck me harder, then," I groan.

His eyes flare, and he begins moving his hips faster, harder, driving into me with such force that my head bumps back onto the tiled wall. I come within three pumps, and I scream out my release, crying out his name, and clenching around him. He throws his head back a minute later, and a ragged cry escapes his throat as he explodes into me, pumping his release into my eager body.

"Holy shit," I manage to whisper after five minutes of shuddering.

"Yeah, that about covers it," he croaks into my ear.

He lets me go, and I slowly put my feet back onto the floor. My knees wobble, but I manage to hold myself up. Axel reaches for the soap, and fills his palm. We spend the next hour in the shower, washing each other, touching each other, and just being together for the first time without this wall between us.

It's perfect.

But perfection never lasts.

CHAPTER 25

AXEL

For you I will sacrifice, to show you, love, you are my life.

Meadow gave me the USB. She put it in my hands, and she trusted me with it. It broke down the last walls between us, because I know how much it took for her to give it to me. Her dad gave that to her, with one order. She made a promise, but she ended up being faced with a situation that tested her, and she decided to put her faith in me. Nothing could make me love her more. Nothing.

Finally, I have my girl.

Then it all goes south.

I hear the rumbling of a mass amount of bikes just as Meadow dozes off against my arm later that night. My eyes narrow, and I slowly get up. She jerks awake, and her eyes widen when she hears the noise.

I don't know why the guys would come out here unless something was wrong. Shit, is something wrong? I walk toward the window, and stare out, waiting…Maybe they're just a group of bikes going past? I'd probably believe that, if something weren't clenching in my chest right now.

Something's not right.

"Is that your guys?" Meadow asks, stepping up beside me.

"Don't know, darlin'," I murmur still keeping my eye on the driveway.

I see lights flash, and then the sounds of bikes coming down gravel fills my ears. This isn't right. Something is off. I squint my eyes, and then I see them, and I know right away they're not my guys. My entire body stops for a minute, and fear courses through my veins. That son of a bitch. He must have followed me out here, and then gotten himself some backup. He knew I couldn't call my guys in time; he knew he'd trap me if I were here.

I spin to Meadow. Her eyes are wide and frantic. She's seen who they are too.

"You need to run, and you need to run now. Go, Meadow, don't fuckin' stop."

"I can't leave you here, Axel," she cries, her face washed with fear.

I take her shoulders, forcing my voice to go hard and steely. "I'm not giving you a fucking choice. Go, get onto the road, find a lift. Get my guys. Don't hesitate, don't stop, just do it. If you don't go, and they take us both, then my guys will never be able to get the leads they need to find us. You gotta do this for me. You can't argue with me on this."

"What about Lady?" she gasps.

I shake my head. "She's out, she will be for at least four hours. They won't be here when she gets back. Just go, Cricket."

She slowly nods, just as the bikes come to a skidding halt outside. I rush over to Lady's drawer, pulling out the two guns she keeps there. I thrust one at Meadow, and then I clutch one firmly in my hand.

"Axel…"

I press my finger to her lips. "Don't, just run, baby. Run hard."

She nods, and a tear slides from her eye. She's terrified, but she sucks it in, and turns and rushes toward the back door. I watch her go, and then I turn to where the sounds of boots crunching are coming closer. Holding my head high, I walk out onto the front porch. Beast is standing in front of at least eighty bikers. I hold the gun in one hand, ready to fight with everything I am.

"Nice one, Beast," I grunt.

He grins, and walks forward. "You know me. I don't do anything in halves."

"What do you want? Clearly something, or you wouldn't have rounded up a hundred pussies to do your dirty work."

His jaw ticks, but he keeps his grin. "Big words for a man standing alone."

I shrug, even though my body is stiff and on alert. "Shit happens."

"Where's Meadow?" he asks causally, looking behind me.

"Didn't you hear? Raide took her."

He narrows his eyes, studying to see if I'm serious or not. "Well, that just makes my plan a whole lot easier then, doesn't it? If Raide has Meadow, then we can take you, and I'm sure between the two of them they'll do whatever it takes to get you back. Like, say, give over a USB?"

"The USB has been destroyed, Beast. You're wasting your time," I say, keeping my voice hard, even though I'm racked with fear and rage.

He throws his head back, and laughs. "Now you think I'm stupid."

"I know you're stupid," I hiss.

His eyes grow hard. "As much as I'd love to sit here and talk to you about this, I don't have the time, nor the patience. I know that USB isn't destroyed, and I know you're lying. So, I'm going to take a leap here, and assume Raide or Meadow will come for your sorry ass. Leaving me with only one choice..."

He raises his hand, and a gunshot blares out through the night. My body is shoved back, and a burning pain shoots through my shoulder. It's like being hit with a hot poker. Blood leaks down my arm, and the pain intensifies to the point where a ragged roar leaves my throat, and I drop to my knees, howling in pain.

"Now it's time we do this my way," Beast growls.

CHAPTER 26

MEADOW

As my soul is ripped apart, I will give you, my heart.

I'm drenched by the time a car stops. I've been running for an hour and my legs are aching. I feel sick to my stomach, not knowing if Axel is ok, or if he's hurt. I finally get a lift with a young boy, who drops me directly to the compound. I charge through the front doors, and into the main living area. The moment the guys see me, drenched, panting and frantic, they stop everything. Cobra rushes over first, taking hold of my shoulders.

"Shit kid, what's goin' on?"

"It's Axel," I cry out. "B-b-beast showed up…I don't know what happened, he made me come and get you."

"Where?" he barks.

"Lady's house."

"When?"

"About two hours ago," I whisper.

Cobra spins around. "Boys, get on your bikes. Now!"

Everything happens in a blur after that. The guys get on their bikes, and I hear Cobra barking orders. Soon they're skidding off into the night, guns loaded, ready to find their boss. I am left behind, alone, with only a few strays left hanging around. I go to Axel's room, and crawl onto his bed, letting the tears escape. God, they took him, I just know it. I tremble with fear, and pull out my phone, trying to dial his number. It goes straight to voice mail.

The sick feeling that spreads through my stomach is enough to make me run to the bathroom and throw up.

Please God, let him be ok.

~*~*~*~

MEADOW

The next twelve hours of my life are slow and completely agonizing. I just sit, blaming myself. If I didn't go out there, he would have never had to follow me. It would have never happened. Colt keeps telling me repeatedly that it's not my fault. How can he say that? I'm the one who refused not to listen. I'm the one who ran constantly, making Axel chase me. It is my fault. He's gone because of me. Grief doesn't begin to explain what I'm feeling right now.

I hate myself.

I'm curled up in a corner, just watching they guys run past. None of them have slept. They've been making calls, trying to track cell phones, and doing the best they can to locate Axel. They can't. Beast isn't in his compound. He's not co-operating at all. We don't know where Axel is. We have no idea. It feels like we're banging our heads against a brick wall.

Then my phone rings.

And I see Axel's number.

I can't scramble quickly enough to press the enter button. I hold the phone to my ear, and the entire room stops, watching me, their eyes wide. "H-h-hello?" I whisper, praying with everything inside me that I hear Axel's voice on the phone.

I don't.

"Well, hello, Meadow."

It's Beast. My blood runs cold, and I clench my fists.

"What have you done with him?" I snarl.

"You know, I've thought about this, and it wasn't an easy decision to make. I thought about keeping Axel until I had the USB drive, but then I decided, I really don't want to let him go. Without Axel, that club will go up in flames. They can't function without him. When he's gone they will run off the rails, and the cops will focus on them. I've really only wanted Axel for one thing…the satisfaction of killing him."

"You're bluffing," I stammer.

A cold laugh comes across the phone. "Poor naive little girl, how stupid do you think I am? Axel had the USB on him, and now I have it. I simply have no purpose for him. He's been scum in my life for too long now…"

My body freezes. I gave Axel the USB. Oh God, I gave it to him right before Beast showed up. Tears leak out of my eyes, and fear makes it hard to breathe.

"Please," I whisper, "I'll give you anything, just bring him back."

Colt kneels in front of me, his eyes searching my face.

"Aw, now, your pleading might have worked if I hadn't already killed him."

"You're lying," I scream.

"I have pictures, if you'd like. Please hold; I'll send them through to your phone."

The next few seconds of my life pass by in a blur as I feel my phone vibrate in my hand. With the function of a robot, I move it from my ear and stare down at the screen. My scream escapes, ragged and broken, as a picture of Axel, covered in blood, his eyes wide open, his head tilted back. He looks...dead. No.

No.

Colt snatches the phone from my hand, looks at the picture, and then presses it to his ear. "You son of a bitch. I'll fucking kill you for this. I'll fucking gut you."

Then he sends the phone soaring across the room, but I don't notice. My entire body slumps forward. There's no strength to hold myself up. All I can see in my head is Axel's vacant eyes, and the way his mouth was slightly open. My screams come out high-pitched and violent, unbreakable. Colt leans down, scooping me into his arms. I feel his hot tears drop down onto my cheek. By the time we're halfway down the hall, my screaming has turned to ragged pleas.

"He's lying!" I cry, not believing it.

It can't be over. It's a trick. He's playing with us.

Colt looks down at me, his eyes broken. "I'm sorry, honey."

"No, Colt, he's not dead," I begin to scream again. The pain in my chest is something I can't explain. It's like two hands have reached in, and torn my heart out. Desperation fills my veins, fighting against reality. This isn't real. It's just too easy. It's too simple. Beast wouldn't just ring up and say he's dead. It's not how a man like him works. He wants a fight, he wants our desperation.

It can't be real.

Colt takes me to his room, and lays me on the bed. I clutch him, not wanting to let him go, needing something to take this aching pain in my chest away. Grief wracks my body, causing me to shake and cry so hard my teeth snap together. My mumbled words are not comprehendible to anyone. My lifeline has been torn from me. We never even got a chance. We finally broke down that wall, and then we were left with nothing but emptiness.

My beautiful broken man can't be gone.

CHAPTER 27

MEADOW

Darkness, consume me.

"You need to keep looking, Cobra!" I cry, storming through the club four days later.

I'm sleep stricken, my eyes are burning, and I haven't eaten in days. I know Axel isn't gone, and no matter what everyone is telling me, something doesn't feel right. It's just not in Beast's nature to go down that easily, and after finding out what he did to Axel all those years ago, I'm not convinced he's not doing it again. He'd get off far more by knowing he had Axel, torturing him, while everyone thinks he's dead.

Cobra glares at me. "Fuck, Meadow, I'm doin' everything I can. I can't find Beast. I'm not entirely convinced we ever will."

"You can't give up on him, he's not dead!"

"We saw a damned photo!" he barks, stress consuming him.

"That means nothing, you know that. How can you just walk away so easily?"

He grabs my shoulder, shaking me slightly. "God dammit, Meadow. I've not slept trying to find him. Do you think I'll rest until I at least have his body? Jesus, you're making out like I don't fucking care. He's like my fucking brother."

His voice cracks on the last word, and my heart sinks. God, I'm being such a bitch. He's doing everything he can, but there's only so much they can do without recourses. I step forward, wrapping my arms around his waist. He stiffens, and I'm sure for a moment he won't hug me, but finally he wraps his arms around me. I hold onto him, needing some comfort. My heart is breaking day by day.

I won't lose my fight though.

"I'm so sorry, Cobra," I whisper. "I know you're hurting too."

He pulls back, looking down at me with a hard stare. "You gotta let me work this how I need to."

I nod. "And you have to let me work it how I need to."

He doesn't question me, because quite frankly I think he's gotten so desperate that he needs the reassurance that someone else is out there looking for Axel besides him. I give him a weak nod, and grip the keys to Axel's SUV. I walk out the front door without another look. There's only one person who might be able to help me now, and that's Raide.

The ride over to his office is slow; my mind keeps going to Axel. It makes me sick to my stomach to think about what he's going through right now. I don't even want to think of the situation he's probably in, but I do know I'll fight, just like the guys, until the day I get a final answer. It'll be Axel alive – which I believe he is – or it'll be sighting his body as proof he's gone. I won't stop until I get one or the other.

"Meadow," the receptionist says as I walk through the front door to Raide's office.

"Is he here?" I whisper, exhausted.

"Yes, let me call him."

She's giving me a hard stare; clearly she thinks that I'm having one off with her boss. She has no idea. I hear her whispering something on the phone, and then she hangs up and I see Raide's office door open. At the sight of him, my eyes burn. I don't know why. He's the only hope I've got left; he's the only chance we might have of finding Axel. He walks over, surprising me by taking me in a firm, yet warm hug.

"I'm so sorry, Meadow. We're doing everything we can."

"Can we talk, Raide?" I ask, pulling back.

"Of course, come in."

We head into his office, and I sit on the chair over from him. He looks as exhausted as me, his eyes are heavy and his face is lacking any emotion. I speak before he gets the chance, I don't want to waste anymore time.

"I don't think he's dead," I say, simply.

Raide looks up at me. "No, I don't think so either. It's not the way clubs like Beast's run."

"Axel's guys don't have enough recourses to be able to find him on their own, but I know you do."

He sighs, running his hands through his hair. "I don't have enough information on Beast, without that USB..."

"I have information," I say.

He raises his brows. I exhale loudly. Axel doesn't know it, because he came after me so quickly, but when I got to Lady's house the night he was taken, I looked over the USB drive before giving it back to him. I studied some of the information and locations. I didn't give them to the boys at the club, because they'll only get themselves killed going in. I can't risk Axel like that. I feel safer knowing Raide has it.

"How?" he asks.

"I have seen what's on the USB."

His eyes widen. "Meadow, I can't stress enough how much that information would change this."

"I can only tell you what I remember," I point out. "But I remember some locations."

He nods, and pulls out a pen and paper. "Give me what you can."

I give him every single thing I remember seeing on that USB. When we're done, he assures me that he'll do everything he can to get me the answer I deserve. He knows I need to know. I need closure one way or another. I need to know, more than anything in the world, if Axel is dead or alive.

I need to know if I've lost him forever.

TWO MONTHS LATER

MEADOW

Living without you, is like living with no heart, how will I ever know where to start?

Time doesn't heal wounds. It simply numbs them. In the months that have passed since Axel's disappearance, nothing has changed. I still wake each morning with a hole in my heart, a hole that can't be filled. I walk through my day not feeling, not really seeing—just doing. Then, when night falls, I slide into my bed, and cry myself into a fitful sleep. Nothing will ever feel okay until I know he's okay.

At least until my baby is born.

Staring down at my small, rounded tummy, I know that this baby was sent to me for a reason. I have to believe that. It's the only thing that keeps me going. I'm just about four months pregnant. I didn't even know I was, until my stomach started rounding. Then I realized I hadn't had a period since before I'd been with Axel. The news hit me hard, like a hurricane. I refused to accept it for two weeks, but Colt dragged me to the hospital, and made me get a scan.

Then I saw her.

Okay, I don't really know if it's a her, but to me...that's what she is.

Everything changed for me when I laid eyes on that tiny beating heart. She is the only part of Axel I have right now, and I'm not going to give up on her. It doesn't take the pain away, though. Each day is still a mission to get through.

I live with Lady now. She's the only person who I trust enough to take care of us. The guys visit me every day. They've claimed me as a part of their club, even though Axel never patched me in.

They're my rocks.

Not a day goes by that they don't fight. They've been searching for Beast for months now. Raide hasn't stopped; he's had his team on it, wanting closure for all of us. If he's gotten any leads, he hasn't let me know about it. He won't give me false hope unless he knows something for sure. I know they all won't stop until they find Beast, and when they do, they'll make him wish he were never born.

I don't blame them for that.

"Meadow? You in here?"

I lift my eyes to see Colt walking into Lady's living room. I'm sitting, staring out the window with my hands on my belly, like I do most days. I give him what used to be a smile, and he takes a seat beside me, his gaze searching my face.

"It's been so hard around the club lately, so we thought tonight, we'd do a cook-out. We're just tryin' to piece together what was broken. I want you to come."

I shake my head. "No thank you."

He reaches out, taking my hand. "You know I'm not going to force you, Meadow, but I need you to try for me. You have to try. You can't live your life sitting here."

My eyes grow hard. I can feel them. "What will you have me do, Colt? Pretend like he's not trapped and probably being tortured? Pretend like his baby isn't growing in my belly?"

His eyes fill with guilt. "Shit, no, of course not. I just…I'm just trying to help."

I squeeze his hand weakly. "And you know I am grateful for it, but I'm not ready to face the club. I can't…I can't go there if he's not there. Not right now. I'm barely holding it together. I'm sorry, Colt."

"I get it," he says, leaning back in the chair. "Every day I walk in there. Feels like my heart's being ripped out."

My eyes burn with unshed tears. "It doesn't get easier," I say, in a weak voice.

"No, it doesn't."

I lean into him, and he wraps an arm around me. The other hand rests on my tiny baby bump. "How's this one going?"

Colt has been super-supportive of me since the day I found out I was pregnant. He dragged me to the doctors, got me my prenatal vitamins, and made sure I had everything I needed. Without him, I would have crumbled.

"She's okay. I think I felt her move the other day, but I can't be sure."

He smiles, but his eyes are sad. "I'm glad. I have to get going, I just wanted to check in on you while I was going past. Are you okay? Do you have everything you need?"

"I do," I say in a weak, strained voice.

He nods at me, flashes me a sorry smile, and then leaves. I'm used to it. I know I'm not easy for them to deal with. They never know what to say, or how to act around me, and I can't blame them. This is the easier way.

For everyone.

~*~*~*~

MEADOW

I lift the washing basket, and walk out the front door. A light drizzle of rain has begun to fall. I walk down the front steps, holding the overly full basket, and heading out to the back washing house where there's an indoor clothesline. My hair sticks to my face in seconds, and my entire body breaks out in a shiver.

It takes me a moment to realize that shiver is a feeling of unease. I glance around, unable to see anything through the mist.

Is someone here?

My heart begins to speed up, and I back up toward the house. That's when I hear the sounds of boots crunching. Oh, no. Has Beast come back for me? Fear pulsates through me as I turn, and head back toward the stairs, rushing as fast as I can. When I reach the bottom step, I hear the broken, crackled voice. "Stop."

It can't be.

My entire body stops working, and slowly, I turn, feeling my knees already beginning to wobble. Out of the mist steps a dark figure. As he nears closer, his features become clearer. Aqua eyes are all I see before my knees give way, and I go down with the washing basket. A ragged cry leaves my throat as reality hits me hard, and for a moment, I wonder if I'm hallucinating.

It's Axel.

I feel arms wrap around me, and a hand takes my chin, tilting my head up. I can't see him through the rain and the tears, but I can smell him. Only one man smells that way. In a pitiful voice, I cry out his name, and press my hands against his chest. I'm sure this isn't real. I feel a steady, pounding heart beneath his shirt. I also feel that he's lost a lot of weight. Slowly we begin moving up, until we're on our feet. I blink rapidly, needing to make sure this is real.

Then I see his face, and a strangled cry wrenches from my throat. It's him. It's really him. He's here, standing in front of me. His face is slightly sunken, and he's got fading bruises, but there's no missing those eyes. I lift a trembling hand, and I stroke his heavily stubbled cheek. He closes his eyes, and his hand goes up, covering mine.

"It...you're...you're...I didn't know if you were dead, or alive, I..." I rasp.

"I'm here, I'm here," he murmurs, his voice crackly.

"B-b-b-but..."

My voice breaks, and I begin to sob again. Axel's hands slide down over me, as if he's checking I'm all there. When his hands slide over my belly, he stops moving. His eyes lift up to mine, and in them I see a question. I nod weakly, trying to smile between sobs. He drops to his knees, suddenly, heavily. I hear him thump onto the ground before his hands cup my belly, and he presses his face against it.

This only makes me cry harder.

I tangle my fingers into his hair, feeling his body shaking with emotion. Then he wraps his arms around me, and I take his head in my hands, holding him with everything I am. He slowly slides up my body, and envelopes me in a hug so tight, and so warm that it takes my breath away. I cling to him, never wanting to let him go, but not understanding if this is real or if I've completely lost my mind.

"Are you real?" I whisper.

"I'm real. I'm here."

He slowly pulls away from me, and takes my hand, leading me up the front stairs and inside the house. The minute we get into the light, I see him. Really see him. His clothes are hanging on his frame, and his skin is pale. He has bruises up his arms, and dark, angry red scars around his wrists. His eyes have fading bruises, and his lip has been split a lot, because a jagged scar runs down the bottom left corner. His cheeks are sunken, and his eyes are dull. But it's him.

He steps forward, and swipes a tear from underneath my eye as I sob wildly. I clutch his hands, and meet his eyes. "What happened?"

He takes me over to the couch, and pulls us both down. Then he wraps me in another hug, squeezing me until I can't breathe. His hands are on my belly again, his fingers lightly grazing the bulge. "How far?" he croaks.

"I'm nearly four months."

His eyes show a sparkle of light when he looks back up at me. I reach across, touching his sunken cheeks that are covered in rubble. "I was starting to think you were dead, but I didn't want to give up," I whisper.

"I know, baby," he says, looking away.

"He sent me a photo, and…"

"I know," he grinds out, cutting me off. "I know what he did. I heard you scream on the phone…"

"H-h-h-how? Oh God, Axel. We left you there…we…we thought…"

He presses a finger to my lips. "Hush, you didn't leave me. I know the guys didn't stop looking for me. I know *you* didn't stop looking for me."

"But we didn't find you."

He shakes his head. "I'm here now. The rest doesn't matter."

"How did you get out?"

He tucks me into his arm, and then begins speaking in a low, heavy voice. "Raide got me. He found out my location, and he took most of the club down, killing a majority of them. The rest he took into custody. He didn't plan on killing them, but when he found my location, he made sure he had full re-enforcement. He knew Beast would come out, guns ready, and he did. He shot at them the minute they arrived, but Raide was prepared. He pulled me out."

Raide saved him. My heart swells.

"W-w-what did Beast do to you, Axel?"

He looks me in the eye. "Nothing he didn't do before. Only this time there were no girls, just beatings. He could have killed me when he told you I was dead, but he enjoyed watching me suffer and starve. I'm only sorry I didn't pull the trigger that exploded his brains."

I take his hand, squeezing it. "I'm so sorry."

"Don't you say sorry to me, Cricket," he says into my hair. "Never say sorry."

"The photo?" I croak.

"He shot me twice, and just as I threw my head back and opened my mouth to wail in pain, he took the photo. He was going to send it as a torture picture, to make sure you all gave him the USB, only he found out I had it on me, and decided the photo would work to prove I was dead. It was a freak shot; he got lucky."

It was a freak photo? My mind spins, and I shake my head over and over. Axel shifts in the chair, and leans down, cupping my face.

"The only thing I saw in that place was you, Cricket. You saved me; you kept me fighting. I realized what a complete fuck-head I've been, when faced with the reality that I might never see you again. I don't care what happens from now. I want you, and I'll make you mine. I'll cherish the fucking ground you walk on. I love you, Meadow. I should have told you sooner."

I feel tears tumble down my cheeks again. "I love you too," I croak.

"Then marry me, don't waste another moment away from me."

I nod, cupping his face, and pressing my lips gently to his. He kisses me softly, before pulling back and looking into my eyes.

"You saved me. You gave me hope when I had none left. You're the reason I kept breathing, Cricket. The reason I kept fighting instead of giving up. I won't live another moment of my life without you by my side. From this moment on, I claim you. I swear to everything I have inside that I'll take care of you, and our baby. I'll love you until the day I'm a bunch of ashes in the ground."

I smile, and make a loud hiccupping sound. "Don't you worry about that, biker," I laugh and choke at the same time. "I'm never letting you go again."

A small, weak smile plays across his lips. "If you ever run from me," he murmurs, leaning down to my ear. "I'll chase you, and I'll always find you. You belong to me now."

My smile gets bigger, and my eyes twinkle. "Damn right I do."

EPILOGUE

COBRA

There's no room for two.

Her eyes meet mine from across the room, and a wobbly smile spreads across her lips. I return it, only mine is harder, far more gruff. We lock gazes, and she knows as well as I do that there's something here. Since the moment she walked into the club, all broken and fragile, she called to me. The minute I saw those feral yellow eyes, and she clutched my hand in fear when I took her to her room, I knew she was mine.

Even if that was wrong.

Then Jax came into the picture. Seems he felt the same pull. Now she looks at us both with confusion, and deep lust. Her eyes travel longingly over my body, but they light up when he walks in the room. We're the yin and yang, the complete opposite to each other. He's the good, I'm the bad, but she's the line in the middle. She wants a little something of both, and I can already see how this situation will end.

Badly.

I get out of my chair anyway, walking toward her. The minute I stop in front of her, I see the flush fill her cheeks. She pulls that plump little bottom lip between her teeth, and those cat's eyes lock on mine. I give her a lazy half-grin, and her flush deepens. "Hi, Cobra," she murmurs, looking at the tattoo on my neck. Now, her cheeks are flaming red.

"How you doin', darlin'?"

"I'm doing real well," she says, meeting my gaze.

"You bein' treated well?"

She nods, quickly. "Always."

I nod, letting my gaze slide over her long, slender body. "Seems you're gettin' comfortable in my club?"

She darts her eyes around, like I've just insulted her. "I'm sorry...I..."

I lean in closer. "I never said it was a bad thing."

She trembles, and lifts her face so we're nearly nose-to-nose. "You don't mind me being here?"

"Makes my fuckin' day."

She swallows, and her eyes drop onto my lips. Fuck, I want to lean down and claim those lips, kissing her until she moans my name.

"Ivy?"

She flinches at the sound of her name, and I grumble low in my chest, lifting myself up straight to see Jax walking in. Ivy smiles, her eyes lighting up when she sets her gaze on him.

"Jax," she breathes.

He grins, stopping beside her. He flashes me a warning expression, an expression that says she's mine. We'll fuckin' see about that. I take a step back, watching him help her off the stool.

"You ready?"

"Where you goin'?" I snap.

Ivy looks up at me, and a flash of guilt crosses her pretty features.

"We're just going for a ride," she says.

I nod, because there's nothing else I can do. I'm not going to make a song and fucking dance in the middle of the club. Jax gives me one more hard glare before taking Ivy's hand, and leading her out the door.

Fuck; just fuck.

I want her, he wants her, but the cold hard truth is...

Only one of us can win.

THE END

Now the prologue from my newest book due out March 2014 –
NUMBER THIRTEEN.

Please note – This book won't be a BDSM romance, but it will be quite dark!

PROLOGUE

My boots crunch in the yellow autumn leaves as I walk towards the school yard. I didn't want to come today, but Momma told me I had no choice. She said school is for smart kids, and if I don't, then how am I ever going to get smart? I could get smart, the man on the television tells me everything I need to know. But she claims that I can't make friends with the man on the television, that the only way to make friends, is to go to school. I could have told her that I don't need friends to be successful, but she'd only tell me I'm being silly.

So I came to school.

I didn't tell her that there are bullies here, that every day they push me around and shove me into lockers. That would make me sound weak, and now that my dad is working, and my brother is in college, I've had to be the man of the house. There's no room for weak. Momma tells me bullies pick on the kids who are victims. I think she's wrong. I'm not a victim, I'm just a kid. They pick on me because I'm *different*. I don't look at the girls like they do, I don't try to sneak out to parties. I'm just there to learn, then I go home and I take care of my family, because, I'm the man of the house.

Like I said.

The shrill sound of the school bell ringing, tells me I'm late. I pick up into a jog, rounding the corner and into the school yard. It's a cool winter day, and I have to pinch my coat together to stop it from flapping in the icy breeze. I can see the students piling in the front doors, and I turn my jog into a run. I'm focusing so heavily on the doors, that I don't see them. A strong hand lashes out, catching hold of my sleeve and tugging me into the alley way that runs down beside my school.

I always knew this alley was dangerous.

My body is slammed against a hard wooden fence, and I set eyes on my bullies. Four of them. They're all bigger than me, all of them on the football team. They're in the grade up, and they've just turned sixteen. The leader of the group, Marcel, steps forward first. He scrunches his nose in disgust, as if I've just dragged myself out of a gutter, as if *I'm* offending *him*. He leans in close, and I can smell cigarettes on his breath.

Smoking is not cool.

"You've been trying to avoid me, Will. Did you really think you could hide at home with mommy, and never have to come out again?"

I stare at him, wondering why he chose me to pick on. I didn't even know his name until he flagged me down and shoved my head down a toilet six months ago. I was just a kid, keeping my head down, studying and learning like I should. Now here I am, pressed against a fence, wondering why they decided I was good enough to take extra special effort to attack. I don't bother answering him, it'll only make him worse. My answers won't make a difference. If I answer, I'm *wrong*. If I don't answer, I'm *wrong*.

"Are you fucking mute, you little cunt?"

My body jerks. I hate that word, it's so...vulgar. I let my eyes move to the four other guys standing like protective pack animals around Marcel. I don't know their names, they're not significant enough. The tall boy with orange hair looks nervous, like he knows what's about to happen could put him in a world of trouble, but he's still here, still making the choice to stay. The other two guys are stony faced, and fully aware of their part in this attack.

I still don't answer him. If I just let them beat me, it'll go away quicker.

"You're a freak, *Will*, do you know that?" Marcel hisses, leaning in closer.

Of course I know that. I wouldn't be pinned against a fence if I didn't know that.

Bullies are so dumb.

Marcel raises his fist, and brings it down over my face, cracking my nose so hard blood spurts onto his shirt. I don't cry out, because that's what he wants, but the pain radiating through my head is nearly enough to make me beg. *Nearly.* Marcel takes hold of my shirt, and his grey eyes scan my face. He's panting, as though I've shoved *him* into an alley and challenged *him*. Like this is *my* fault. The world is twisted like that, and it's a lesson I've learned the hard way.

"You know," he growls, locking eyes with me. "I heard my girl saying how handsome you were the other day. Do you know how much it sucks to have my girl saying that a freak, is handsome?"

No, I don't. I don't have a girl.

Again, bullies are dumb.

"Don't answer me, you little twerp. It doesn't matter. I will make sure by the time you leave this alley, you're not handsome anymore. I won't have my competition being some little weasel that can't even speak."

I taste blood filling my mouth, and my nose is pounding so

283

heavily I'm almost sure I can hear my own heart in my head. I don't take my eyes from Marcel. They say look danger right in the eye, it gives you power and strength. I don't feel powerful right now, in fact, I don't really feel anything. Someone like me doesn't fight, I'm the underdog, and underdogs are weak. Everyone knows it.

Marcel reaches into his back pocket, and pulls out a pocket knife. The heart that feels like it's in my head, begins thumping even harder. I try not to show fear, I try to stand tall and take what he dishes out with strength, but that's not so easy when your attacker is waving around a pocket knife.

"She said it was your eyes," he begins, lazily tracing circles on his palm with the blade. "She said they're the most stunning eyes she's ever seen. Like the ocean."

I didn't know my eyes were like the ocean.

He takes hold of my shirt, yanking me close. "No one is more appealing to my girl, than *me*."

They say bad things happen in slow motion, they're right. I feel Marcel throw me down onto the floor. I feel every movement as my body is slammed into the dirt. I feel his body weight coming over me, his knees pinning me down as I squirm. I feel his friend take my arms, pulling them above my head, while another puts a hand over my mouth. With my nose pouring with blood, that makes it difficult to breathe.

But what I know I'll remember until the day I die, is the

moment he drives the knife into my eye.

I don't feel pain, not right away. Instead I hear the popping sound, as his blade pierces right through. Then I feel pressure as he twists. It's only when he yanks it out of it's socket, that I start to scream. Then the pain is unlike anything I've ever felt. Words cannot begin to explain the horror I feel as darkness begins to envade my body. I know my face is covered in blood, because it drips down to soak my hair. I know I bite his friends hand so hard I nearly take off his finger.

I don't know what they're saying, or even acknowledge the moment when they run away. All I know was that I am bleeding to death in an alley, missing an eye. Red fills my vision as the blood begins to cover every part of my face. I know I'm still screaming, even though I can't hear it. All I can hear is an excessive ringing in my ears. I can't even move my hands to cover my eye, in an attempt to protect the empty socket. I can do nothing but lay and scream, witnessing a pain that I'll never witness again in my life, and wondering what I did to deserve it.

No one deserves to die.

But I do die that day.

And in my place, a monster is born.

6484679R00169

Printed in Great Britain
by Amazon.co.uk, Ltd.,
Marston Gate.